M000031303

Stay smart!

signature

Mama's got a brand new job

Mama's got a brand new job

JANIS POWERS

Mama's got a brand new job by Janis Powers. Copyright © 2013 Powers Enterprises, LLC.
All Rights Reserved. No part of the book may be reproduced
in any manner whatsoever without written permission.

ISBN 978-0-9892037-0-8

Printed in the United States of America
Design by Bella Guzmán, Highwire Creative
Author Photograph by Carrie Biggar Photography

For more information, visit www.mamasgotabrandnewjob.com.

My mother for her moxie

My father for Jacques

V and B for the inspiration

Laura Burns, Diana Clukey and Jamie Reidy
for telling me I wasn't done yet

"You have to make your own luck."

–Ernest Hemingway

1

Patent Number 9175638

Collapsible Jogging Stroller/Backpack

Company: Infant Ingenuity, LLC

"*Love it!*" I hunched closer to the monitor in my office, as if the six-point text on my screen would magically transform into the as-yet-to-be-sanctioned baby gear. It wasn't clear from the patent application how this contraption was going to function. It didn't even have consumer regulatory approval. But with the right marketing campaign, its first production run would sell out from advance purchases on amazon.com before a prototype hit the floors of Babies "Я" Us. And I would be making one of those advance purchases.

I wasn't even pregnant yet, but that was beside the point. I live in Manhattan. In a New York nanosecond, my conventional existence as a patent attorney could be thrown into chaos by a financial crisis, another terror attack, or worse yet, the arrival of a new upstart associate. I had to use the means at my disposal to position myself for success. In this case, that meant trolling the United States Patent and Trademark website looking for next-generation baby paraphernalia.

I jolted up when I heard a tap on the glass wall of my office. It was my admin, Joy. Joy noticed everything and today that included my new lavender dress suit. She tugged on her jacket near the shoulder and gave me a thumbs-up sign. Then she grabbed her earlobe and looked at me curiously. I felt my own earlobes. Only one of them had an earring.

I mouthed the words "thank you" and then patted the clean blotter on my desk in a futile attempt to find the missing earring. As the panic subsided, I realized that the earring was probably still at home. I had been distracted while getting ready, the flustered result of a dreamy early morning wake-up call administered by my husband, Dale. I removed the other earring, ostensibly restoring symmetry around my brain. Perhaps that's what I needed to get started on billable work.

I paged through the spammy emails on my computer, looking for something important. I kept my eyes on the monitor as I picked up my cell phone. It was pulsating with the White Stripes' "Seven Nation Army." Dale was calling.

The time was 9:20 am. My conversation with Dale would be brief, since the opening bell on Wall Street was set to ring in a few minutes. And once it did, Dale, armed with a tricked-out mobile device, a tailored Joseph A. Bank suit and an attitude, would step into the role of white collar combatant.

"You make it to work O.K.?" From the breathy undertone in Dale's voice, it seemed as if he were doing some sort of ritualistic preparatory maneuver, like one-armed push-ups.

"Yup!" I said confidently, ignoring the missing earring issue. "All good. What've you got going on?"

"Interesting you should ask. . ." His voice trailed off, and then he told me to wait a moment. He didn't put me on hold, which would have been a courtesy, considering the tirade that streamed through the receiver. "Did you *fucking* read the research on Inter-Tech? And what the hell is this graph? Go update the data for Christ's sake!"

Foul language was definitely the norm for the bankers downtown, but at McCale, Morgan & Black, it was grounds for a professional demerit. I put my hand over the face of the phone, trying to muffle the sounds.

"Jesus Christ!" groaned Dale, finally resuming the conversation. "No one can concentrate now that O'Shaugnessy announced he's having another kid."

Patrick O'Shaugnessy was one of Dale's colleagues, someone who had elevated buffoonery to an art form. And now, this clown had replicated his DNA for a fourth time. "God help humanity," I said.

"Maxine, we have got to get going with this parenting thing. I can finally get into the club."

My forehead wrinkled. "Club? What club?"

"The club of dads at Worthington Investments."

"What are you talking about? That's not a real club, is it?"

"No. It's not," he said in an excited whisper. "But this O'Shaugnessy thing is a real eye-opener. Clearly, the guys with kids are the ones who get ahead."

"I thought you got ahead by making gobs of money for the company," I said coolly.

"Right. And the rainmaker around here is Bobbie Macaluso, and Bobbie Macaluso has kids. So any excuse to ask for parenting advice is also an excuse to get some trading tips from the master."

I swiveled my chair and looked out the window at midtown Manhattan. From the 35th floor, the steam puffing out of mechanical towers on the roofs of nearby buildings belied the fact that it was an early spring morning. "So you're saying that a baby will help your career because you'll have more face time with your boss?"

"Yes. Totally! I can't believe I didn't think of this before!"

"Yeah. Me neither." Perfect. I'd do all the heavy lifting, and Dale would reap the benefits. Maybe I needed to start a club of moms at McCale, Morgan & Black.

"Maxine, I gotta go. Good luck at your meeting tonight, O.K.?"

I was shocked that he remembered. But then again, I had been going on and on about tonight's culminating session with a potential new client, Parfum Aix. I was about to thank him for his thoughtfulness, but he had already hung up. I wouldn't talk to him until the afternoon, after the market closed. Non-work related calls and texts were too distracting for Dale, who was busy monitoring real-time updates of financial information. No big deal, though. If I wanted to know how Dale was doing, I could just check the NASDAQ.

I spent the rest of the day plowing through research materials. Anyone who had flipped through the pages of *Vogue* knew that Parfum Aix was an elite brand. Their perfumes and skin care products commanded incredibly high prices due to their unparalleled quality. It was a brand any woman dreamed she could afford; most would have to satisfy themselves with a $35 bar of Parfum Aix soap.

Over lunch at my desk, I read about how the company had been independently owned and operated since its inception 50 years ago. Parfum Aix's superiority was driven by a meticulous product sourcing department. Elaborate deals were structured for herbs and flowers indigenous to countries all over the world. Roses from Bulgaria. Patchouli from Indonesia. Even frankincense from Somalia. Coordinating these international agreements was a legal fee goldmine.

Fortunately, our McCale team wouldn't have to do the hardship travel. When necessary, we would probably just do site visits to the company headquarters in Grasse, France. Maybe we would take a ride over to Aix-en-Provence to validate the organic cultivation of the company's signature ingredient, lavender. After all, it was a major component of their best-selling product, Eau de Vie.

As exciting as working for a company like Parfum Aix might be, the real carrot was the fact that if we won the business tonight, I would share lead billing credit. No other senior associate was even close to achieving such a milestone. At this rate, I might even make it to partner at McCale before Dale got promoted at Worthington.

Joy tapped on my window and waved good-bye. It was five o'clock and my desk was a mess. I stood up, calling out the items I needed for the meeting as a means to help me focus. "Pen. Notes. Phone."

"To whom are you speaking, Maxine?" The unmistakably gravelly voice belonged to Caine Seaver, McCale's lead partner for Consumer Business Services. He was also my dinner date for the evening.

"Sorry," I stammered, "I was try. . ."

"Did you do something wrong?"

"No."

"Then why are you apologizing?" Caine took pleasure in literally interpreting colloquial terms. I resisted the urge to clock him with my phone. "Never mind," he said. He bared his teeth—two sets of rectangular enamel. He looked like he had just eaten a row of piano keys. "I presume you are preparing for the meeting?"

"That's right."

"Very good. I will meet you at Reception in five minutes. We can strategize in the car." With his staccato list of instructions complete, he turned on his heel and vanished down the hall.

Some at McCale, in fact many, would describe Caine as brusque. The younger associates dreaded an assignment with him. I had, too, but after years of being paired together, Caine and I had developed a tacit rapport based on our mutual knowledge of his hopeless social ineptitude. Regardless of which breach of social etiquette Caine would commit tonight—and there would be many—I would be on point to fix the situation with my wit and charm.

I had a seasoned set of redirection tactics for these strained social moments. Sometimes, I might interject a scintillating factoid about the stock market. I might bring up something relevant that I had just read in *The New York Times*. And it was always a safe bet to comment informatively about the wine we would be drinking, particularly if Caine was kind or oblivious enough to allow our guest to select it.

Topics I tended to avoid were children and spouses. Here I was—married and child-less at this biologically critical juncture known as the Early Thirties. It was nobody's business that I had laid off the birth control, and I certainly wasn't in any rush to show up at McCale in a maternity jumper. My master plan for pregnancy involved having sex with my husband. And if, God forbid, that method failed, I could revert to fertility drugs, artificial insemination, surrogacy, or maybe even adoption. Regardless of the procurement method, I failed to see how any of these topics were appropriate for dinner conversation.

As for the spouse, that was also delicate territory. If Dale had been a doctor or a teacher, things might have been easier. But few professions (barring mine) generate more scorn than that of the Investment Banker. Upon hearing the news that my husband was "one of them," I was immediately cast in the shadow of evil and greed, and any attempt to explain otherwise was futile.

In any event, sidestepping a discussion about family was not just about reducing potential awkwardness for me. Family was an equal-opportunity topic. Everyone at the table was expected to participate, and that included Caine. His stock contribution, "I am married with two daughters," was perfunctory and unemotional. At least, I would remind myself, we could be perceived as lawyers—not mothers or fathers, wives or husbands.

2

The horns honked outside the windows of our Town Car. Caine tapped his Cross Pen on the door handle. Although we were only blocks from our destination, I knew he would fidget the entire way. I hoped that his nervousness wouldn't ooze over to my side of the car.

He peeled his eyes off the window. "You said you met Deschemel at a charity fundraiser?"

"Right. A Memorial Sloan-Kettering Cancer Center event."

"Do you think he has cancer? Maybe he's dying. Did he look well to you?"

"No, I don't think he has cancer. He looked perfectly healthy to me. Sprightly, in fact, for a 70-year-old man."

Caine shuddered as a bicycle messenger sped by, barely evading the side mirror of a neighboring taxi. "Why would he attend such an event? Don't they have cancer fundraisers in France?"

All of these irrelevant and previously discussed questions were just a smokescreen to obscure Caine's anxiety. Caine was baffled that, through casual conversation, I had generated a business lead. All of his "new business" came from referrals from existing McCale clients. For Caine, embarking on a social situation like tonight's, with so many unknown variables, was professional torture.

And since it was my lead, I didn't feel like playing the "work wife" to coax Caine back into his comfort zone. Uncharacteristically, I was on edge too. I scanned my notes one more time, hoping that I was prepared.

I heard some stifled tapping noises, an indication that Caine had busied himself with his cell phone. Despite years of typing on a hand-held device, he still lacked the finesse of a seasoned user. While he wrestled with his keypad, I took the opportunity to mentally remove myself from the car, and revisit my first and only meeting with Jacques Deschemel, founder and president of Parfum Aix.

Truth be told, I had been bored out of my mind when I met him. Dale had dragged me to the Sloan-Kettering fundraiser, one in a long line of events we attended so he could glad-hand anyone with wads of cash at their disposal. My job had been to survey the silent auction tables and see who was bidding how much on what. I had only agreed to it because it gave me the chance to look over some of the items myself, which I had planned to do anyway.

While the men bid on restaurant gift cards and professional sports tickets, the ladies focused on the jewelry and spa treatments. I put in a bid for a spa package for two at the newly opened Tribeca Day Spa. After I pledged $500, I realized that I could probably get all the services through a Groupon for half the price. But then again, this was a charity event. But then again, I had no business blowing $500 on a massage and pedicure. I backed away from the table, hoping that someone would outbid me. Then I noticed Bidder 714. He was older than the average attendee, probably in his late 60's or early 70's. His gray hair was cut short and he had a trim-cut mustache, which was also gray. He wore an impeccably tailored tweed sports coat with dark gray slacks. The monotony of color was broken up by an evergreen bow tie and sparkling hazel eyes.

I nursed my Stoli Orange and soda while I watched this curious man's process. He spent well over 10 minutes reviewing the wines and spirits available. After careful consideration, he placed his bids—but only on half of the offerings. Once he left, I made my own inspection of the potable goods. To avoid suspicion, I placed a bid on a bottle of Dom Pérignon that I knew Dale would like.

I noted that this man, Bidder 714, had pledged $1,300 for a bottle of French dessert wine, Chateau d'Yquem. I had only seen a bottle of it once before, while shopping for Christmas gifts at Sherry-Lehmann. According to the store's Bordeaux expert, the grapes used to make Chateau d'Yquem were still picked by hand, but only when they had ripened to an almost mold-like state on the vine. Apparently, this "noble rot" was the key to Chateau d'Yquem's legendary reputation. It sounded like a crazy marketing scheme to glorify the bizarre, but since I hadn't tried it and certainly couldn't afford it, I was in awe of it.

Meanwhile, an over-served, under-dressed party-goer stumbled up to the auction tables. He placed a bid on every wine and spirit available. This prompted Bidder 714 to return to the table to defend his territory with even higher bids.

The Dom Pérignon was now out of my range. At $180, it was just over the retail price. I was happy to let someone else buy it, and even more relieved that I was no longer the open bidder for the spa package.

But a few hundred dollars was chump change compared to the current offer for the d'Yquem, which was now going for $1,700. I couldn't take my eyes off the bottle. The color of the wine had darkened, which I knew was typical for a wine of its age and character. The dimmed lighting at the event made it hard to tell for sure, but it seemed like the top of the bottle looked crusty. As I pondered the condition of the wine inside, an announcer requested that final bids be placed, as the silent auction was set to close in two minutes.

"Excuse me," said Bidder 714, holding his pen. "I would like to place a final bid on that d'Yquem in front of you. That is, unless you are interested in it . . . ." His voice was laced with a French accent.

"Oh, no," I said. "I'm not interested in bidding on it." Bidder 714 smiled curtly, waiting for me to move. I hesitated, adding, "In fact, I don't think you should bid on it either. I think it's corked."

"No! *Impossible!*" He grabbed the wine and inspected it himself. As he held the neck of the bottle, the foil over the cork loosened and fell off. He examined the cork, which was heavily stained and damp. He placed the bottle back on the table and motioned for me to follow him to the window.

"What an outrage!" he said, waving his arms in disbelief. "That d'Yquem; *qui ne vaut rien!*" I knew the French were passionate, but this guy was downright emotional. His bowtie had turned slightly askew, and he was rubbing his chin so intensely, I could hear the sound of the stubble against his fingers.

"Do you think it was stored poorly?" I asked.

"*Bien sûr!* The wine must have been stored, eh, vertically." He struggled a bit with the word and then made parallel chopping movements with his hands. "*Alors*, the cork dried out, and when the bottle was laid down, it started to leak. *Quel dommage!*"

I had some idea about how to store wine, but Bidder 714's expert explanation was both entertaining and edifying. I struggled for something to contribute. "I can't believe they didn't do a better job vetting the donations," I offered.

Bidder 714's shoulders rose in agreement. "*Exactement!* I am disappointed with the standards. Now, I will have to reject anything I may win tonight, just on principle." I wondered if, legally, he could do that, but Bidder 714's aspect seemed too lofty to be bothered by such details. He extended an arm out formally. I shook his hand as he said, "*Merci beaucoup, mademoiselle*, for your excellent observation. My name is Jacques." He did not give his last name. I forgot to ask what it was when he said, "*Enchanté*," so beautifully after I introduced myself.

We exchanged pleasantries, I gave him my card, and we parted ways. It wasn't until later in the evening when Dale debriefed me about the players in attendance that I realized that my evening's entertainment had been supplied by the founder of Parfum Aix, Jacques Deschemel.

Dale was thrilled that I had given him my card, undoubtedly hopeful that he might score some business from the old chap. But when a representative from Parfum Aix called me the next day inquiring about our company's services, I referred the call up the chain at McCale, Morgan & Black, rather than downtown to Worthington Investments.

3

To the untrained eye, Bertran may have been hard to spot. The building's columned portico and stone exterior looked like any of the other brownstones on the street. The exception was the shiny navy blue door over which was posted a white sign with brass letters bearing the establishment's name.

I took for granted the entrance's speakeasy atmosphere because I had been there so many times with Dale and the Worthington crew. Bertran was one of the few places north of 14th Street that attracted the Wall Street crowd. The ambiance was clubby and decidedly old school, the décor accented with centuries old wainscoting and glass cases filled with ship models.

The atmosphere was great, but more importantly, Bertran was

renowned for their fresh oysters. Sure, it would have been more conservative for me to book a dinner with Jacques Deschemel somewhere French, like Restaurant Daniel. However, I was betting that Jacques would enjoy top quality, regardless of the cuisine.

And then there was the bar. New York classics like the King Cole Bar and 21 could choke on the neckties of their midtown stuffiness. Bar Bertran had it all. Its glass shelves were crowded with bottles of myriad sizes and shapes, most notably: vodka (my favorite), gin (nowhere near as versatile), whiskey (Dale's choice), cognac (bought by the bottle after a good day at the market), and tequila (done by the shot after a bad day at the market). If Jacques Deschemel labored over wine and liquor at a silent auction, he'd be a kid in a candy shop at Bar Bertran.

I spotted him immediately, posted at the bar in his signature tweed jacket. I waved enthusiastically. Caine was several paces behind, cleaning the lenses of his glasses, despite the fact that they weren't dirty. "Maxine!" smiled Jacques, as he double-kissed my cheeks.

"So," I asked with anticipation, "what do you think of Bertran?"

Jacques made little fists of joy as he half turned in deference to the spirits behind him. "It is wonderful. I am not sure where to start!"

Anticipating this exchange, I had done quite a bit of homework about the preferred spirits of the French. I learned that the French had a marvelous array of regional liqueurs, each steeped with its own ritual for serving and imbibing. In Provence, Deschemel's territory, the anise-flavored pastis was the beverage of choice. Pastis was served with four parts water to one part liqueur, and the resulting cocktail bore an unfortunate resemblance to Milk of Magnesia. How anyone could find such a concoction even remotely appetizing was beyond me. But then again, I was the last person to pass judgment on anyone else's alcohol-related cultural mores. I was the undisputed champion of Quarters in my class at law school.

In any case, this was my chance to try it, and I had called in advance to ensure that Bar Bertran served pastis. I was about to order three when Caine appeared with the maître d'. "Shall we sit?" It was a question stated in the declarative.

Not missing a beat, I ushered Deschemel to follow along and then instructed the maître d' to bring us our pastis *toute suite*.

The ceiling in the Bertran dining room was about 10 feet higher than in the bar. Three large brass chandeliers illuminated the space. Starched tablecloths hung down to the well-worn wooden floor. The heavy white china and no-nonsense glassware were plentiful, and regularly broken. Our ears were filled with the sounds of shellfish shucking, silverware clanking, and diners chattering.

Caine, meanwhile, struggled with the wine list, which was about an inch thick. I wanted to grab it from his clutches and hand it over to Jacques, who was clearly more qualified to perform the wine ordering duties for our table. But ceding the menu would have meant ceding control. Caine bumbled through the pages, which was excruciating to watch, since I knew all the white wines he should have been considering were listed at the front of the book.

The waiter arrived with a tray of glasses. Each of us was served a small glass of ice water, a smaller glass filled with a thick clear liquid, and a spoon. I watched as Jacques poured out the thick liquid and gently stirred it, transforming the ice water into a murky, mysterious pastis on the rocks. Jacques and I shared a smile as I took a sip. It was lovely—a fresh blend of spices, herbal essence and licorice.

Caine had taken a gulp, not a sip, which had rendered him useless in the wine-ordering department. Jacques was happy to pick up the slack and ordered some esoteric Chablis that earned a knowing nod from the waiter. I drank more pastis.

Finally settling in, Caine initiated some technical legal commentary. It was all politely acknowledged by Jacques. Of course the man knew we were a good firm. Aside from our reputation, Caine had sent Parfum Aix as much due diligence about us as the FBI might provide for a RICO case.

Caine then tried an alternative tack and described some of McCale's relationships with clients similar to Parfum Aix. Unfortunately, due to client confidentiality, Caine couldn't mention any of their names. Comparing Parfum Aix to a "large multi-national consumer goods manufacturer," as evidenced from Jacques's disgusted expression, bordered on the insulting.

But rather than verbalize his discontent to Caine, Jacques went to town on the waiter, who had arrived to take our dinner order. I was so grateful that we had one of the veteran Bertran servers because Jacques would have eaten a novice alive. He didn't even look at the menu. He had an idea of the kind of oysters he wanted to eat, and to find them, he squeezed every ounce of molluscan knowledge from the mitochondria of our waiter's brain. When all was said and done, we were treated to a spectrum of flavors and textures that I never could have imagined existed in that family of bi-valves.

I began to wonder if the labor-intensive activities required for the consumption of oysters had proven too distracting for a business meal. Much of Jacques's attention seemed focused on the food on his plate. I tried my best not to stare, but his process was riveting. First, he stabbed the oyster meat with his seafood fork. Then he turned the fork—delicately, but assertively—about 90 degrees until the meat popped off the shell. Then he smelled it.

I couldn't imagine what fragrances were even detectable, but if any nose in the world could ferret them out, it belonged to Jacques Deschemel. I was about to ask him if the oysters were up to snuff, so to speak, when I heard the shrill bellowing of my name across the

Bertran dining room. "Maxine! Is that you?" Jacques, Caine and I turned to see a man shuffling towards our table. He was about 5' 6", with cropped red hair and pale, freckled skin. The knot of his Brooks Brothers tie was wide and loose, demonstrating more of an inability to tie it correctly, than an air of casual, post-work relaxation. Patrick O'Shaughnessy had arrived to crash the party. "Oh, thank GOD! I totally need your advice!" he blurted out, finally reaching the table.

Caine shot me a look that easily translated into, "Get rid of him—NOW."

"Hello, Patrick," I mustered the patience to say. "I hear congratulations are in order." I turned to Jacques and Caine, and in an effort to explain Patrick's inebriation, I said, "Patrick works with my husband, and he's just learned that he and his wife are expecting their fourth child." I forced myself to smile, despite my disgust at the notion.

"Yup. We just keep pumpin' 'em out." Patrick gave the two gentlemen a small nod of acknowledgement and then hunched over my shoulder.

I could smell the alcohol on his breath. "Patrick, I'm in a meeting. Can't this wait 'til later?"

"Oh, sorry. Sure. I just need to know the name of that gin that you always have at your apartment. The one in the black bottle. It looks like a medicine bottle?" Patrick looked up and said a bit more loudly, "You have got to have cocktails at Dale and Maxine's apartment. Seriously, this woman knows more about alcohol than anyone I know. And believe me, that means a lot!"

Caine's face reddened. Patrick continued, totally oblivious of his unwelcomed presence. "Gin, vodka, rum. I had no idea there was so much to know. I would argue that the volume of Maxine's vodka collection might rival that of an amateur wine collector."

Patrick's last comment, the most eloquently stated, really

chapped me. My 30-odd bottles of vodka were always a source of amusement for the visiting Worthington staffers, and the wine collector joke was a staple of bar talk at our home. Leave it to O'Shaughnessy to pawn off someone else's joke as his own, while making me look like a lush at a critical moment in my career.

I answered testily, "The gin is Hendrick's. Good-bye, Patrick." I turned my back on O'Shaughnessy, who stumbled off to annoy someone else.

I patted down my hair and said to no one in particular, "I apologize for the interruption. Please continue."

"Hendrick's?" Jacques repeated, rolling the "r" so much, the word didn't sound English anymore.

"Yes!" I said, laughing from both amusement and relief. "It's almost like vodka. Very crisp, usually served with a cucumber." I rattled on, my nerves getting the better of me. "But gin is so English. I can't imagine it's widely popular in France." Jacques didn't have a response. I couldn't believe he didn't have anything to contribute, so I just kept on talking. "Well, I'd think, given your enjoyment of pastis, that of all the gins out there, you'd be a fan of Bombay Sapphire."

"The one in the blue bottle?" he asked.

"Yes!"

Jacques sat back in his seat, in contemplation. It seemed like he was trying to remember the taste, the flavor profile. His brain had to be jam-packed with an encyclopedic record of scents and smells.

Kind of like mine.

I jolted up in the chair. I waved the waiter over to our table, and asked him to bring me something from the bar. Within moments he returned with a light blue glass bottle and put it on the table. I picked it up, cradling it like a newborn baby. "Maybe you have noticed this before, but I think it's just delightful." I pointed to raised impressions in the glass down the side of the bottle. I flipped the bottle around, pointing to similar etchings on the other side. "These pictures show the herbs and spices used in the production of Bombay Sapphire. Angelica. Coriander. Juniper berries."

Jacques examined the bottle with pure joy. I let him admire it for a bit and then said, "Can you imagine a bottle of Parfum Aix with etchings of the flowers and herbs that you use to create each fragrance? Wouldn't that be fun?!"

"Certainly," said Caine, "but you would need a lawyer to make sure you did not get sued for trade dress infringement."

"Impressive. Very impressive." Then Jacques sat up in his chair and buttoned his sports coat. "Monsieur Seaver, you have demonstrated that your company has excellent professional qualifications. Maxine, you have now proven to me that you understand—and passionately appreciate—the *essence* of Parfum Aix. Congratulations to you both. Parfum Aix is pleased to select you as our new legal counsel!"

I couldn't stop smiling when I heard the news. Caine got right down to business, committing the firm to providing all kinds of documentation, which he delegated to me. Of course I would present Caine with draft material the next day. Of course I would ensure the contract was signed by the end of the week. This deal was my baby, and nothing was going to stop me from closing it.

4

"*I'm not sure how you did it,*" said Caine, "but on behalf of the partners at McCale, Morgan & Black, congratulations on helping us to expand our global reach by signing Parfum Aix."

I stood in the conference room surrounded by the firm's illustrious leadership. Applause filled my ears. It was the weekly partner meeting and I had just concluded a rudimentary overview of Deschemel's company. As far as I knew, I was the only one of my peers to have been an agenda item for the weekly power session. I graciously thanked Caine for his support and attempted to exit the meeting with dignity. I think I may have skipped out the door. I'm not sure.

I high-fived Joy on the way to my office, where I tried to compose myself. It was a completely ridiculous notion, because it was 1:15 on a Friday afternoon. Too mentally fried to undertake anything challenging, I opted to make a phone call.

Dale would be a great person with whom to share my professional success. But he wouldn't answer his phone since the market was still open. My mother would be proud of me, but in an abstract way. Proud as she had been when I received an "A" on my senior thesis at Yale, "The Electoral College as an Anti-Democratic Construct." She could understand the concepts, but was too removed from the experience to give me the affirmation that I needed. Which brought me to Paola.

Paola was my best friend, a bond that developed when we had attended the same elementary school in Manhattan. It was a small, Upper East Side private school that my parents struggled to afford and ultimately led to our decampment to the suburbs.

While my family was moving out, Paola's was moving in. Her father had moved everyone up from Mexico City so he could open an American office of his successful investment firm. Paola and I had remained friends, I believe, due to our separation. Pre-teen jealousy over Paola's position of privilege was replaced by ties of sisterly solidarity, a joy in maintaining a friendship outside either of our social circles.

As the years had progressed, Paola and I had also developed a pseudo-sibling rivalry, career-wise. Paola was a successful management consultant, who, like me, was closing in on making partner at her company. But she had one thing that I did not: a child. Conversations with her of late were a combination of therapy for her, education for me, and a little competition for us both.

Paola traveled during most of the week, enabled by the support of a battery of nannies, her mother's seemingly unlimited availability, and a husband with a flexible work schedule. On Fridays, she worked out of her apartment in what I considered a futile attempt at maternal bonding. Taking a conference call while nursing an infant? That was Paola's definition of multi-tasking. I called Paola at home, hoping that her daughter wasn't hungry since just thinking about nursing made me want to buy stock in Enfamil.

When she picked up the phone, I could hear the sound of a baby crying in the background. As Paola started to speak, the sound grew louder. "Hi," she huffed into the receiver.

"What are you doing?"

"Amanda is teething really badly and she can't fall asleep. Sorry, but I have to pick her up." The child's screams were quite loud.

"Oh, I guess this is a bad time. I can call you later," I said, anxious to get off the phone.

"No, no, no! All good. I'm glad to have an actual conversation. I've been on conference calls all day." Paola's voice was shaking. "Sorry, I've got to rock her back and forth."

Just listening to her was making me tired. Paola, poor thing, still hadn't lost the baby weight she had gained during pregnancy. Any attempts at maintaining a fitness regime, which was not her strong suit to being with, went out the window with the arrival of Amanda. Less time for herself and for her friends seemed to be the post-baby mantra.

She may have been busy, but I wanted to go out and celebrate my win. "So, is there any chance you can grab a drink? I know you're swamped, but we need to hang out!"

"Uh, yeah. Sure. Sounds fun." Pause. She had nothing to add. The usually chatty Paola Brighton wasn't saying a word. Either she was jealous, or her child had to be doing something to distract her from listening to me. How annoying.

"Everything O.K. with you?"

"Oh, *dios mio*," deadpanned Paola. This couldn't be good. Paola breaking into Spanish was a bellwether for an impending crisis.

"Oh, my GOD," she repeated. "You know, I have seen some pretty gruesome stuff on YouTube before. But nothing compares to this. I am holding Amanda's bottom right now, and she is squeezing out the nastiest poop. I have to go. I'll call you later. You need to come over. Visit me!" Then she hung up.

I hadn't seen Paola in a while, but the image of watching a baby take a bowel movement wasn't exactly the enticement I needed to set up a play-date. Besides, I had more mundane things to deal with, like clearing out my over-stuffed inbox. I was determined to address all the loose ends at work. I didn't want anything hanging over my head for the weekend.

At the top of my inbox was a series of emails marked "urgent." They were all from Nancy Lallyberry, a female junior associate, just one year behind me but gunning for Caine's job. My back stiffened as I prepared to read her barrage of missives.

A quick scan of the first six messages revealed that nothing was truly urgent, but that fact was irrelevant to Nancy. She had probably set a default in her email so that all of her messages would be tagged as "urgent." That, however, would have suggested a sense of efficiency, and Nancy was not one for that.

The flutter of emails was related to the law school clerk program. Nancy was in charge of overseeing the mentoring program for the prospective attorneys and was pulling together a meeting to brainstorm about improvements to the process. Although the timing for the meeting was almost ludicrous—the clerk program wasn't supposed to start for three months, yet the meeting was next week—I put it on my calendar anyway.

Further down the inbox were several emails from Caine. He was still in the partner meeting, which was scheduled to end at 2:00, so I had some time to react.

Now that the engagement letter was signed, Caine was wasting no time in charging ahead with the Parfum Aix relationship. I, of course, was the team lead. Caine had assigned Horace Blankenfield, a junior associate of moderate capability, as support.

I dialed Blankenfield's extension so I could get him up to speed. I scanned more messages as his phone rang four or five times. Finally, Horace picked up. "Hi, Maxine," he said cordially.

"Hey, Horace. Did you see the emails from Caine? We are going to be working together on Parfum Aix."

"Yeah. Congratulations. I heard you got to present at the partner meeting. I guess that's kind of a big deal."

"Thanks," I said. Word was out in the office about my awesomeness. "I know it's Friday afternoon, but I want to debrief you before the end of the day so we can get a jump on things Monday morning. What are you working on right now?"

"Well, I'm just finishing this clerk presentation for Nancy. She wants it by the end of the day," he said. I could tell from the laconic tone in his voice that he was bored with the scut work with which he had been assigned.

"Is that for the meeting next week?"

"Yeah. But you know Nancy. She likes to see everything in advance," warned Horace.

I tossed my pen onto my desk. "Whatever," I oozed. "This is billable client business. It takes priority over internal projects. Can you come to my office please? Thanks."

I pulled together a few documents and emails for Horace while I waited. He showed up with his legal pad, ready to take notes. I began the discussion, outlining the Parfum Aix relationship and my expectations of Horace. I didn't get very far before a tiny head topped with mousy brown hair popped by my office. The head belonged to Nancy Lallyberry, as did the rest of the 5' 5", 110-pound spindly body.

"Oh, hello, Maxine. I was just walking by and I thought I would congratulate you on presenting at the partner meeting today." Although the comment was civil, I could almost hear her teeth grinding behind her smile. I reminded myself to be nice because, after all, I was her superior.

"Thanks, Nancy. So what can I do for you?"

"You've probably seen my emails. I'm working on the clerk program this year, so I am really busy with that. Horace is working with me on it." Then she shot poor Horace a look that masterfully combined pity, anger and authority.

"Caine has requested that Horace assist me with Parfum Aix," I said, coming to Horace's rescue. "Prior to the weekend, I felt that it was important for us to debrief, so we can get rolling on Monday. I understand that he has some commitments to you and the clerk program. I'm sure you'll be able to find someone else to help you." In an act of consolation, I added, "I will be at the meeting on Wednesday to help, though."

"O.K. then. Thanks." She backed out of the office and marched off to deal with the next bit of pressing business.

Horace laughed uneasily. It appeared he didn't want to take sides. "What am I supposed to do about the work I was doing for Nancy?"

"Well, finish what you were working on for today, but starting Monday, I'll need you full time." I thought that was a reasonable. Horace and I concluded, leaving me with my glorious inbox.

Within a few minutes, my office was filled with noise from the break-up of the partner meeting. I caught the eye of a few folks as they walked by my office. Some of the partners smiled in acknowledgment. I even got a few waves of congratulations, which was satisfying.

At the end of the pack came Deirdre Morgan, a named partner

of the firm. She was slowly walking down the hall while checking her phone, the classic multi-tasker. Deirdre's uncanny legal and political instincts had propelled her to the role of Assistant District Attorney in Brooklyn by age 30. At that point, Deirdre was already married with two children. Soon afterwards, Deirdre left public service and started this company with two other distinguished professionals, Richard McCale, and Paul Black. I admired her immensely.

Deirdre stopped in front of my office door. She started speaking before she finished reading what was on her phone. "Maxine, I am the office partner responsible for the clerk program. I have asked Nancy Lallyberry to coordinate the effort on my behalf, and have given her access to the resources she requires. None of us has the time to sort through this sandstorm of emails from Nancy regarding your commandeering one of the resources." She looked back at her phone and read another email while she waited for my response.

My eyes darted to my computer screen. From what I could tell, Nancy had sent a slew of emails to the partner group first, and then forwarded the sent emails to me. By doing so, she had ensured that any response to her messages from a partner would not be seen by me. It was a classic tactic to let me know that she was going over my head, without giving me the capability to defend myself . . . unless I were to stoop to her level and start emailing all the partners directly myself. What a preposterous waste of time.

"Well. . ." I started.

Deirdre, still engaged with her phone, opted to summarize the situation. "From what I have gathered, you were proceeding as instructed by Caine, and a simple staffing snafu has been elevated to me. So now I have to over-ride Caine and discipline you, all while making Nancy look like a winner." Deirdre stepped into my office. She hunched down a bit, and raised her left eyebrow. "She hasn't even copied you on any of these emails."

"She forwarded them on to me after the fact," I said. "I figured client work should take . . ."

Deirdre cut me off with the wave of her hand. "I know, Maxine. You did a nice job at the presentation, and we're all very excited about the Parfum Aix account. But let me give you some advice. You can bring in the most business at this firm, but to be really successful, you have to control people's opinions of you and not the other way around." She took a few steps back, thereby ending the moment of mentorship. "Give Horace back to Nancy. Talk to Staffing and find somebody new." Then Deirdre whisked out of my office, leaving me wondering how something so small could have made such a big mess.

5

I almost tripped on the cleats when I walked into the apartment. I regained my balance, and then stumbled on the lacrosse stick on the floor. Dale bounded out of the kitchen and caught me before I face-planted into his equipment bag. At 6' 3" and 200 pounds, Dale was hovering close to the fitness level he had attained as an All-American lacrosse player in college. Fortunately for me, that also included fine-tuned reflexes.

With one hand behind my back, he guided me away from his gear and into the living room. He ran his hand up the back of my neck and loosened the clip that held back my hair. He kissed me, while simultaneously unbuttoning my blouse.

I was overwhelmed by the sense of touch—and smell. I pulled

away, trying not to grimace. "Mr. Pedersen," I started in a mock judicial tone, "There is a clothing disparity between yourself and Mrs. Pedersen. You are attired in a mud-laced cotton jersey, while your counterpart is wearing a white silk shirt and power heels." I started backing towards the bedroom before I was ambushed. "Can you explain this disparity to the court?"

Dale skipped over an ottoman before I could remove my suit jacket. "If it pleases her honor, I submit that the disparity could be alleviated if all clothing were removed." And then he took off his shirt. Usually, one glimpse of Dale's bare chest was an instant aphrodisiac. But the pungent aroma of his manliness was unbearable.

I dropped the judicial charade and asked a legitimate question. "Dale, why have you been playing lacrosse on a Friday afternoon? Does Bobbie Macaluso play lacrosse? Are you trying to get 'trading tips from the master' in between body checks?"

Dale threw his shirt on the floor and walked off towards the kitchen. "I told you this morning that Bobbie wants everyone at Worthington to do some community service. I got this afternoon off to run a lacrosse clinic in Harlem." He flicked open a Coors with his thumb and took a swig. "Yes, I smell. But you need to get your head out of a perfume bottle and take a whiff of reality."

It was a valid point, so I headed to the bedroom to clear the air. I put on my analog to Dale's outfit—Hanro pajama bottoms and a Yale Tennis t-shirt. Then I went straight to the dining area to kick off the weekend with a glass of vodka. Maybe Dale wouldn't smell so bad after I consumed a shot of grain-based alcohol.

All of my choices were neatly arranged in the cabinet I had specially made for my 30th birthday. Any custom furniture is a luxury, but I had managed to triple the cost by insisting on the use of Russian larch wood. Sure, I could have trimmed the project budget by downgrading to larch wood from Canada. But that would have been like wearing Victoria's Secret instead of La Perla. I had standards.

The cabinet itself was about five feet wide, with two sets of doors on each side. A six inch high banding was mounted to the bottom of each shelf to ensure that the bottles wouldn't fall out should the cabinet doors be opened too brusquely. Dale declared that these retainers had "drunk-proofed" the cabinet. I disagreed, noting that the real problem was not inadvertently knocking over a bottle, but drinking a rare and expensive one. So I "drunk-proofed" the cabinet by installing a lock on the entire lower section.

I entered the requisite digits into the lock, and the cabinet doors gently sprung open. Front and center was the pride of my collection: over a dozen bottles, each one from a former United Soviet Socialist Republic country. Belarus. Georgia. And about eight countries ending with "-stan." Novelty, not quality, was the driver in assembling that lot of spirits.

My favorite bottle was an unopened Communist-era bottle of Stoli. It had an image of Lenin on the back label and all the markings were in Russian. It was a tribute to a bygone era, and I wondered when I'd ever open it. Maybe when I made partner at McCale, Morgan & Black. Next to the Stoli was Blue Ice, an unorthodox potato-based vodka, from, of course, Idaho. Then there was Belvedere, with its dreamy palace etched on the frosted bottle.

"What's it gonna be?" Dale had snuck into the dining room and stood behind me, whispering in my ear. His cheek lingered against mine, and I could feel the damp residue from the shower that he must have taken. He was crafty, determined, and convincing. Inspired by his overtures, I grabbed a French vodka with the image of frolicking polar bears on the bottle.

"Balinoff?" I offered. I quickly poured out two glasses. Dale drained his, grabbing my waist before I could make a toast, or more importantly, take a sip of the drink. He kissed me, the taste of the spirit still on his tongue. I pulled back, surprised at the unpleasant residue in my mouth. I smelled the liquid in my glass.

Undeterred, Dale started kissing my neck while I drank the Balinoff. It was sour. I didn't understand. Vodka was supposed to be smooth, subtle, crisp. I wriggled free, staring at the glass. "Does this taste weird to you?" I asked.

He backed off, his hands in a position of surrender. "Maxine, what is wrong with you? You're acting all weird with the smells and everything. What are you, pregnant?"

We stared at each other, mouths agape. I did some quick mental math, trying to pinpoint key milestone activities, i.e. ovulation, intercourse and my last period. Thoughts of sperm motility and pH levels passed through my mind. As did the lack of birth control.

Dale eased the glass from my hand before I could drop it. "Do you think you're pregnant?"

"Uh . . . well . . . I should have gotten my period by now, but with all the distractions from work, I had forgotten all about it."

"Does that mean you're pregnant?"

I took my drink back from Dale. "Probably," I said, and then I downed the rest of the vodka.

He looked down at me cautiously. "Can we still have sex?"

"Now?"

"Yes. Now." Dale adjusted his towel, which had almost fallen off. A drop of perspiration slid down from his neck and disappeared into the tuft of hair on his chest. If I really were pregnant and all the rumors were true, then the spontaneous glee of my sex life was about to transmogrify into a scheduled nuisance. I had to forestall the inevitable as long as possible.

I pulled off Dale's towel. I could get a pregnancy test later.

I finished the second of a bottle of water we had purchased while Dale unlocked the door to our apartment. Inside, he dumped five different kinds of pregnancy tests onto the kitchen counter. I looked at them with nervous fascination. All I had to do was add a little bodily fluid and we'd learn if there was a little Pedersen on the way. I crunched up the empty bottle and said, "I'm never going to be able to pee enough to use all of those tests at once. Maybe I should have some more water."

"I don't think so," said Dale. "If you keep drinking, you're going to dilute the test results."

I didn't know if his point was valid. I did know that drinking more water was a stall tactic. I had always told myself that I wanted to be a mother, but now the reality of the responsibility was starting to sink in.

We both opened a box. I unraveled a wad of instructions and started to read them. Dale pulled out the contents of his box, a plastic stick with a little window on one end and a brushy plastic tip on the other. He elbowed me and said, "I think you just pee on this part."

I looked at the rest of the contents of my box, which was basically the same thing. "I think I pee on this one too." I took it, as well as Dale's, to the bathroom.

"What about the other tests? Don't you want those?"

I called out from behind the bathroom door. "Two has to be enough. And if I'm not pregnant, we can save those other tests for next month." I went about my business in silence, but I could hear Dale deciphering the result indicators for the different tests.

"So listen. On one of those, if there's a cross in the middle, then it means you're pregnant. No cross means you're not pregnant. The other one has a dot instead of a cross to show that you're pregnant. Got it?"

I wasn't really listening. I just wanted to get out of the bathroom as quickly as possible and see the results. "Hey, can you get a paper towel? I don't want to put urine on the counter."

Dale pulled a bunch of sheets from the roll, folded them up and placed the mound on the counter. I tried to place the two active sticks on the paper towels, but they kept sliding off. I grabbed one of the tests and pounded it down on the paper towels.

"Hey! Hey! Hey!" he said, his voice rising. "Be careful of the test! You don't want to mess it up!"

We both checked the stick to make sure it wasn't broken. Apparently, it was fine, because a tiny red cross appeared in the plastic window. Dale picked up the other test and showed me the result, a tiny red dot on the plastic stick. My mouth opened. No words came out.

"Double confirmation!" he practically yelled. "We're gonna have a baby!" And then he hugged me so hard, I almost lost my balance. My eyes welled up with tears as he whispered in my ear, "I love you."

Dale, in his current state of wackadoodle joy, took me completely off guard. I reminded myself that he had been pressing for kids for quite some time. The beginning of his paternal pangs seemed to correspond to the start of his volunteer work running lacrosse clinics around the city. Dale Pedersen was Daddy Dale for one afternoon every month, and I think he found satisfaction in the role.

I fell into a stool by the counter. My most prominent emotion was womanly pride. Without much fanfare at all, I (with Dale's help) had become pregnant. It seemed like a natural course of events. I was about to produce a child, thereby perpetuating the human race on planet earth.

Philosophically, I loved the idea. But from a tactical standpoint, I had no idea what I had gotten myself into. It was hard to be joyous when facing the unknown. I assumed I would warm to the idea; in the meantime, Dale was more than over-compensating for my lack of enthusiasm.

"So, check it out," said Dale. "I know things are going to get really complicated and I am committed to helping. I already ordered dinner!" And on cue, the doorbell rang. Dale sprang to answer it. Within seconds he deposited a white plastic bag on the counter marked Upper East Side Sushi, my favorite take-out. "I ordered it on the way to Duane Reade. I knew you were pregnant; the tests just confirmed it. Anyway, I wanted to get something that you like to celebrate. What do you think?"

As he unloaded the order, the first waves of pregnancy paranoia rolled in. "I don't think I'm supposed to eat sushi when I'm pregnant. I remember Paola telling me that she couldn't have it."

Dale ate a piece of pickled ginger. "Maybe she has an allergy." Then he offered me a piece of spicy tuna roll, which I refused.

"Seriously, I think there's something with the raw fish. I should look it up."

I wanted to do just that, but Dale's glare paralyzed me. "Why don't you ask the inhabitants of the island nation of Japan what they do?" he stated sarcastically. "Sushi's got to be bad for you because, you know, the Japanese are known for their poor health and lack of intelligence."

I cracked a smile and then had a piece of *toro*. But I googled "sushi" and "pregnancy" anyway. I read from my phone. "O.K. You're right about the sushi. I can eat it, as long as it doesn't have high levels of mercury." I put the phone down incredulously.

"How am I supposed to know how much mercury is in the fish?" I didn't get a response as Dale was typing into his phone. If he was communicating with the outside world, it had to be about his impending admittance to the club of dads at Worthington. "You're not telling anyone yet, are you?!"

"What?!" he squeaked. Then he tossed his phone on the counter, as if the surrender of the device nullified what he had been doing two seconds prior.

"Dale, can we just wait a bit until we start blabbing to the world? We should go to the doctor and get everything checked out before we start telling people. It's nobody's business but ours right now."

Dale cocked his head sideways. As he spoke, his voice went up an entire octave. "Just a few people? Please?"

I took a seat, suddenly overwhelmed by the myriad changes about to foist themselves on my already over-committed life. I had nine months—or was it eight months?—to grow a baby in my stomach, prepare a household for its arrival, hire a nanny, stay fit, maintain my obligations as a wife to Dale and a friend to many, and somehow make partner at McCale. The fewer number of people who knew about my situation, the lower the odds that any changes to my behavior would be noticed. I hedged and asked, "Can we hold off on saying anything at least until we go to the doctor?"

"Fine," said Dale, as he gorged on a spider roll. A couple of deep-fried crustacean legs were still sticking out of his mouth when he said, "But we're going to have to tell your mother."

6

"*Yes, Mom. I'm pregnant.*" I abruptly pulled the phone away from my ear. From across the living room, even Dale could hear the feverishly loud shrieks through the receiver. I put my hand over the mouthpiece and whispered, "Maybe we should have waited. She's freaking out."

Dale flipped a page in the Marketplace section of *The Wall Street Journal* and smiled uneasily.

As the only child to Anna Marie and Stephen Nichols, I should have better anticipated my mother's joy-meets-hysteria reaction. After I explained to her that Dale and I had confirmed the results with two pregnancy tests, she finally settled down. That meant she could focus on the questions.

"So, eight months from now puts the baby due in the winter sometime. That's a good time to be pregnant. You're going to be so swollen and it would be so much worse in the humidity of the summer."

"I didn't think about that, Mom."

"Although I am concerned about you spending the last trimester on the subway, pregnant, during the busiest shopping season of the year. You'll have to just take a cab." Mom wasn't one for dirt and grime, which is why she lived in Westchester.

Thankfully, my dad interjected. "Does that mean the baby is coming in December or January?" This was a critical question to both my father, a tax accountant, and to Dale. An interest in numbers was about all that the two of them had in common, and I was surprised how much mileage could be derived from discussing the IRS tax code.

"We're thinking December. And yes, Dale is thrilled with the potential tax benefit."

"Well done, you two!" I didn't thank him because I hadn't planned it. And seriously, how could anyone think about taxes at a time like this?

"So when are you finding out the sex of the baby? When do they do that these days?" asked my mom.

"Uh, I'm not sure when we can find out." I sat back down on a broad chair in the living room and said, both to the phone and to Dale, "We definitely want to know the sex of the baby." Dale flapped his paper in agreement.

"When are you going to the doctor?"

"I don't know. I just found out I was pregnant like, ten minutes ago."

"Well, you better get there A.S.A.P. You have a good O.B./ Gyn., right? You need to get those visits scheduled immediately, especially with your crazy schedule."

My head was getting fuzzy. "Right, Mom. Whatever."

She huffed haughtily through the phone. "You know that Dale needs to come to the appointments too. That's what Nan Smithfield's son-in-law did. She said it really helped her daughter relax. And he's a better father because he was such an active participant in the pre-natal process. Is Dale there?"

I looked over at my husband, who was really challenging himself intellectually by adjusting his scrotum and reading the paper—at the same time. I handed him the phone. It seemed as if he were still reading as he graciously responded to what could only have been some bossy directives from my mother. He handed the phone back without smiling.

"Well, Dale seems very excited," said Mom. "He's going to take good care of you."

"What does that mean?" I asked. "I'm not an invalid."

"Actually," noted my dad, "you are technically categorized as 'disabled' by most health insurance companies."

My mom jumped in. "What I mean is, Dale can take care of you and the baby. Financially."

"Are you kidding me? I'm not quitting my job!" I let out a loud, nervous grunt. The notion of quitting work to be a stay-at-home mother had not even come up in conversation with Dale. I made a reassuring shrug in my husband's direction and then tried to explain a few things to my mother. "Mom, I didn't go to law school just so I could walk away from my job a few years later."

"But Dale makes a lot of money," said my mother, missing the point entirely.

"We're supposed to be equal contributors. We bought this co-op based on that assumption. Dale and I are in no shape to just eliminate a chunk of the household income."

"Well, maybe you shouldn't have bought the apartment until after the baby. If you had waited, you wouldn't be in this predicament."

"But we bought the apartment so we could have room *for* the baby." I went into the kitchen. I started to clean up the sushi debris as noisily as possible.

Dad broke in. "Well, it sounds like you're busy. Let us know when you go to the doctor so we know everything's O.K. Love you." And he hung up the phone. I wished I could do the same.

"You don't have to get so sensitive, Maxine. Although the hormones do go crazy when you're pregnant."

I crushed the Styrofoam containers and wadded up the plastic bags. "Got it, Mom. Thanks," I said loudly. "I'll talk to you later!"

"I'll call you at work tomorrow morning. We love you. And congratulations, dear."

Dale and I had collectively strategized to identify the optimal date and time for our first appointment with the obstetrician. He wanted a date shortly after an important Inter-Tech announcement. According to him, trade activity on one of his key stocks was the lightest a day or so after big news was released. I, on the other hand, was more concerned about the time when the appointment would be set. Anything scheduled over lunch would raise the fewest eyebrows. And since I wasn't telling a soul at McCale about my impending motherhood, I'd have to play the extended lunch card as long as possible.

All that coordination was for naught when we arrived at the obstetrician's office and were informed that the doctor was at the hospital. "One of her patients went into labor," explained the receptionist. "It can happen any time!" she said gleefully.

Dale and I stared at each other, in complete alignment over the fact that "anytime" was fine, as long as it didn't interfere with "our time."

"So, what does this mean?" I asked. "How long is she going to be?"

"I'm not sure," was the inconclusive response. "It usually takes about two hours, but since it's twins, it may take longer." Sensing our growing frustration, she offered, "You can sit right over there. We've got some bottled water and free Wi-Fi."

The syllables "Wi" and "Fi" seemed to send an electric shock up Dale's spine. He propped himself on the counter, his torso half way inside the opening to the receptionist's area, phone in hand. He was logging on to the system. "I see you don't utilize a system password for your network," he said, in a mildly scolding tone.

"Is that a problem? I'm sorry. I'm not responsible for the network! That's not my job!"

"Of course it's not your job," said Dale, as he loaded something onto his phone. "Your job is to ensure that my wife and unborn child get access to the best medical care your office can provide." That was probably over-stating and slightly misrepresenting her job description, but the receptionist wasn't provided the time to form a rebuttal. Dale shoved his phone in front of her face. "You see this?"

"It's a graph," communicated the receptionist flatly.

"You are correct. It's a graph. And it represents my job." A woman, way more pregnant than I was, entered the office. She waited to check in, but Dale was oblivious. He had a special gift for convincing others of his professional superiority, yet still inspiring empathy for the hard work required to maintain it. I turned to the woman and shrugged. She, like me, was going to have to wait.

Dale handed the receptionist his phone, imparting to her a level of trust, and more importantly, forcing her involvement in the conversation. "That graph shows the real-time performance of the stocks I monitor."

Her eyes glazed as she responded, "Wow. That's amazing." In truth, it was amazing. Bobbie Macaluso had commissioned the design of some proprietary stock-monitoring software for all the Worthington associates. It had a battery of alarm settings, customizable for the user. In other words, if Dale's stock fell below a given threshold, his phone would alarm, regardless of where he was. And that included the bathroom at Worthington, or so I had heard in gross detail from O'Shaughnessy.

Dale explained the features of the program to the receptionist. He showed her the downward trend of Inter-Tech. He instilled panic in her mind over the fact that, if the stock continued on its current trajectory, Dale could potentially lose millions of dollars for investors over the next few hours if he were trapped in a doctor's office, unable to react. This seemed ridiculous, and I surmised that Dale was showing her a graph of historical trading volume, not real-time information.

Nonetheless, his scheme started to work. She handed the phone back to Dale. "I'm not sure what I can do for you, Mr. Pedersen. Dr. Armstrong won't be back for a few hours. Do you want to reschedule? Or maybe you'd like to see Dr. Patel?" She started clacking on her keyboard. "Yes, Dr. Patel could see you right now. Come right on in." She buzzed the door and let us into the interior waiting room.

There was a reason Dr. Patel could see us right now. She was new. Her bio had been forwarded to all patients of the practice, undoubtedly in an effort to offload the workload of the other partners.

Dale played on his phone while the nurse collected all the

requisite diagnostic information: blood pressure, heart rate, weight, etc. When I disclosed the date of my last period, the nurse quickly deduced that the embryo inside me was probably around eight weeks old. She told me all about the fact that the "baby" was now a bunch of replicating cells about the size of a small kidney bean. The head and major organs had already started to develop. Next month, it would have webbed hands, maybe even fingernails. I looked down at my stomach, and all I could see was a tiny bit of bloating.

Logically, none of it made sense. All this stuff was going on at a microscopic level inside my body, yet I had no direct supervision over any of it. Not like I was qualified to oversee the physical development of the fetus. *Grow arm, here! Make legs longer!* While this little thing toiled away on its own schedule, my job was to be an enabler. I was supposed to give it everything it needed to fulfill its purpose, to grow into a healthy person. *Eat right.* Check. *Don't smoke.* Check. *Don't drink alcohol.* Uh oh.

Vodka, wine, probably a few cordials . . . all consumed after conception. Had I already impaired the development of my poor child's brain? Had I already done irreversible damage to the heart and the spinal cord?

Addressing the alcohol-consumption-before-knowledge-of-conception issue soon became Topic #1 to discuss with Dr. Patel. Dale and I were a bit impatient, as even though Dr. Patel had been billed as available "right now," it took her fifteen minutes to join us.

The door opened slowly, and Dr. Patel entered slowly. She had the gait and the frailty of an 80-year-old woman. Her metabolism likely rivaled that of a growing turnip. Her wrinkle-free complexion was the most telling indicator of her age; she had to be in her late 20's. Which meant that she was fresh out of her medical residency. My immediate thought: no matter how inexperienced she was, she couldn't screw up an ultrasound.

Her elocution was painstakingly deliberate. If this was her pace of delivering patient care, she'd have a short-lived practice in New York City. "So, Dr. Patel. I have a question about some of my behavior prior to learning that I was pregnant."

"Please lie down, Mrs. Pedersen," instructed Dr. Patel, patently ignoring my question. "I am going to perform a pelvic examination. Please relax."

"Why are you doing that?" asked Dale, his voice a squeamish panic. "Can't you just do an ultrasound?"

Dr. Patel probed around my private parts with surprising and much appreciated efficiency. She removed and discarded her rubber glove, and then helped me sit up. "Everything seems normal," she said. Now that the invasive patient interaction was over, an air of relief seemed to infuse her with confidence. "And it is too early in the process for an ultrasound. You'll get one some time in the next trimester. There's nothing to worry about."

"Are you sure about that?" I asked. "I was eating and drinking all kinds of things before I knew I was pregnant. How am I going to know that the baby is O.K.? What if something's wrong?"

Dr. Patel entered some data into the laptop in the office and addressed my concerns with what seemed like the canned answer for every other mother who had come in with the same freaked out questions. "At this point, you know to avoid alcohol while you are pregnant. The nurse will give you a packet of information about all the important pre-natal activities, food choices and supplements you should take." She shut the laptop. "Right now, you're going to get some blood work done. That will tell us if there are any major problems, genetic issues, etc."

"And how long does that take to come back?" asked Dale, always anxious for data.

"About three business days. We'll contact you if there are any problems."

Not satisfied with that answer, Dale followed up with, "How much would it cost to get the tests expedited?"

Dr. Patel looked at her watch. Then she gave Dale and me the once over. "You two look very healthy. Is there a history of Down's Syndrome in either family?"

"No," we replied.

"Developmental delays, physical or mental?"

"No."

"Autism?"

"No."

"Spinda Bifida?"

"What?"

She put her hand on the handle of the door. "My best advice for you is to not go looking for problems with the baby. Your blood pressure is excellent. You're close, but not yet 35, so you are not a high-risk pregnancy. Your family history is solid. I can't make any promises, but it looks like this will be a very ordinary pregnancy. Any other questions?"

Dale and I had none. But for the first time in my life, I was happy to be average.

7

"*So This is where* you practice your magic!" Jacques Deschemel was standing, unexpectedly, in my office. I glanced out to Joy and then winked in appreciation. Other secretaries might have pulled the gate-keeper card, eliminating any sort of impromptu interruptions by unannounced guests. Joy, however, was shrewd enough to allow select people the privilege.

I couldn't have been happier to see him. Our McCale team had exceeded Jacques's expectations, and I was proud to be leading the charge. Working with a pioneer like Deschemel was a rarefied experience. Here was a man, who, in the twilight of his years, was on the cutting edge of innovation. Jacques refused to let his company stagnate. And the innovations kept coming: new products, new markets, new ingredients. Happily, I, along with my team, was there every step of the way to legally protect him.

He gave me a kiss on both sides of the cheek.

"*Merci* for stopping by, Monsieur Deschemel. *Assiez-vous, s'il vous plaît.*"

Jacques sat down, as I had offered. "Your French is flawless, Maxine. Did you study in France?"

"I did take a semester in Paris, while I was in college. I was researching France's role in the American Revolution. Le Marquis de Lafayette, Ben Franklin. That whole crew. Practicing the language was an added bonus."

"Well, if you ever get tired of New York, you could always work in France. The lifestyle is much more, eh, civilized." While I did love my time in France, Dale and I were committed to raising our family in Manhattan. Besides, Dale would go bonkers transitioning from the global eminence of the S&P 500 to the regional coterie of the CAC 40. I acknowledged Jacques's comment with a sustained smile and then inquired as to the purpose of his visit.

Jacques opened the leather case at his feet. "I have some news," he said. He pulled out a small bottle, about half the size of a soda can, and put it on my desk. "I'm also here on unofficial Parfum Aix business. Well, sort of Parfum Aix business, but not exactly."

He seemed nervous about something, which was completely adorable, so I eased him through his befuddlement. "O.K. First tell me about the official Parfum Aix news."

"That is simple. I am returning to France."

I was shocked. Well, sort of shocked. Why would I be shocked? Jacques Deschemel was French. He lived in France. Of course he'd be returning there. "Well, of course you are," I said. "We will coordinate with whomever you designate as your local representative and liaise with you while you are back home. You're returning to Grasse, or

Paris?" It didn't really matter where he was going. I was running at the mouth on lawyer-speak auto-pilot, trying to determine how his departure was going to affect McCale's effectiveness as corporate counsel.

"Vivienne Suivant is the acting head of the American offices for Parfum Aix. I believe you have met her once or twice." Vivienne was hard to forget. Glamorous, flirtatious and creative, she was the yin to Caine Seaver's yang. Vivienne's introduction to the scene would complicate my job ten-fold. Exactly what I needed now that I was with child.

'Yes. Vivienne will do a wonderful job," I lied. "So what is the non-Parfum Aix news?"

Jacques pointed to the bottle on my desk. "That." I picked it up, assuming it was a prototype for a new line of Parfum Aix perfumes. I was about to take a whiff when I was cautioned by its creator. "It may not be what you think."

I sniffed the contents of the bottle. My eyes moistened from the pungent, alcoholic aroma, my face contorting in confusion. "Is that . . . gin?" I sniffed it again, now with a clearer expectation of what was in the bottle. It smelled botanical and floral, but had an unpleasant isopropyl undertone.

He hunched over in his chair, giving a few furtive looks around the empty room. "No one can know about it!" I felt like I was in a bit of a gray area. He had said this wasn't Parfum Aix business, yet he was confiding in me. About alcohol.

I hunched back. "No one can know about what?"

"*Créneau!*" he exclaimed.

"What?" I asked, trying to translate the term.

"*Créneau*! It means to put something in reverse. It's what I am calling the gin you just sniffed."

I looked back at the bottle. "You made this?" He nodded.

Now I really wanted to try it. I felt like I was supposed to take a surreptitious sip in the office. Ordinarily, I would have done it. But I was anything but ordinary now—I was pregnant. "Wow," I said, stalling. "I would love to try this, but. . ." And I waved at Joy, who had been watching the entire exchange through the glass window.

Jacques collected himself. "Well, of course not now! That's the last thing you should be doing in the office! Someone might smell it on your breath and then the secret would be out." In more ways than one, I thought. "Let me explain. I was so inspired by your exposition on Bombay Sapphire gin that I decided to try to make it myself. I started backwards, though, with the herbs first, not the alcohol. So I made it in reverse!"

"And that's where the name came from? *Créneau?*"

"*Exactemente.* It's just a side hobby right now, but I thought you would be the perfect person to test-taste my prototypes. But I don't want to over-step my bounds . . . ."

Pregnant or not, this was one opportunity that I wasn't going to let slide. "You're not over-stepping, and I can't tell you how much I appreciate your respect for my opinion." I wrote down my home address on a card and handed it to Jacques. "You should probably send the prototypes to my home, rather than to the office. It's just simpler that way."

Jacques stood up to leave. "Wonderful. I am excited to learn your opinion of the first prototype. A woman of your age has the perfect palate!"

Like alcohol, caffeine was to be avoided during pregnancy. However, the time had come when I had to decide whether the miniscule odds of negatively impacting the fetus's development by drinking a cup of coffee would outweigh the joy and relief I would attain if I could just have a bowel movement.

So I drank that cup of coffee. And nothing happened.

I was tempted to drink another when I pulled on my last pair of "fat pants," only to learn that I could barely button them. The metal clasp that was supposed to reinforce the button had bent 45 degrees when I tried to secure it. Did I finally need maternity clothes because I had gained baby weight, or was it because I was constipated? The answer was irrelevant. Shopping for maternity clothes was a loathsome indicator that my body was changing, probably altered forever, and I had to buy a whole new wardrobe just to clothe it.

Bloated from the early summer heat, I hopped the Lexington Avenue subway line downtown. It was Saturday, which meant no commuters, so I could sit down for the short ride. I planted myself on an orange molded seat next to a window. Whizzing by the blackened steel columns of the NYC subway system was hypnotic and strangely calming. It was a helpful aid to sorting out the myriad issues on my mind. And maybe the vibrations from the train would help me go to the bathroom.

I got off at 59th Street and headed towards a cluster of maternity shops. I glanced through the shop windows of each one, ranking them by apparel style, selection, and most importantly, a minimalist approach to decorating with pastel colors. After all, maternity clothes were for me, not the baby. A new shop, Mother of Manhattan, won the prize. I entered forthwith.

I was immediately descended upon by a perky young associate. Judging from her size zero capri khakis and skin-tight halter top, this sweet young thing was probably just out of adolescence. I felt fatter already. "Welcome to Mother of Manhattan! Are you shopping for yourself, or for a friend?" That must have been MoM code for, "I can't tell if you, dear customer, are pregnant. So better to err on the side of a well-placed compliment if you are, and avoid an insult if you're not." Christine, as her name tag identified her, was now on my good side.

"I'm the pregnant one," I admitted. "I haven't been shopping for maternity clothes, so I have no idea what size I am."

Christine smiled broadly as she sized me up. "How far along are you? It must be early, because you don't seem to be showing."

Yes, an un-tucked ruffled tunic and tights can do wonders. "I'm just entering the second trimester."

Christine seemed genuinely surprised. "Really? Well, you look great." More points for Christine, as she insightfully guided me past the casual clothes up front to a section with fashionable (at least by maternity standards) professional attire.

I gestured at a few items that seemed to suit my style. Almost everything was black. Some of the dresses were brighter, but considering that I would be sporting the clothes through the fall and winter, I communicated my interest in just accessorizing with color. For me and my growing belly, black was beautiful.

After trying on the first pair of pants, I realized that I was too large for the first trimester line of clothing. Christine expertly spun this in the positive: I had saved several hundred dollars by avoiding the purchase of a set of clothes that I could no longer wear.

At that point, I stopped looking at the price tags. It was hard enough to look in the mirror. Despite Christine's excellent salesmanship, my style of dress had transitioned from tailored and chic to comfortable and utilitarian. The concept that I had already saved money, coupled with my sudden urge to speedily remove myself from Mother of Manhattan, fueled one of my most expensive shopping sprees to date.

Sensing my tension, Christine noted that one of the benefits of buying such good quality maternity clothing was that I would be able to wear it all again when I got pregnant with my next child. I had to applaud her optimism. But I had other plans for the clothes after I gave birth, and they did not include taking up my precious Manhattan closet space. A bonfire on my apartment rooftop with some stretchy maternity pants as tinder was more like it.

I texted Paola while Christine rang up my purchases. I had finally been able to get her to commit to a social outing by telling her that I was pregnant. I guess she knew my days of socializing were numbered. Distracted by the logistical gymnastics required to schedule a date with Paola, I inadvertently handed Christine my business card, rather than a credit card.

"A lot of customers tell me that the most stressful part of pregnancy is organizing their household to prepare for life with baby." Christine handed back my card.

Flustered, I juggled my phone and wallet. I wasn't sure how to acknowledge her comment, since I hadn't even begun to deal with what she was talking about.

"I've heard of some pretty good nanny agencies if you're interested."

"Really? That would be a fantastic help!" I sputtered.

She closed out my transaction, and then wrote down a few names on some receipt paper. "I hear about these three all the time. I can't vouch for any of them personally, but this one is supposed to be the most comprehensive." She placed her pen next to the first name, NYC Baby Prep.

"By 'comprehensive' do you mean 'expensive'?" I was only half joking.

"I don't know. Check it out for yourself." She walked me to the front of the clothing store and winked. "It might be a good fit for you."

8

Visiting McCale on the weekend was like working at a different company. The lights were dimmed, the air was stagnant, cubicles were empty. My heart-rate always slowed a few beats as my body acclimated to the space. Occasionally, I would see someone, but any interaction was brief as conversing would have lengthened the amount of time both parties would have to spend at the office. Everyone at McCale knew that mindless chit-chat negatively impacted billable hours, even on the weekends.

I settled into my desk and immediately started doing things completely not associated with Parfum Aix, administrivia, or anything else related to my job. Rather, I went straight to the mommy-prep websites recommended by Christine. I spent a solid hour comparing the offerings between them. It seemed that conducting a nanny search was the main focus of these organizations. Some offered a simple matching between an online questionnaire and the nannies they had on staff. Most agencies provided a full background check and health inquiry for each potential employee. Then there was NYC Baby Prep.

NYC Baby Prep took the nanny search to new horizons of simplicity and convenience. They offered a version of interviewing in a speed dating format. They had an in-house decorating staff. They had lactation consultants, life coaches, therapists, yoga instructors, dieticians. While I doubted that I'd need all of these services, it was nice to know there was a one-stop shop for all of my needs, should they ever arise.

Fully convinced that NYC Baby Prep was the right choice, I clicked on the tab marked "Pricing." They offered package pricing and à la carte services. Unfortunately, no prices were available online. Rather, an application had to be completed so the agency could customize a program just for me. Once the application was completed, I would qualify for a free consultation, and then learn about the cost.

NYC Baby Prep's approach seemed somewhat obnoxious since other agencies had posted their rates online. I could only imagine that NYC Baby Prep's rates had to be astronomical. But there was only one way to find out. I clicked on the "Start Application" button.

A workflow graphic topped the page. Apparently, the application was lengthy enough to necessitate a picture to help potential customers know where they were in the process of completing it. Bubble #1 on the workflow, Family Information, only required about 10 minutes to complete. It was basic contact information, employers, etc. Bubble #2, Parental Profile, necessitated more time. It required a description of my job and Dale's, and a summary of any challenges these positions placed on rearing a child. Bubble #3 covered Parenting Philosophy and #4 was Financial Information.

There was no way I would have the time to complete the application at this point, as #3 required some thought and #4 required Dale. I printed out the remaining questions as a physical reminder that I was close to qualifying for my free consultation with NYC Baby Prep. I figured they'd hound me electronically, too, now that I had set up an email password.

On the way out of the office, I stopped in the break room for a bottle of water and some pretzels. I heard a dragging, scratching noise along the hallway near the elevator. The sounds of a mother scolding her child became increasingly loud, as the two approached my location. I knew before she rounded the corner that Nancy Lallyberry and offspring were about to make an entrance.

"Oh, Maxine! What are you doing here on a Saturday?" Nancy and her little charge stopped dead in their tracks when they saw me.

"Hey, Nancy. I'm here probably doing the same thing you are—cleaning up odds and ends." I looked down at her son. "And how are you doing . . . uh . . ." I couldn't remember the boy's name. Nancy was so busy fluttering around the office that she almost never talked about her son.

"Troy. And he's three."

I straightened up and said more authoritatively, "So what's up, Troy?" He ignored me, preferring to roll the train in his hand squarely across the cabinets in the break room. Nancy's arm lurched out, grabbing the toy before any damage was done. Not to be out-maneuvered, Troy took the train in his other hand and dragged it across the stainless steel refrigerator door. I winced.

"Troy is going to watch a show while I attempt to catch up on some work," said Nancy. She dropped her satchels and muscled the train out of Troy's hand. "You want to watch Handy Manny?"

"Handy Manny! Yeah!" Troy jumped around exuberantly.

I knew practically nothing about children's programming. Here was a chance to get a leg up on it from a true fan. I bent over and asked, "So who is this Handy Manny person? Is he as cool as Dora the Explorer?"

Troy dropped his shoulders in disgust. Even Nancy rolled her eyes. "Dora's lame! Handy Manny is awesome!"

It may not have been the most descriptive explanation, but Troy made his point. If I were pregnant with a girl, I'd be wise to avoid purchasing a Dora the Explorer bumper set.

Troy started rifling through Nancy's satchel and pulled out her tablet. "C'mon Mom!"

"Just a minute, Troy! Wait until we get to my office!" The sternness of her voice upset the boy, and he immediately broke down in tears. Nancy stood there unemotionally, like this had happened a hundred times before. After about 10 seconds of wailing, which seemed like 15 minutes to me, Nancy got to her knees and gave Troy a hug. That reduced the wailing to whimpering.

She stood up and put her back to Troy. Frustrated by what I had to assume was a lack of attention, he ran his arm along the top of the break room table, knocking everything to the floor. My papers were strewn everywhere, and Nancy and I scurried to pick them up. It was then that I realized that Troy had papered the room with my partially completed NYC Baby Prep application.

Nancy was gleefully scanning the pages. I was so grateful that I hadn't filled out any of the financial information. It was bad enough that she now knew my secret. But she would have been intolerable if she had seen Dale's salary. It had to eclipse her husband's electrician's paycheck by at least five-fold. She collected what she had and handed the pile to me. "You're pregnant?" she asked.

"Indeed," I admitted.

"Are you serious? You're pregnant?!"

"Yup," I reiterated patiently. "I'm in the second trimester right now."

Nancy went over to the counter and gave Troy a bag of pretzels. "You know, I thought something was up when you started wearing sweaters and jackets more often with your suits. And you looked so tired over the last few weeks. I knew it! I knew you were pregnant!"

I casually tried to look down at my belly to see if any evidence of a bump was present from under my loose-fitting top. There was, sort of. I had to stand up straight to get rid of it. None of this was lost on Nancy, who could not stop talking.

"So, what are you going to do? Are you going to work? I mean, you're so successful. I can't imagine you'd ever quit. What would we do without you? What would I do without you? I need another working mom around here."

I picked up my bag, hoping to demonstrate my desire to end the conversation. "Well, yes, I'm going to continue working. We've got the nanny search going . . . ."

"Oh, nannies!" exclaimed Nancy. "We had such a problem with that. So hard to find someone reliable. And it's expensive! But you guys can afford it. Dale's a banker, right? You're so lucky."

If I were so lucky, then why did I have to stand there and feign interest in her gossipy drivel? I reminded myself to remain professional. If I was going to be a partner at McCale someday, I needed to cultivate my counseling capabilities. "Well, Nancy, I could probably get some advice from you. You'll have to tell me sometime how you manage it all."

"Yes! I'd love that! We should do lunch!"

"Sure," I committed as evasively as possible.

"What about next week? Maybe Monday?"

The last way I wanted to start a work week was a lunch with

Nancy Lallyberry. "I'm kind of buried in Parfum Aix right now, but maybe when the dust clears, we can do something fun. I'll get back to you."

As I gathered my things to leave, I caught a bitter scowl on Nancy's face. I reminded myself to follow up with her on Monday, just to make sure I hadn't burned any bridges. Hell hath no fury like a Nancy scorned.

9

Dale and I were running close to half an hour late for cocktails with Paola and her husband. Despite my newly augmented wardrobe, I just could not find anything to wear. I finally threw on the simplest thing I could find, a black, Empire-waist dress. It made my boobs look gigantic. Dale assured me that they, I mean I, looked fantastic.

When we arrived at Osetra, Paola waved us over to her table. Dale and I weaved through the maze of lacquered white bar stools and lacquered black table tops. Maneuvering over the marble floor in heels was treacherous, even when I wasn't pregnant. That, coupled with the red walls and excessive gold decorative accents, begat an environment far from calming. But with less than five months of child-free days left in my life, I wanted to seize every opportunity I could to enjoy the Manhattan nightlife. So what if it was only eight o'clock and I was ready for a nap? I couldn't drink the cocktails at Osetra, but I could soak up the atmosphere.

"Sorry we're late!" I apologized and blamed it on the traffic.

Rather than hug me, Paola grabbed my arms and raised them out to either side of my body. That constricted my dress, revealing a slight bulge in my tummy. "Oh, my God! You're showing already!"

Nelson, Paola's husband, made her put my arms down. "You look beautiful," he said and gave me a hug. Then he gave Dale a heartfelt and very manly handshake. "You ready for this?"

"I was born ready," replied Dale in mock seriousness. "This is going to be a breeze."

Nelson, about the same height as Dale but without the muscle tone, puffed out his chest. "You'll be singing a different tune at three o'clock in the morning when you have to get out of bed to change a diaper."

Dale shrugged. "Are you kidding me? Maxine's gonna do that."

"Dale, are you in for an awakening!"

"In more ways than one, right?!" Dale forced out a laugh, but no one was laughing with him. His expression morphed to conciliatory. He draped his arm around Nelson's shoulder. "C'mon, professor. You know I'm just busting on you."

I knew he was busting on Nelson because he always busted on Nelson. Nelson was an irresistible target for Dale's residual frat boy mischief. What surprised me was Nelson's continued gullibility. He always seemed to fall for Dale's predictable gags. And of all people, Nelson should have been able to identify such behavior—he was an Associate Professor of Anthropology at NYU.

We all took a seat, and I took a menu. Osetra specialized in serving miniature versions of classic Russian and Eastern European fare, tapas style. Also available was a full caviar menu. Sadly, caviar was discouraged for pregnant women. Maybe there was something karmically wrong with eating the unfertilized eggs of another species while my own inseminated egg bloomed inside of me.

Osetra also offered a wide array of vodka, spirits and Champagne. The bar was renowned for its specialty cocktails and between the four of us, we had tried them all.

Paola spoke up first. "I know we have some toasting to do with regards to the little Pedersen that's on the way . . . ." She smiled so infectiously that I found myself grinning happily too. "But first of all, I'd like to know how Maxine is surviving without her beloved vodka. Seriously, honey, I would have expected you to get a surrogate just so you wouldn't have to give up the habit."

"Ha. Ha. Ha," I acknowledged. "Mother Nature is awesome. I have no interest in drinking. Just the thought of it makes me ill." It was true. Over the last few weeks, my stomach roiled at the thought of drinking even a sip of vodka. I amused myself by ordering virgin Seabreezes—cranberry and grapefruit juices, both of which were highly recommended by Dr. Patel.

"Fine then," said Paola. "Tell me what you think I should get."

I studied the menu. There would be no Sputnik, a drink that featured grain alcohol, a.k.a. moonshine, for me. Nor could I have the cocktail I had created after a work week from hell, the Gulag. The Gulag looked like blood in a Martini glass, which, to the trendy New York cocktail crowd, was something to embrace. By popular demand, the Osetra management had added the Gulag to their menu.

Dale must have noticed me reminiscing because he said, "Well, I'm going to have a Gulag."

"Me, too," copied Nelson.

"What does it say about a person, Nelson, if he voluntarily

orders a drink named after a miserable work prison?" asked Dale curiously.

Nelson was happy to oblige that question with a long-winded answer. I studied the menu, knowing full well what Dale was up to. Half-way through his oration, Nelson realized that Dale had only asked the question so he could sneak a peek at his phone.

Last New Year's Eve, the four of us had made the regrettable pledge to not use our phones for an entire year when we went out together. At the time, under the influence of Champagne and revelry, it seemed like a great idea. Unfortunately, Nelson was now the only one of the group who still wanted to abide by the commitment, and he wasn't going to let any of us renege.

He leaned forward onto the table like he was studying a primate. Dale kept clacking. "And what does it say about a person, DALE," he said loudly, "who utilizes the tools of deception to indulge a habit of rudeness and forfeit his end of a social contract?"

Dale may have been the first at the table to break the rule, but Paola was hot on his trail. "Look!" I re-directed, "She's doing it, too!"

There she was, scrolling through her own device, all within inches of Nelson's right elbow. "You've got to be kidding me, Paola!"

"I'm sorry, but we are supposed to hear any time now whether we won this huge proposal I've been working on. It's worth about $100 million!"

A figure in the millions of dollars was mentioned. Dale's Pavlovian response kicked in and he perked up immediately. "Is that 100 million in one year or over the span of years?"

"It's over five years," Paola admitted. "But still, 20 million in revenue is great for the company."

Dale nodded in concurrence.

"I should say so!" Nelson's reaction was probably a mix of pride in his wife's potential achievement and perplexity that such a huge sum of money could be thrown around while people were starving in America.

The server approached to take our orders. Dale leaned his head back and said, pointing to himself and Nelson, "We'll have two Gulags."

Paola was still absorbed with her device. "Now you're driving me crazy," I said. It was time for some cocktail warfare. I turned to the waitress and said, "You ready for this? I'm going to give you something new. She'll have one part Absinthe, two parts ginger beer with some vodka and . . ." I thought for a moment about how to bring the flavors together. I needed something sweet, but not sugary. ". . . And a dash of grapefruit bitters. Have the bartender correct it." The waitress nodded in compliance and headed off. It was fun being a regular at Osetra.

"How did you come up with that?" asked Paola.

Dale stepped in with an explanation. "Maxine has every wine and liquor app ever created. Seriously, if she were allowed to use her phone, *Nelson*, she could show you."

"Nope," said Nelson, sounding superior. "I'll just try the concoction when it gets here."

"O.K.," said Paola. "What did you get me?"

"I just made it up. Whatever it is should make an impact because Absinthe is supposed to make you crazy."

"They should call it the Nut Job," offered Dale.

"That doesn't sound very Russian," I said, although I had to laugh at the thought of ordering one.

"Then how about the Chernobyl?" said Paola.

Nelson rubbed his chin. "Interesting. What about the Moscow Meltdown?"

I ordered a bunch of plates while the rest of the group debated the name for the new cocktail. Once a consensus was reached—Chernobyl was the winner—a silence draped the table. Dale and Paola seemed handicapped without their phones. Despite the periodic buzzing, no one dared reach for their device—Nelson was hell-bent on enforcing the rules. The polite thing was talk about the baby.

10

"*So Nelson,*" *said Dale.* "Tell me the top three things I need to know about being a great dad." And he meant it. Despite his habitual ribbing on Nelson, Dale actually respected the guy's opinion.

"Well, first and foremost," began Nelson, "Never tell Maxine that she looks fat."

Paola almost fell off her stool. "Oh, my God! Never do that!"

Did that mean that I was going to look fat? I felt fat. And I had barely started gaining weight. I looked desperately at Dale. "You don't look fat," he said.

"Next," continued Nelson, "This is a good one. Every now and then, surprise Maxine and take the baby out of the apartment so she can take a nap." He leaned across the table towards Dale. "Major points for that one, believe me."

Paola smiled sweetly at Nelson and rubbed his hand. "Just because Amanda is almost a year old doesn't mean that you can't still surprise me, honey."

"Yes, well, the need was more acute right after you gave birth. Now, thankfully, we have help. Which brings me to my final, and maybe most important piece of advice: get as much help as you can from as many sources as possible. Turn no one down. Call in favors. Engage parents. With two people working, you guys are going to have your hands full." Nelson squeezed Paola's hand. "I don't know what we'd do without your mother helping out."

I perked up, feeling that I might actually be ahead of the curve because of the research I had done about nanny agencies. "Did you guys use a nanny search agency? Have you heard of NYC Baby Prep?"

"NYC Baby Prep?" asked Paola incredulously. "You mean NYC Wallet Dump? That place is expensive."

"Yeah, but have you seen what they provide? And you don't have to buy the full service package."

Dale pulled out his phone. "What's the place called?"

"No, no, no," warned Nelson. We agreed we weren't using our phones."

"C'mon, Nelson. This is different. Hell, I'm just trying to follow your advice."

Nelson conceded, while Dale mouthed the words to the agency as he typed the address. "I think you'll be impressed, Dale," I offered. "I already started filling out the application. We get a free consultation."

He was barely registering my comments. Dale scrolled through the website with one hand while taking a huge gulp of water with the other. Then he put the phone down, put his hand on his neck and gesticulated in his chair like he needed the Heimlich. Nelson perked up and then realized that Dale was kidding. Sort of. "Holy shit. You have got to be kidding me. This place is ridiculous."

"I can't comment because I don't have the prices yet to compare them to the other agencies."

"Newsflash: this place will drain our retirement fund." Dale looked back down at the website and read, "'NYC Baby Prep Astrological Chart. Provide us with a small branch of your family tree and a few key dates, and we will leverage the heavens to read your baby's future!'" He tossed the device on the table. "Give me a fucking break."

Mercifully, the server arrived with our food—teacups of Borscht, mini Chicken Kiev appetizers, a cucumber-dill salad. My eyes started watering. Instantly, I wondered if a pregnancy-induced hormonal imbalance had triggered my tear ducts to start working. But then my mouth and tongue gushed with water, and I started gagging. I grabbed a napkin and ran straight to the bathroom.

Actually, I ran and walked. The stimulation of running seemed to bring up the contents of my stomach, but walking wasn't going to get me there in time. I thought everything was under control when I got behind the door of the ladies' room. However, the relief of being able to throw up in private seemed to encourage the act of reverse peristalsis.

For the next few minutes, I learned just how well the Osetra janitorial staff cleaned the toilets. It was enough to make me puke.

After my episode, I washed my hands and my mouth. There was no evidence of any vomit on my dress, which was fortuitous. I wiped off my face and proceeded back to the table as if nothing had happened.

Dale got up and helped me to my stool. "Are you all right? Is this a pregnancy thing? I haven't seen you throw up before."

Paola chimed in. "You haven't mentioned any morning sickness."

"How can she have morning sickness when it's nine o'clock at night?" asked Nelson.

I settled back in. "I'm fine. No big deal. I thought nausea was supposed to happen in the first trimester, so it will probably just go away." Still uncomfortable, I looked about the table for the problem. "That," I said, pointing to the pickled cucumber salad, "has got to go, though."

Dale immediately whisked it away, dumping it onto the un-bussed table behind us. "By the way," he said, "your phone has been buzzing like crazy. Maybe the battery is low or something. You should check it out." Dale looked impishly at Nelson.

"Permission to view the phone," I said to Nelson in a robotic tone.

"Permission granted. But just to turn it off."

I couldn't believe my eyes when I saw the screen. I had received a battery of emails and texts all on the same subject, "Re: Maxine Pedersen is expecting a baby!"

"What the. . . ?" My voice dropped off as I tried to find the original message.

"Holy shit!" said Dale, craning to read my phone. "What's that about?"

Nelson's neck grew about two inches longer and he said, "O.K., O.K. I can see it's not broken. Put it away."

When I saw the author of the initial message—the message that had generated everyone else's responses—I almost threw up again. But I should have known. Nancy Lallyberry.

Nancy had sent an email to the entire staff at McCale, Morgan & Black announcing my pregnancy. As an added bonus, she had entreated everyone on her list to email me so they could congratulate me personally.

I was too flummoxed to read any of the responses from the continuous pinging of messages. And if my email was getting stuffed, then so was almost everyone else's. The majority of the messages I received had been tagged "Reply All." Anyone who received the original message was now also receiving congratulatory messages meant for me, but for some unknown reason, everyone else needed to read. The partners—Caine and Deirdre in particular—would be furious with the distractions. I hated "Reply All." And I hated Nancy Lallyberry.

Dale sat up and apprised Nelson of the goings-on. "It's just a bunch of congratulatory emails for Maxine from everyone at work." Then Dale asked me, "Did you send out an announcement right before we came here or something? Why are they all coming now?"

I dropped my phone on the table and took a small sip of Dale's Gulag. "No, I didn't send anything out. That wench Nancy Lallyberry announced my pregnancy without my permission in an email to the entire office."

"You haven't told your office yet?" asked Nelson. "Don't you think everyone already knows at this point?"

"Why are you on her side?!" I almost shouted. I desperately looked to Paola for support. Unbeknownst to the rest of us, she had taken the opportunity to check her own phone and was just placing it back into her purse. Her eyes were bulging as she tried to control herself. "What?!" I demanded.

"Nothing . . . . It's nothing." She let out some of her breath but still looked like she was going to pop.

Dale leaned onto the table. "You got that job, didn't you? The $100 million contract, right?!"

"Yes!" Paola pumped her hands in the air in an annoying raise-the-roof-type send-up. "We totally did! Can you believe it? I am so psyched!" And then she put her hands together and rambled off some stuff in Spanish.

Ordinarily, I would have been very happy for her. I tried to smile enthusiastically. But having Nancy Lallyberry take control over my personal announcement had made my blood boil.

Nelson, ultimately proud of his wife's achievements, waved over the server. "Hey there! We need some Champagne to celebrate some exciting news. How about a bottle of Dom Pérignon?"

"Absolutely! And congratulations!" The server looked at me when he said it. Immediately, I realized that he thought we were getting Champagne to celebrate my pregnancy.

"Oh no!" I said, as he started away.

"You don't want any Champagne?" He looked crestfallen by the loss of his tip for bringing it over. Meanwhile, everyone else just looked annoyed at my lack of excitement for my friend's incredible professional achievement.

Pregnancy was not an excuse for cattiness, I thought. Nancy Lallyberry's stupid antics shouldn't ruin Paola's moment. I carried on bravely. "I meant, no, we don't want the Dom. Bring us something better. Do you have any Cristal?"

11

When I arrived at the office, Joy was already there. My trusted administrative helper had a huge basket of baby goodies on her desk, which she ceremoniously presented to me. The most striking thing about it was its size. Joy took the subway from Queens every day, and I couldn't imagine her trucking this thing around Penn Station during rush hour. No wonder she had come in early.

Inside the basket, which was covered with thick plastic wrap, was an array of unisex baby sundries. There were brands I had heard of—Johnson & Johnson, Carter's—and then some words that were totally unfamiliar, like "layette." I wasn't sure what to make of everything that was in there, but the gesture was touching.

Thank goodness I had given her a bottle of wine for her birthday last month.

I put the gift on the credenza in my office. Joy shifted into professional mode and reported, "The Parfum Aix meeting will be upstairs in Conference Room B."

"Right. I'm headed up there right now." I looked at my watch, noting that I had about two minutes to get to the meeting before Caine would start it punctually at nine. Nonetheless, I had to duck into the bathroom beforehand, so I grabbed my meeting items and took care of business.

I charged out of the ladies room and collided with Jacques's replacement, Vivienne Suivant. Unfazed, she just stepped back to allow me some room. Then she smiled, her grin unfurling in a controlled, almost theatrical movement. As we greeted each other, I couldn't resist admiring her outfit. She was fantastically chic.

On top, she was wearing a black chiffon blouse. Ruffles along the bateau neckline gave way to a delicate, but striking, pavé diamond and emerald necklace. The translucent three-quarter sleeves of the blouse revealed a solid gold Cartier Tank watch on one hand and what had to be at least a 20 carat, emerald cocktail ring on the other. The flowing chiffon of her blouse was counterbalanced by her tailored black leather pants. With the aid of her three-inch black leather boots, she almost met me eye to eye.

My nose started to twitch. I scratched it, which had to have been a no-no in Vivienne's code of grace and beauty. "How are you, Vivienne?" I asked, as I started walking towards the conference room. "Has Jacques kept you busy?"

She started to respond, and I stopped walking. I had horrible indigestion, and the pressure of the baby made me feel like someone had opened up an agitated can of Coke in my intestines.

"Are you all right?" she asked.

"Yes, I'm fine," I reassured her, my mouth starting to water. "It's just the baby."

Vivienne's eyes lit up, and she put her hands close to her face. Not close enough to smear her make-up, but close enough to be demonstrative. "Oh! You're going to have a baby! How exciting!" Her face also showed some signs of relief as the pregnancy was obviously the explanation for my dowdy outfit.

Caine stuck his head out of the conference room. His gaze was like a magnet, sucking us into the meeting. I sat down at the table, dizzy and disoriented. Vivienne took a seat next to me, thereby engulfing me into her cloud of perfume. The back of my blouse was stuck to my skin, so I leaned over in my chair in a futile attempt to circulate air around my body. She asked me again, "Are you all right?"

"That's not Eau de Vie, is it?"

"Maxine!" scolded Caine, obviously more concerned about the client than me.

"Maybe you just need some water," offered Vivienne. She poured me a glass from the pitcher on the conference room table. I watched the ice cubes bob up and down in the water as Vivienne brought the glass to my lips. She put her arm on the back of my chair, the scent of her perfume overwhelming me.

Then like a heroic soldier holding a grenade, I glanced desperately at Caine, and threw up into my hands. In the process, I had managed to elbow Vivienne in the arm, dumping the entire glass of water onto her blouse. It was probably the best thing that could have happened. Vivienne jumped back with such alarm that Caine tended to her, rather than to me. I pushed back my chair and ran out of the conference room, trying my best not to leave a trail of vomit in my wake.

Joy was a complete saint. After my cursory pass at cleaning myself up in the bathroom near the conference room, I scurried back to my office to hide. Joy took me to the ladies room again and somehow managed to remove most of the vomit from my top. Then she loaned me her scarf to cover up the rest. Although "loan" might not have been the right word as I couldn't imagine she'd ever want the scarf back again. I would have to buy her an Hermès as a replacement.

I sat down at my desk, hoping to figure out a plan. Was I supposed to go back upstairs? Or should I just text Caine first and ask for permission? All of my questions were answered when I looked up to see Caine standing in my doorway. "Can I have a word with you?" he asked as he took a seat on one of my office chairs. I just nodded. "First of all, are you feeling all right?"

"Yes. Absolutely. I'm fine. Happens all the time."

Caine repositioned himself as far back in the chair as he could while I realized that I had just said the dumbest thing possible. I unclenched the fists I had made to try to gain some composure. I also glanced around to locate the garbage can, just in case I lost control again.

"We've put the meeting on hold so both you and Vivienne can collect yourselves."

"Is Vivienne all right?" I had to imagine that it would take her about 45 minutes to re-assemble herself. Maybe some of the water I had dumped on her had washed off some of her perfume. That would be a huge relief because I dreaded going back into that conference room.

"Vivienne's fine. She was quite composed, actually." I thought

I detected a longing sigh, but Caine snapped himself straight. "I have communicated to Vivienne that you will not be attending the meeting. For obvious reasons." I didn't say anything because if I opened my mouth, I wasn't sure what was going to come out. Caine folded his hands in his lap and declared, "To take your place, Staffing has assigned . . ."

I slouched in relief when he did not say Nancy Lallyberry. I didn't care who was going to the meeting in my place as long as it wasn't her. Although it would have been fun to see how long it would take Vivienne to chew her up and spit her out.

"Caine, I am so terribly sorry for what happened. It came out of nowhere. I don't know what fragrance Vivienne was wearing, but it really got to me. Next time, I just won't sit next to her."

I was still talking, but Caine put his hand up. "There's not going to be a next time."

"What?"

"McCale, Morgan & Black prides itself on providing the best representation to our clients. Given your delicate condition, you are no longer able to do so for Parfum Aix."

"Are you kidding me?!" I tried to stand up in defiance, but the casters on my chair were positioned the wrong way and I couldn't move.

"I am re-assigning you to another client. You will need to transfer all of your materials over to the new resource. The change is permanent and effective immediately."

I rolled around until I could get up. "Look. This isn't fair. I'm not going to be in a meeting room with Vivienne every day for the next few months. And I'm not going to be pregnant forever. You have to let me stay on!"

Caine walked to the doorway in finality. "Maxine, I understand your disappointment. But we do not know whether you will come in contact with this sort of thing again. It's too risky for you, the client, and everyone else to potentially expose you to such a situation."

I could understand his point of view, but I still held out hope that some accommodation could be made. "Well, maybe I could help out on a part-time basis. I would still like to stay involved."

"I appreciate that, Maxine, but I need a resource that's 100% committed right now, especially with the upcoming trip to Provence."

Tears started welling up in my eyes. Trip to Provence? I hadn't heard anything about that! The trip was probably scheduled right around my due date, so even if I were still staffed on Parfum Aix, my pregnancy would prohibit me from airline travel. Why had I gotten pregnant at such an inconvenient time?

I was expecting a moment of privacy so I could cry in peace, but I saw Caine's shiny black shoes still in the doorway. I grabbed a tissue, blotted my eyes and threw my shoulders back.

He waited a moment, his gaze empathetic while he seemed to mull over what was happening. "I am sorry things have worked out like this. Vivienne informed me about the trip this morning. We have to do what's best for the client."

I nodded.

"Deirdre Morgan has an interesting project underway, and she needs a senior resource like you. After the meeting this morning, I will formalize the arrangements. In the meantime, please prepare to transition your materials."

He made a curt smile, and then walked out of my office. I just stood there, half wanting to scream, half wanting to cry.

Caine may have booted me from the Parfum Aix account, but he wasn't going to ruin my relationship with Jacques. Without involving Deschemel in an office imbroglio, I had to explain my situation to him before Vivienne had the chance. Deirdre Morgan had counseled me on it, and Nancy Lallyberry had reminded me of it: I needed to be in control of what people thought about me, not the other way around.

I whipped off a quick email to Jacques. I explained my recent sensitivities to selected odors and scents, spinning the nausea thing as a pregnancy issue that would be resolved in just a few months. That way, I let him know that I could roll right back onto the team after I returned from maternity leave, whether that was the McCale plan or not.

Then I realized that I had never given Jacques my opinion about his home-made gin. Here I was, attempting to forge a long-term professional relationship with this guy and I had blown him off when he had reached out to me.

Certainly, the pregnancy would explain my reticence at being Jacques's gin sampler. But even though I was pregnant, I could still advise Jacques. So I spent the next hour, which I billed to Caine's Administrative Account, creating an entire gin primer for Deschemel. While I knew a lot more about vodka than I did gin, there was plenty of transferable knowledge.

For research purposes, I suggested that Jacques take a trip to the Plymouth Gin Distillery in England. I knew about the place because the distillery is located in what was once a monastery built in 1431. Centuries later, some of the original pilgrims to America lodged at the site, waiting for repairs to be completed on the Mayflower before their historic journey. Sometime after that, the facility was converted to a distillery. In 1793, gin production began. It was the oldest distillery in Britain, certainly worth a trip for an enthusiast like Jacques.

Then I scanned all of my cocktail apps, focusing on the ones which used gin as a base. I cross-referenced the ingredients to identify the most common mixers with gin. Bitters, citrus and some savory herbs were used most frequently. I hoped this information would help Jacques infuse his gin with some refreshing, distinct flavors.

Once I finished my packet, I was at a loss for what to do next. I had an unscheduled, albeit brief break in between client assignments. That never happened. It seemed like an ideal time to address some of the pressing issues in my life, i.e. childcare.

Despite Dale's protestations at Osetra, he had helped me complete the NYC Baby Prep application. In my mind, that meant I was entitled to my free consultation. I pulled up the company's bookmarked webpage and put in a call for a meeting.

After a brief discussion, I was delighted to learn that NYC Baby Prep could see me in an hour. Apparently, all of my materials had been processed, and a meeting time had just opened up with their director. I loved this place already.

12

"*Mrs. Pedersen?*" A mid-height, mid-weight, brown-suited woman offered me an outstretched hand. "Please come in," she said, as she pulled me through the door. "I am Tawny Sheen, the director of NYC Baby Prep. But, please, call me Tawny."

Had the words "NYC Baby Prep" not been etched in gold on the door, I might have confused the office for McCale, Morgan & Black's. I had expected the décor to be more on the order of a glorified nursery, but instead of gingham, there were pin-stripes. Pink and blue were replaced with burgundy and gold. White-washed wood was nowhere to be found in the dark-stained, oak hallways. Apparently, to Tawny Sheen and the other stoic associates of NYC Baby Prep, having a child was serious business.

We sat down in Tawny's office. Painted directly on the wall behind her desk was the NYC Baby Prep logo, a pacifier inside a briefcase. That oddity was accompanied by the company slogan, "Maximizing the efficiency of your prenatal experience to ensure an optimal transition to motherhood." I repeated the words slowly. My initiation into the cult had begun.

Having arranged herself precisely in the middle of her chair, in the middle of her desk, Ms. Sheen began. "From your application, we have created a list of services which we think best match your needs. Today we will go over the list and agree to which services you would like. After you sign the requisite paperwork, a 50% deposit will be required."

I smiled perfunctorily when Tawny handed me a clipboard and a pen. One piece of paper was on the clipboard. It contained a grid of the NYC Baby Prep services. No prices were listed, and nothing was checked off.

"Well, it seems that NYC Baby Prep can't do anything for me," I cracked.

Tawny cocked her head to one side, barely hiding her annoyance with my interruption. She picked up a pen and dramatically checked off the first box on her copy, which she read out loud. "Nanny Search."

Underneath the box were several bullets describing exactly what was encompassed in the Nanny Search—several rounds of interviews, background checks, drug tests, and impressively, creation of the human resources overhead necessary to manage a household employee. I presumed the bullets were on the piece of paper as a reminder of how much work I was not going to have to do, assuming that I, too, were to check off the box.

"Mrs. Pedersen, as an attorney, you work long hours. Your husband, a banker, works long hours. It should come as no surprise to you that at the very least, you will need an extended care nanny. The best option for you would be a live-in nanny, certainly until the child is enrolled in kindergarten."

My mouth dried out at the thought of having not one, but two more people squeeze into our new apartment. Even if Dale were not the slob that he was, a live-in was absolutely out of the question. "We don't need a live-in," I declared authoritatively. "But we need you to conduct the search. We'll need someone from probably 7:30 in the morning until 6:30 at night." That was 11 hours. Strangely, I couldn't image the last time my commute and work fit neatly and regularly into an 11hour bundle. I'd just have to get more efficient with my time once the baby arrived.

Tawny scribbled something down on her chart. I took that as an acknowledgment of what I had said. "Next is Nursery Design Services." This one got a swooping checkmark from Tawny.

I think the second Dale's sperm fertilized my egg, we started receiving catalogs featuring all manner of infant merchandise. There were countless instant nurseries that I could easily select from a magazine, or even design on-line (although that was never going to happen). "You know, Tawny, I think we've got the nursery covered."

"Really? That's wonderful! What does it look like?"

"Well, I haven't exactly picked anything out yet, but I saw some really cute stuff in the Pottery Barn Kids catalog."

Given Tawny's reaction, I could have said that I had picked up a crib bumper at the Salvation Army. "Mrs. Pedersen. Seriously. You don't have time to be flipping through catalogs, of all things." She slid something from under her checklist across the top of her desk to me. "You indicated that you don't know the sex of the baby, but we at NYC Baby Prep have our own means of discerning such important information. Look at what our designers have already done for you."

I picked up a glossy 8" X 10" photograph. It was a fully decorated nursery for a boy.

"Why do you think I'm pregnant with a boy?" From all I had read, the fact that my butt had widened by about 50% was supposed to indicate that I was having a girl. Old wives' tales had to be more time-tested than undocumented suspicions from an upscale nanny agency.

Tawny waved her hand, like I had entirely missed the point. Which was the photograph. And it was spectacular. All the furniture—the crib, changing table, bookshelf and glider—was a gorgeous cherry wood. Dark blue, hunter green and light tan composed the palette for the carpeting and paint. As I looked closely at the custom bedding and window treatments, I detected a miniature tennis racquet and lacrosse stick motif in the fabric. "This is fantastic!" I whispered, mesmerized.

"I'm glad you think so." Tawny's eyes lit up for the first time, and she actually swiveled in her chair. "I was so thrilled when I read that you had gone to Yale and Dale had gone to Dartmouth. Blue and green! What perfect colors for a boy's room! And the fact that you both played sports . . . well, that really got our designers energized."

I handed the picture back to Tawny. "What if it's a girl?"

"You'll be even more blown away. With girls, the decorating possibilities are endless."

I stared at the photograph one more time. Anyone could have Pottery Barn linens. But only our child could have this magnificent custom zone of elite baby awesomeness. This would have to be my only splurge, I cautioned myself. I justified it by vowing not to redecorate the baby's room again until he or she turned ten. "O.K. 'Yes' to the Decorator Services. What's next?"

For the next half an hour, I tried my best to resist the other fantastic offerings that Tawny described. I really didn't need a custom play-list of classical music to be played to the baby in utero. So what if NYC Baby Prep had determined which composers stimulated the different stages of fetal development? I could download Mozart from iTunes myself.

I did opt for the Custom Registry Creation service, but declined the Product Assembly Option. I figured this was a great way to get Dale involved in the baby process. Watching him try to put together something like a baby swing would be worth the entertainment value alone.

After all the boxes had been reviewed, Tawny presented me with an updated checklist. Except this time, the agreed-upon boxes were checked off and the prices were filled in. When I spotted the total, I gasped. It was twice what I had estimated.

Tawny was well-prepared for my reaction. "You must remember the peace of mind you will have once you engage NYC Baby Prep. No one can put a price on that." Well, she just had, and it had just crossed the five digit threshold.

She stood up and presented me with a bound document entitled, "Weekly Activity Schedule: Mrs. Maxine Pedersen." "This is complimentary with all of our packages. Please review it while I get you something—some water, perhaps?"

I nodded robotically and opened the book. There was a section for each week of pregnancy and a page for each day of the week. The top of each page described the state of the baby's fetal development, and a handy diagram displayed the baby's growth pictorially on the right-hand top corner. I wondered if I could create a quick cartoon by flipping through the pages really fast.

My work schedule was listed for each weekday, as well as one trip to the office on the weekend, just as I had communicated in my application. Aside from that, there were a slew of new activities and appointments that I hadn't even considered scheduling. And of course, there were referrals and contact information for each recommended vendor at the back of the book.

Why hadn't I gone to any pre-natal yoga classes yet? What about my weekly pregnancy massage treatments? Yes, I had scheduled doctor appointments with the obstetrician, but not with a dermatologist. I hadn't even thought about the need to prevent stretch marks, freckles and . . . melasma. I didn't even know what melasma was, but now I knew I had to do everything I could to avoid catching it.

Tawny returned to the room with a bottle of water and a glass of ice. "That's a pretty helpful resource, isn't it? Most of our clients think it's worth the Baby Prep fee all on its own."

"Really?" It was impressive. I closed the book, knowing that it was yet another sales tactic meant to overwhelm me into signing off on the exorbitant fee structure. Maybe my re-assignment from Parfum Aix was causing me to act impulsively. Hesitantly, I pulled my chair up to the awaiting documents, which Tawny had slyly laid out for me to sign.

"And for your convenience, the entire schedule listed in the book is available for you to download directly into your calendar, onto your phone, whatever medium works for you."

I rubbed the cover of the book with the palm of my hand, still considering what to do. "So, after I upload the data in this binder, I can pull up some future day and see . . ." I opened the book to a random page and read the first thing I saw, which was, "Sexual intercourse with spouse. Position D." My words slowed as I completed the sentence. Tawny resumed her place behind her desk.

"Oh, those are just the scheduled intimacy sessions."

At least it hadn't read, "Make love to spouse." Dale would have had to incinerate the book just for bad phraseology.

Still, it was weird.

"Let's keep it simple here, Tawny, and just call it sex." I slammed the book shut. "You can't possibly think that your clients really need you to tell them when to have sex, can you?" And as I said it, I realized that I hadn't had sex in a month.

"Please don't be alarmed. We have a physician on staff to advise us on the medical aspects of your pregnancy as it relates to your lifestyle. And studies show that regular intercourse during pregnancy exercises the vaginal . . ."

"Please!" I stood up, determined to walk out of the office. "Thank you very much, but I understand the physical and mental benefits of pregnancy sex. Let's just stop there."

"But I haven't told you what Position D is."

"Let me guess. I can download sexual positions for the entire alphabet once you get my deposit." Now maybe that was something Dale might enjoy. The Kama Sutra meets Lamaze.

Tawny tapped the top of the contract with her fingernail. "Mrs. Pedersen, one of the aspects of preparing for childbirth is achieving a sense of comfort with your body. As you will discover in your binder, there will be numerous opportunities for you to download video providing realistic and," she paused for dramatic effect, "*graphic* depictions of childbirth scenarios. There's just no way to know where you'll be when your water breaks, how fast the baby's going to come, how much pain you'll be in . . ." She kept talking, even though my heart had basically stopped beating. "Mrs. Pedersen, a woman like you should appreciate that your best chance at a successful delivery is through education and preparation."

That last tactic—the scare tactic—seemed to be the most effective in convincing me to make the commitment. Once I realized that almost anything could happen with the birth of my child, it became paramount that I control everything else. My brain told my hand to pick up the pen and sign the papers. With a deposit of $6,000 out the door, I wondered why no one had told me how expensive it was to have a baby.

13

I looked past the raw silk curtains of our bedroom window. The morning haze was dissipating, giving way to a beautiful sunny Saturday. I watched a couple of birds flit through the air as I slid off our bed. My bare feet hit the wood floor. I groped around for some tissues as I skittered into the bathroom, bumping into the bureau on the way. Naked and seven months pregnant, I just didn't have the grace I was used to.

"Be careful," cautioned Dale as he turned on the television. "You don't want to hurt anything in there."

"You should have thought about that a few minutes ago while we were doing Position J."

Dale chuckled. "We're going to have to get a move on if we're going to get to Position Z before you have the baby. And if I didn't say so before, that pre-natal yoga is definitely helping with your flexibility." After all his whining about the rigorous mandates of the NYC Baby Prep schedule, Dale had become a major convert for the sole reason that he knew he was going to get laid.

After cleaning up, I fished around my closet for a robe. As I put it on, a limb, perhaps an elbow, raised the skin across my tummy. The bulge moved from one side to the other and then disappeared.

"He's moving again. I think he likes sex."

"Of course he likes sex, he's a guy." Our recent trip to the O.B.'s office had confirmed what NYC Baby Prep had predicted: I was going to have a boy. I thought I knew a lot about the male gender, i.e. the aforementioned pre-occupation with sex.

But as an infant, a boy was a baby with a penis. And I had no personal familiarity with the parts from a practical, behavioral standpoint—circumcision, standing urination, and inevitably, pubescent "activities." I guess Dale was going to earn his place in parenting heaven because these topics fell squarely in his area of expertise, not mine.

I sat down on the empty side of the bed. I started sorting through the magazines piled on the bedside table, reminding myself that anything that could be done to move the apartment towards a more orderly environment was a plus. As one of the magazines fell onto the floor, I leaned over to pick it up. I couldn't reach it. It was geometrically impossible, no matter how much yoga I did. I heaved myself back up and then got off the bed to retrieve it.

It was a copy of *Wine Enthusiast*, with a cover story about running marathons through wine regions around the world. A trip like that had been on my life-long to-do list, but there was no chance in the immediate future that I might ever check it off. As I admired the photos of the picturesque towns and the well-tended vineyards, I had a strange pregnancy-induced reaction. I started to cry.

Dale put ESPN on hold. I looked up and saw his head hanging over me. "Please don't tell me that I messed up Position J, or I am going to be very upset."

I got up from my knees, laughing at his joke, but still upset with my condition. Dale patted the side of the bed and I crawled back to where I had been just a few minutes before. He untied my robe, just enough to get a look at the baby moving while still maintaining some of my modesty.

As the baby shifted under Dale's hand he said, "So I guess Position J was effective."

I closed up my robe and looked up at the ceiling. "I didn't realize that the objective of sex was to make the baby move around."

Dale rolled onto his back and grabbed the remote. "Well, if he's moving around, then it had to work for you too, right?" I wasn't sure whether he wanted an answer because he turned the TV back on.

In truth, while it was underway, Position J had been effective. Pre-natal sex had been living up to all of its internet hype. A surplus of random hormones swirling around the body had definitely contributed to a gratifying conclusion.

But then there was the involvement of the third party, the fetus. While I knew that he didn't know what Mommy and Daddy were doing, *I* knew what we were doing. And as the baby continued to grow, his presence became exponentially more bizarre and emotionally uncomfortable for me.

I didn't wait for a commercial to speak. "So you don't think it's weird to be having sex when the baby can feel it?"

"Are you asking me a question? Or are you telling me an answer. I just want to know so I can answer the right way."

"There's no correct answer when I'm asking you about your feelings," I clarified.

Dale got out of bed and pulled on a pair of boxer shorts from the floor. I got up and tightened the sash on my robe.

He walked by me on the way to the kitchen and said, ignoring my last comment, "I'm going to make some coffee."

When I walked into the kitchen, Dale was drinking his coffee and reading the paper. Water was boiling for some decaffeinated tea for me, a considerate gesture that I acknowledged with a terse smile. I cruised to my computer so I could pull up the calendar and see what had been planned for the day. Without looking up, Dale said, "We have the baseball game today." My heart sank. I remembered that I hadn't put it on my schedule so I could forget about it.

I had just a few months of freedom, and the last thing I wanted to do with my precious time was spend it at Citi Field with Dale and his Worthington comrades. I referred to the calendar, like it was a crucial piece of evidence in a major case. "But it says here I'm supposed to swim today. Exercise is good for the baby."

Dale got up and pulled some eggs out of the fridge. "You're not getting out of it, Maxine. And besides, sex burns a lot of calories, so you can check off exercise from your to-do list today." He started cracking some eggs into a bowl. "Isn't it a great feeling to be ahead of schedule already?"

I took a frying pan out of the cabinet and tossed it onto the cooktop. I leaned up against the counter, arms crossed over the baby bulge. Today wasn't just a baseball game. Today was "Beat the Boss," a major rite of passage for anyone who worked under Bobbie Macaluso.

I didn't understand all of the rules, but the Boss (Bobbie) and his crew were in competition to determine who could most accurately predict the outcome of the baseball game. The exercise was supposed to simulate trading at the market. If the guys studied up on their companies, then they should be able to quickly react to the day's trading events and turn a profit. And in Beat the Boss, if they knew all the players and the right statistics, then they should be able to accurately predict what was going to happen in the game.

The entire notion seemed ridiculous and that opinion was validated every year when Dale would return from Beat the Boss. Drunk, tired and angry at losing, he would crash in the bedroom until about noon the following day. With so much to look forward to, why shouldn't I want to take my pregnant self out to the ballgame this year?

In any case, if anyone actually beat Macaluso, the winner would get to shadow Bobbie on all of his deals for a year. The opportunity all but promised a huge bonus for the winner. Of greater long-term value was the long list of contacts to be made through Macaluso's web-like affiliations with almost every major player in the high-tech industry. Dale told me that the last guy to beat Bobbie now runs his own investment fund, with over $10 billion in assets.

Considering this, I began to realize how beneficial it could be for Dale to win this year. We had the expenses for the baby covered with our two jobs, but it would be nice to have a bigger cushion for unforeseen events. I put some bagels in the toaster and switched gears.

"Fine. Who else is going?"

"Well, Mike, of course. And he's bringing a date."

Mike Simonson was Dale's best friend. He was bright, reasonably good-looking and totally commitment-phobic. Married guys lived vicariously through him since he was always dating a hot bimbo.

"Oh, good. What does this one do? Is she another model? Budding actress? Or does she have an actual profession like, say, massage therapist?"

Dale laughed as he whisked up the eggs in a bowl. "I think this one is a towel girl at his gym."

"Don't you guys go to the same gym?"

"Yes."

"Then you know her, too."

Dale flipped on a burner on the cooktop. "Let's just say you two are probably not going to have a lot to chat about."

I closed my eyelids, trying hard not to squeeze the ocular fluid out of my eyeballs. "Please don't tell me that O'Shaughnessy's wife is coming. All she talks about are her kids. I know we're having one, too, but I don't need any of her unsolicited advice."

"You're off the hook there. Patrick said that between the three kids, there were two birthday parties, a swim meet, and try-outs for the soccer team. And his wife's not handling her pregnancy all that well." Dale smiled at me and said, "She doesn't look anywhere as good as you do."

It was a sweet comment, and I had to applaud Dale's positivity around my swelling body. But I still would have preferred to stay home. If O'Shaughnessy's wife could get out of going, then so could I. "You know, I think I'm going to sit this one out. You go have a good time, O.K.?" I pulled the bagels out of the toaster.

Dale looked up in a panic. "Oh, no! You have to come! I told Bobbie that you were coming! His wife's been asking about you and I told him you would be there. If she comes and you're not there, I'm screwed!"

"O.K.! O.K.!" I said. "I didn't know it was such a big deal." I opened the fridge. I impatiently shoved jars of olives, cocktail onions and assorted half-eaten condiments around until I found the cream cheese. I couldn't believe he had committed me to this all-day event without my clearance. I really wanted Dale to do well in his career, but there had to be a better way for me to help. I dumped the cream cheese onto the counter. "What's his wife's name again?"

"Helen. Helen Macaluso." Dale took the frying pan off the cooktop and served the eggs.

"Oh, right. Helen." I had spoken to Mrs. Macaluso on several occasions at the Worthington holiday parties. She was pleasant enough, but with three kids in college, we didn't have much in common. Instead, we'd talk about our husbands and how dedicated and busy they were. After about a half a Screwdriver, I'd usually excuse myself and go to the ladies room. This time, there'd be no Screwdriver to dull the pain. But at least I'd have my pregnancy to justify impromptu trips to the bathroom.

14

"*Check this out!* Mike just sent this to me." Dale gave me his phone. It was tough to see the screen with the glare of the sun in the ballpark, but I could make out a disproportionately endowed girl standing near a concession stand in a bra.

I shrugged, more annoyed than threatened by the photo on my husband's phone. "So what?"

Dale gestured towards the end of the row. "That's what." Mike Simonson entered the section, followed by the girl from the picture. At least now she was wearing a shirt.

"That's Mike's girlfriend? Melanie the towel girl?"

"Yup. Mike texted me and said that she had showed up in a

Yankees t-shirt. Total ditz! And so he bought her a Mets shirt, which she put on *right in front of everyone!* Fucking classic!"

I handed the phone back to Dale. "God help me," I thought, as I said it out loud.

I smiled as politely as I could when Mike introduced me to his date. I must have appeared rude, since Dale whacked me in the ankle with his shoe. I extended a hand for Melanie to shake. Confused, she looked to Mike, who assured her that it was not a sign of aggression. Her hand felt like a soggy clump of over-cooked spaghetti. I made a mental note to find some Purell before I touched anything else.

Melanie was the first to speak. "So why aren't we up there?" she was pointing to the skyboxes. "I thought you said you worked on Wall Street. Can't you guys afford a couple of those just for one game?"

Remarkably, she had an excellent point. With full bars, an array of hors d'oeuvres and a private bathroom, the skyboxes had been developed for companies just like Worthington. But for some inexplicable reason, we were seated with all the regular fans, right along the first base line. "Yeah, what's with the ring-side seats down here?"

"Bobbie used to be a minor-league baseball player," explained Mike. "He likes to sit in the stands since it's a more authentic experience." I had to wonder if it was because he was really just a cheap bastard, but I figured I'd keep that comment to myself.

Dale took out his tablet from the bag of gadgets he had brought along. "Well, I'm going to get some last minute cramming in." Dale had been studying baseball statistics for months in preparation for today's game. He flicked the screen a couple of times and then landed on an app that flashed pictures of baseball players along with their relevant data.

I decided to sit down, too. I was half-way into the chair when Mike pulled me out by the arm. "Hey, be careful! You don't want to sit on the DEDs!"

Dale jerked upright. "Yeah! Be careful!" He pulled his bag from my chair onto his lap and started inspecting the items inside.

"Sorry," I said. "What's in there? What's the big deal?"

Dale took out an oblong, gun-metal plastic object and held it with reverence. "This is a DED." I must have looked as baffled as Melanie. "DED," repeated Dale. "Data Entry Device."

"What's that for?" I asked, wondering what else was in Dale's magical bag of tricks.

"It's for entering data, right?" asked Melanie proudly.

Mike smiled patiently and started speaking slowly. "The DED was created by some genius MIT intern a few years ago. He developed the software that will enable each of us to enter our bet for each pitch of the game."

"That sounds fun," said Melanie sincerely. "The guessing part, that is."

Mike raised an eyebrow and continued. "Simply put, each of us will bet on whether each pitch of the game will be a ball, a strike, a hit, or an out. The player who has the best guessing percentage wins Beat the Boss."

Dale piped up from his chair. "You didn't mention the upgrade to this year's DED. There's a timer in there now that's going to get synched up to all the plays in the game. Any entry made after a play has been made will be detected, and the answer will be counted as incorrect. Anyone who gets over five violations will be disqualified."

Melanie turned the DED around and around, inspecting it from a variety of different angles. I wondered if it was the first time she had seen a rectangle. "So where do you guys buy these things? I've never seen one before."

The clunky DED really did look like a calculator from 1975. I couldn't understand why Mr. High Tech himself, Bobbie Macaluso, would develop a piece of software in-house and then slap it in some obsolete bar of plastic. "You know, couldn't you guys have just put an app on your phones with the program that's on the DED here?"

Mike snatched the device back from Melanie. "Listen. Bobbie went old-school with the DED. The software's hard-wired to the hardware and that prevents theft and manipulation of the program."

"Yeah. So does a patent," I said. And then I realized something else. "But what if someone loses their DED?"

"No one loses the DED," responded Dale and Mike in unison. It sounded like a hazing term that was ingrained onto the cerebral cortex of every Worthington employee.

"Sounds like a cult, doesn't it?" Helen Macaluso warmly touched my shoulder. I turned and smiled, relieved another woman had arrived to serve as a buffer between me and Towel Girl.

"I've never come to Beat the Boss," I confessed. "I had no idea how deranged these guys would behave."

"Well, you're in for a treat, I'll tell you that!" laughed Helen. "Dale, Bobbie wants you to distribute the DEDs. Everyone's here now." Dale mobilized immediately, distributing the DEDs to what I assumed were his peers at Worthington—Mike, O'Shaughnessy, a few other nondescript looking fellows and notably, no women. Dale continued through the section, making his way towards a scene I couldn't believe I had missed when I had come in. Melanie must have been rubbing off on me.

Just a few rows up was a makeshift table loaded with enough computer equipment to drain the power from the massive Citi Field video screen. A tall, thin, Indian man-child, wearing noise cancelling earphones and a tee shirt that read, "Tech Finance is the new Hedge Fund," was overseeing a pile of metal before him. He looked like a DJ at an MBA Finance Club party.

I stepped closer to Helen and laughed. "Are you serious? That guy is a VP? What is he—12?"

Helen cocked her hip and put her hand on her chin in mock curiosity. "12? No. But hopefully over 21, because once O'Shaugnessy starts drinking, everyone gets sucked into the funnel."

Dale rushed back to his chair, his face sallow. "Are you all right?" I asked. "Did you get electrocuted by all the gear up there?"

"Look, don't get me all wound up now. Rajeev has gone *loco*. All the computer crap he has there is, supposedly, a dynamic version of the DED. If it works, it will make this piece of shit," and Dale held up the DED, "look like an abacus."

"I don't understand."

"There's not much of a difference between entering our data into this device, rather than writing it down on a piece of paper, right?" he explained hurriedly.

"Yeah. I got that."

"We all come to the game with our data files and binders. But everyone knows that once things get underway, all the suppositions go out the window." He yanked at the collar of his Worthington polo shirt. "Things happen. Players get injured, the crowd gets excited, whatever. By the fourth or fifth inning, we're all just guessing our asses off, hoping to win."

"So that's why Bobbie usually wins? He understands baseball?" It was a valid point. It seemed like the deck was stacked against everyone besides Bobbie. "But what has that got to do with Rajeev and his portable disco over there?" I looked back at Rajeev again. His eyes darted around the ballpark, as his hands typed wildly. "What the heck is he doing, anyway? He scares me."

Dale exhaled impatiently. "Well, he's probably loading ballpark attendance and weather patterns into his model. He's already incorporated thousands of variables into the thing. All he has to do now is load every play after it happens. Then the model will compute the most likely outcome for the next play. And that he enters into the DED."

"That sounds absolutely ridiculous," I scoffed.

"It's not ridiculous if he wins."

"That doesn't really seem fair, to have all that help. Don't you guys have some rules around this thing? How far you can go to win?"

"Good God. You sound like the Securities & Exchange Commission."

Snarky as his comment was, I resisted the urge to respond. I usually won our verbal arguments, and I didn't want Dale feeling like a loser before he started playing Beat the Boss.

Helen, sensing the tension, said, "So, shall we get this party started? We might as well go for a beer run before the game begins."

When we came back with the beer, Dale had repositioned himself next to Bobbie. If I hadn't known Dale better, I would have thought that he was trying to sneak a peek off Bobbie's entries into the DED. Dale did have a penchant for pushing professional boundaries, but he also loved competition. In the end, my husband would want to win on merit alone.

I handed Dale a beer, and he thanked me graciously. I offered one to Bobbie, who declined. That must have been his secret to winning every year: sobriety. Helen took the beer for herself confiding, "Bobbie's a little concerned about losing to Rajeev, so he's been an absolute pill."

An unhappy Bobbie seemed the kind of person who could suck the energy out of a nuclear generator. But Dale seemed unfazed by

Bobbie's moodiness, which is probably why they got on so well. Standing together, the two men were a study in contrasts.

Bobbie was about as tall as Dale, with broader shoulders and long arms. His chest was sort of hollow and he had a small bulge protruding over his belt. It seemed that over the years, gravity had redistributed his body mass southwards. Nonetheless, he stood erect and seemed fairly fit.

While traces of youth were evident in his physique, his face showed a different history. He had thick lines under his eyes from permanent bags which were the war wounds from years of stress and fatigue. Two more lines from the corners of his mouth to the bottom of his chin engulfed a cleft in the middle. This jaunty feature, along with his bright eyes, enlivened an otherwise somber expression.

If Bobbie's physique was any indication of what Worthington was going to do to Dale, then I couldn't feel too bad about what pregnancy was going to do to me.

15

The National Anthem had been sung, the players announced, and the Mets pitcher wound up for his first throw of the game. All the Worthington heads dropped as they entered their bets. Dale entered an S, which I presumed meant he thought the first pitch would be a strike. With all the guesses entered into their respective DEDs, the Worthington heads bobbled up in eager anticipation. I couldn't believe that this ritual was going to repeat itself for every pitch of the game. I had under-estimated how hideously boring this was going to be.

"It's gonna be a strike, right?" said Melanie. Everyone stared at her for speaking during the moment of silence between when the ball was pitched and when the pitch was called. But she turned out to be right: the first pitch was a called strike. Dale appeared both happy for guessing correctly and annoyed with Melanie's vocal participation. He glared at Mike, who pouted at Melanie. "What?!" she said defensively. "Don't you guys know the next pitch is gonna be a ball?"

The next pitch was a ball. Melanie clapped enthusiastically. Helen stepped in to intervene, or at least to investigate. Melanie the towel girl apparently had some hidden talents—the kind I was interested in hearing about, anyway.

"Melanie, I had no idea you were such a baseball fan!" she said, trying to engage Mike's date.

Melanie was on her toes looking out to the field. "I think this one's a hit," she decided and then turned to Helen. "I was a semi-pro softball player before I started working at the gym."

I scanned her physique again and decided that she must've gotten the boob job after she retired because there was no way she'd be able to swing a bat with those things in the way. "What position did you play?" I asked.

"Catcher." Sure enough, the next pitch was a line drive between first and second. "Hey, I'm three for three! Hey, Mikey! You get all those?" Mike cupped the DED to his chest and smiled.

As the next batter came to the plate, Dale spoke up. "Dude. That is not fair. You're totally cheating!"

"How is it cheating if everyone can hear what Melanie's saying? And don't you even start comparing Melanie to that," and he pointed up at Rajeev.

Bobbie glared at Helen, who had apparently not dealt with the situation to his satisfaction. Helen shrugged her shoulders back.

"You know, maybe you need your own DED, Melanie," Helen offered. "That way you could keep track of everything without influencing the play of everyone else. And who knows—maybe you could be the first woman to win Beat the Boss! Can you imagine?!"

"No," demurred Melanie. "I can't. That DED thing looks too hard to use."

"It can't be that hard," I said. "Patrick's using it."

"It doesn't matter," interjected Dale. "We don't have any more at the ballpark."

With all the commotion about Melanie the Ringer, all the guys had failed to enter their bets. That translated into an automatic incorrect guess for everyone. Sensing Bobbie's irritation, Helen herded me and Melanie to a different part of the section. "There are about 250 pitches thrown in a baseball game," she said. "Statistically, getting one wrong shouldn't mean a lot, but these guys are rabid. We need to separate ourselves from the mayhem."

Melanie looked disappointed. "Well, that sucks," she stated crudely but accurately. "I don't understand why I am penalized for being better than everybody else. It happens all the time." I held back the laughter as best I could. She stood up defiantly. "I'm out of here. Tell Mike I'll be back later. Maybe." Melanie took off towards the Promenade, with the ultimate goal of probably trying to find a way to sneak into the Mets locker room.

As the innings progressed, the fiber of the Worthington masses started to unravel. Not surprisingly, the leader of the pack was O'Shaughnessy. I had almost made it safely back to my seat from the bathroom when Patrick ran into me during the seventh-inning stretch. He bumped my tummy with his own distended gut and then made an exaggerated tumble backwards. The juniors were highly amused, especially after he fell down and knocked a Slurpee on his pants.

I tried to walk over him, but he was up in a flash, draping his arm over my shoulders. I slunk down, trying to escape his sweaty armpit, but he started talking. To Helen. About me.

"You know, Mrs. Macaluso," he slurred, "You and Mr. Macaluso have got to have cocktails at Dale and Maxine's apartment. These guys have a huge collection of vodka, gin and rum. It's just mind-blowing!"

Patrick's antics had now caught the attention of Dale, Bobbie and everyone else in the Worthington section. I kept trying to get free, but Patrick clamped down on my shoulder. Now that he had everyone's attention, he wasn't about to wrap it up.

"You know, I would argue that the volume of Maxine's vodka collection might rival that of an amateur wine collector." Patrick rubbed my shoulder a bit and then plopped into his seat. I had trouble reciting the "amateur wine collector" comment, even when I was sober. When Patrick gave me a good-natured smile, I realized that the extent of his drunkenness was highly overblown. Still, his back-handed compliment, while friendly in intent, only tempted me to give him a massive middle-school style redneck as I stood behind him in the aisle.

Meanwhile, Mike seemed to be using every electronic means possible to locate Melanie. Heaven forbid he actually leave the section and go look for her. Dale and Bobbie were engrossed in some technical discussion about Inter-Tech. Ordinarily, I would have let them continue, but I was curious to see how the boys were doing.

"So—how is it going? You enjoying the game?" I posed the question to anyone who might answer.

"I think I'm doing pretty well," admitted Dale. "But Rajeev has turned very cocky." Indeed, Rajeev Gupta had taken the seventh inning stretch to literally put his feet up on his table and take a cat nap. "He says his model has worked perfectly. So who knows—maybe this year someone will bring down 'Big Mac.'" Dale grimaced nervously as he absorbed Bobbie's glare. Nobody used Bobbie's Triple A nickname without permission.

I asked Bobbie, as a former pitcher, how he thought the Mets pitching staff was performing. In doing so, I realized that he wouldn't answer, as his opinions would jeopardize his own attempts to win the competition.

An awkward silence ensued. Helen arrived bearing beer, much to everyone's relief. While people snatched up the drinks, I could feel Bobbie's eyeballs boring into the top of my head. He rubbed the lines around his mouth until his thumb and forefinger met at the bottom of his chin. He repeated this a few times while we all waited for him to speak.

"Dale has told me about your interest in spirits and liqueurs, Maxine. We might be able to utilize your expertise for a gala that Helen is planning. What would you think of that?"

Bobbie was very crafty. He had maneuvered me into a position where I'd have to commit to helping his wife, even though the scope of the activities had not yet been agreed upon.

Dale was more than happy to declare my complete availability. Helen looked like she had just won a cruise to the Bahamas on a game show. I decided right then and there to never go to a baseball game again.

Bobbie took a manly slug of his purified water. "Helen is President of the Long Island Heritage Society. Every year the gala committee is supposed to come up with something original for the menu. Helen can tell you all about it." And with that, he resumed his conversation with Dale. Helen whisked me back to our seats as the game got back underway.

"So what is this gala you're planning?" As I said the words, I realized that Helen would be the ideal party planner. She was considerate, tactful and fun. And she seemed to have amazing tolerance for alcohol because she was on her fourth beer and wasn't slurring a word.

She spent the rest of the game describing the event. I was only half listening, because the baseball game was tied. I dreaded the notion of sticking around for extra innings. At the top of the ninth, the Cardinals didn't score, so the Mets got their turn at the plate to win the game. "What happens if the game goes into extra innings?" I asked Helen. "Does the DED self-destruct?"

Before she could answer, the crowd erupted. It was a lead-off home run, putting the Mets on top, four to three. Game over.

All the DEDs were summarily handed to a neutral tabulation party, i.e. a set of up-and-coming junior associates tapped by Bobbie. While Dale and Mike nervously shuffled around, Rajeev sauntered over, dragging his worn flip-flops with confidence. "So, Mr. Pedersen," he said with an Indo-British accent, "what is the highest winning percentage ever posted in this competition?"

Dale puffed out his chest and crossed his arms. "I'm not sure. Maybe Macaluso got close to 30% once?"

Rajeev bent over and slapped his knee with phony laughter. "30%? That's it? I totally won this thing this year. My model had almost a 90% prediction rate."

Dale released his arms and let them swing in front of his body. He squinted his eyes at Rajeev and said feebly, "I don't believe you."

"Yeah? Well, we'll see!" he cackled. And within moments, the Worthington cell phones all started to buzz. Everyone feverishly scanned their devices with such focused attention I thought the Fed had lowered the interest rates.

Dale's mouth slowly started to open. He couldn't take his eyes off his phone. Mike slapped him out of his trance, literally, and gave him a huge man-hug.

"Congratulations! Holy shit! You won it, bro!"

Dale became flushed and he smiled at me through the onslaught of congratulatory handshakes and high-fives. Macaluso shook Dale's hand solidly and said, "You eked it out there, Dale. You beat me by two one hundredths of a point. But in this game, the margin doesn't matter. There's only one winner—you." Then he hugged Dale briefly, whispering something into his ear.

I supposed I should have been squealing with joy over Dale's victory. I was truly proud of him, but I felt oddly deserted. If half of what Dale had said was true, then he would be spending much more time with Bobbie than with me. How was he going to help me with the baby if he was working all night with his boss?

I didn't know what to say when Dale gave me a hug. Everyone else applauded, and I got a reprieve when Rajeev came pushing through the crowd, holding his laptop.

"Bobbie! Look here! My model had a 91.23% accuracy rate. Why does the email say that the DED I used had a 12.87% betting rate? Everything from my model was entered exactly into the DED. I should be the winner!" He pointed at the junior techs that had uploaded all the DED data. "You guys screwed this up completely!"

Bobbie held the laptop in one of his hands and started scanning through it. Almost immediately, he pointed to something on the screen and said, "These are the results you entered into the DED?"

"Yes! And they are correct! Don't you remember DeSauza striking out to end the 8th inning? That's what that is!"

Macaluso rubbed his chin, analyzing the data. "Rajeev, that result says *K*. Did you enter *K* into the DED for a strike?"

"Yes! Of course! *K* is for strike-out, right? Look at the scoring guidelines in the program!" Rajeev had the day's program rolled up in a tube, which he was swirling around his head.

"Yes. *K* is for strike out, when the batter strikes out. But even in professional scoring, you don't use a *K* for each strike, which it looks like you did in your model. You were supposed to enter an *S* into the DED for every strike, not a *K*." Bobbie kept paging through the spreadsheet, looking for more corrections. "See? You did the same thing here with Marbry's walk in the 5th. You put a *BB* in the DED. *BB* is for base on balls, or a walk. You were supposed to enter *B*, even for the final called ball."

Bobbie shut the PC, having resolved the confusion. Rajeev slumped into a chair and uttered the words, "mother fucker." Somehow they didn't seem so coarse when he said them with a British accent.

Dale opened the PC back up and looked through the model himself. "The amazing thing is that the model actually worked. Rajeev just messed up the letters. I feel like I won on a technicality, Bobbie." Dale shoved his fists into the pockets of his shorts and kicked an empty plastic cup from under a chair.

Rajeev stood up straight, adjusted his shirt and said, "That's bullshit. You won, fair and square, Pedersen. Think about it. If Bobbie had given me $10 million to invest in stock SAS and I put the money in ASS, I would have screwed up royally. This is the same thing." Rajeev extended a hand. "Don't worry. I'll fix the model, and then next year, I will kick *your* ass!"

Dale and Rajeev shook hands, and then Patrick capped off the afternoon by pouring an oversized beer on Dale's head. And now that Dale was officially Bobbie's slave for the next twelve months, I figured the indentured servitude extended to me as well. I gave Helen my card and offered to help her with the gala dinner. In one afternoon, Dale and I had earned two more additions to our family: Bobbie and Helen Macaluso.

16

The most striking element to Beat the Boss was the camaraderie it cultivated among the Worthington staff. We at McCale had none of that. Maybe it was a cultural difference in industries; lawyers weren't known for their work-hard-play-hard character. Nonetheless, we are an ambitious lot. And in order to be successful, I needed not only talent (which I had) and luck (which I couldn't control) but also a mentor (which I had to cultivate).

Dale had Bobbie. I had Caine. Sort of. He was my designated human resources partner, the one who was supposed to guide my career by staffing me on projects that would showcase my skillset. Of late, he had fulfilled these mentoring duties by booting me from Parfum Aix and giving me zero guidance on the working mother transition. As a man, he wasn't really qualified for the latter role, so I needed to move up the chain to Deirdre.

I simply needed some dedicated time with Deirdre to lay the foundation for her mentorship of me. Therein lay the challenge, as Mrs. Morgan was militant about controlling her time. For all I knew, she could have been the surreptitious author of the NYC Baby Prep Schedule of Activities, because she accounted for every minute of her existence. But the woman had to eat, even if she did so at her desk. And that seemed like an opportune time to initiate a call to mentoring.

I gave Joy a mission: she had to get me on that calendar. For each day of the upcoming two weeks, I gave Joy an excuse for why Deirdre's assistant should work me in. Depending on when the lunch took place, we might be discussing the anniversary of a landmark case, an announcement from one of our client's top competitors, or the introduction of the latest legal app.

Within 10 minutes, Joy excitedly buzzed into my office. She held a notepad and pen right under her chin when she said, "You're on. Today!" She looked down at the pad and followed with, "You're supposed to be talking about the new shipping regulations for containers arriving from Hong Kong into the United States."

"Awesome! Joy, you are the best."

"I know, right?" she flapped her pad coquettishly and then sauntered out of the office.

I knocked gingerly on Deirdre's open door. Stacked in one hand were two salads from her favorite deli; the other held a tote with my phone, laptop, notepad, pens, and whatever else I might need. I had already emailed her the information about the shipping regulations, so she could easily pull it up on her own PC. If nothing else, I was prepared.

I waited a few moments until she finished up. "Good. Done." Abruptly, she stood and scooted around her desk to help me. "Maxine! Thank you for organizing this meeting." She took both salads and placed them on the coffee table in the conversation pit of her office.

"Well, I know you're busy, so I was glad to just get on your calendar." I settled onto one of the pewter and green upholstered chairs. She sat on a pewter and black couch.

"I read the information about the shipping regs," said Deirdre as she cracked open the plastic container of the salad. "I'm glad to see that you are so on top of the issues concerning HKI."

"It seems like the major implication is going to be labeling and packaging modifications for the products they're sending over here. More administrative than technical, but important nonetheless." As clients, Parfum Aix and HKI couldn't have been more different. Parfum Aix was a leading edge, family-owned company known for impeccable quality. HKI was a pseudo-government conglomerate with an expertise in manufacturing knock-offs. If I thought too hard about it, I could draw the parallel between being a trademark lawyer for HKI and a defense attorney for a felon: everyone deserved legal protection.

"You're right. But that's just the tip of it. The client situation is getting complicated, so we're bringing on a new resource to the team." Deirdre dug into her salad with a plastic fork. "I was hoping you could help out. You know, perhaps serve as a mentor for him."

"Sure! No problem!" If Deirdre thought I would be a good advisor for someone new, then she'd be sure to support me. "When is he rolling on?"

"Today," said Deirdre. "And from what I understand, he's going to need some help."

"Help? What kind of help?"

"He hasn't passed the bar exam yet."

My first reaction was that this guy must have been fresh out of law school. McCale had hired me before I had passed the bar; that was common industry practice. "So? What's the big deal?"

Deirdre put her salad on the coffee table. "He's failed it twice already."

I put my salad down, too. "Forgive me for asking, but with the labor market as it is, why would McCale hire someone who's failed the bar exam—twice?"

"Paul Black is really high on this kid." Paul Black was one of the other named partners at the Firm and although his name was last on the marquee, he was widely regarded as the lead partner at the firm. Deirdre explained the situation with measured words. "Jeffry Hsu, the new associate, is fluent in Cantonese. He didn't just take it in college; he was raised in Hong Kong. As a result, he's got family connections back home that may prove to be helpful as developments with HKI unfold."

I stuffed a fork full of greens in my mouth so I could process her comments. I had hoped that the conversation would have focused more on me: work-life balance for a new working mother stuff. But Deirdre was giving me a unique opportunity that acknowledged not only my technical capabilities as a lawyer, but also my strong personal relationships with the staff. Given that, the idea of discussing nannies, or sleep deprivation, or nursing at the office seemed trivial.

"I'm guessing he's going to need some help with his working style," I started. Deirdre nodded. "And I know I can give him some excellent pointers on passing the bar. I'm assuming he's just failed the summer exam?"

"Yes."

"So we've got to get him filed for February by November."

"Exactly."

Like most lawyers who'd passed a bar examination, the dates when the test were administered had become ingrained in my psyche. I knew that Jeffry should have plenty of time to study for the next test. But as I pulled the dates together in my mind, I realized that I would probably be on maternity leave during the crucial weeks running up to the February exam date. I'd have to deal with that later. I didn't want Deirdre to entrust this critical responsibility to anyone else besides me.

With Deirdre's meeting objectives satisfied, she began to pack up her salad. She did have the courtesy to ask me some rudimentary questions about how I was feeling and whether Dale and I knew the sex of the baby. She seemed genuinely excited when I told her that we were having a boy. With children of each sex at home, Deirdre advised authoritatively that boys were much easier to handle. "You're lucky," she said. "Boys are much less work when they're young. And you're going to need all the help you can get."

If Deirdre Morgan was intent on maximizing her professional effectiveness, then I, too, decided to be the model of efficiency. I just had to make sure I was comfortable. Pregnancy had brought on a whole range of minor physical issues which required continuous management. I had no idea that being pregnant was such a high-maintenance activity.

At this point, I refused to ignore the need to constantly hydrate myself and its companion requirement, the urge to urinate almost every hour. If meeting times ran over, I simply excused myself, took care of business and came right back. I didn't miss a thing. I wondered why I had ever felt the need to deny myself bathroom breaks in the past. I guess I thought I might be considered rude if I walked out of someone's meeting. Now I thought it was rude if someone let their meeting drag on.

I became a slave to the NYC Baby Prep Schedule of Activities. Personal appointments and activities had been purposefully scheduled several times a week at 6:30 at night. I was forced to re-adjust my work behavior now, while pregnant, so I could become accustomed to getting home by then to relieve my future nanny.

Unfortunately, my individual team members did not have a Schedule of Activities for their lives. I did my best to compensate, and I implemented a rigid workflow of activities for them to complete while in the office. Team meetings were held first thing in the morning. The afternoon was reserved for research, writing and whatever else inevitably popped up. After about a week of griping, everyone realized the benefits of minimizing non-work related activities when they were able to leave the office by 6:00 pm on a semi-regular basis. Everyone, that is, except Jeffry Hsu.

Jeffry's shortcomings had been highly under-estimated by Deirdre. Or maybe she knew what a lousy associate Jeffry was, and didn't want to tell me for fear I would reject the offer to work with him. Whatever the case, she had misrepresented my role with Jeffry. Rather than act as his mentor, I became his disciplinarian. Perhaps this, too, was preparation for my impending parenthood.

First on the docket for improvement was his status report, which typically arrived with dozens of typos. Using the English-as-a-second-language excuse was not going to cut it when his computer had the spell-check function. More troubling was his failure to properly source any of the case law that he had cited.

After re-reading his first few reports, I was relieved that at least he had done the right research. He was just too lazy to bother with the details. No wonder he had trouble passing the bar exam.

I tried my best to provide Jeffry with professional guidance. Every overture I made was summarily, rudely, rejected. The fact that he had to work for a woman—and a pregnant one at that—seemed to be a source of shame for him. If I asked him to move a hefty box of file folders, he would ignore me. If I called a five-minute bathroom break during our team meetings, he would refuse to leave, demonstrating his refusal to comply with the directives of such a weak leader. I remembered his reactions when I corrected his horrific drafts with extra doses of red ink.

I decided that perhaps Jeffry might respond better if he were given some direct responsibility. Our team was to provide Deirdre with case summaries about American factory working conditions, an activity I delegated squarely to him. Knowing Jeffry's poor track record, I had actually done most of the research for him. A second year law student could have picked up where I had left off. I was hopeful he could pull something decent together to impress Deirdre and earn the goodwill of the team.

When the time came to present to Deirdre, even I was shocked by Jeffry's insolence. He had nothing prepared. Accustomed to taking full responsibility for the team's performance, I began to apologize. Then, out of the corner of my eye, I noticed Jeffry push himself back in his chair. He was grinning while scrolling through something on his phone, probably online porn.

That was when I decided to speak to Jeffry Hsu in a language he could understand.

"Jeffry!" I roared. He snapped to attention, almost falling out of his chair. "Deirdre is asking for the comparative case work I assigned you. Where is it?" Our entire team looked over at him in disappointment. It was a public group conviction of his incompetence, further validated by the fact that he hadn't brought anything to the meetingbesides his phone.

Deirdre, not one for confrontations, didn't say a word. Jeffry may have been a full-blown flake, but as team lead, I was accountable for the completion of the work. I finished my apology and assured Deirdre that the information would be completed by the end of the day.

For the rest of the meeting, Jeffry sat at attention in his chair. When the meeting was adjourned, he waited for everyone else to leave and then approached me. Instead of talking, he half-bowed quickly and then raced out the door. As I collected my belongings, I realized that from Jeffry's perspective, a half-bow was the equivalent of a one-page, hand-written apology letter.

My hunch was confirmed at the day's end, when Deirdre Morgan's reports were completed efficiently and accurately by one Jeffry Hsu.

17

"I brought this up for you." Paola handed me a package as she entered my apartment. "Looks like it's from France. Did you order some esoteric baby gadget that's only available in Europe?"

"No. But that is a great idea." I was well into the third trimester of pregnancy, but there was still time to buy more stuff for the baby. One more board book, though, and the anchors for the shelving unit in the baby's room might rip straight through the drywall.

The return address was Grasse, France, without the Parfum Aix designation. I figured it was more of Jacques's gin. Jacques was a scientist, so he was meticulous about keeping Parfum Aix correspondence separate from his other endeavors.

"I thought you said you weren't staffed on Parfum Aix," noted Paola. "Why are you getting something from work?"

"It's not work, exactly. Jacques just likes to send me samples of the side projects he's got going."

"Really?" said Paola, her forehead wrinkling. "Maybe he's got the hots for you."

"No way. He's older than my father." I pulled some inflatable bubble inserts from the envelope. "I bet he would have been a nightmare to date 30 or 40 years ago. He's all over the place with ideas and projects. But now, I think it's charming."

"You're weird."

"No. I'm pregnant." What was I going to do in a few weeks when my built-in excuse for random thoughts and behavior had expired? I'd have to come up with something new, like sleep-deprivation.

Inside the wrapping was a delicate fabric pouch, which covered a polished wooden box, about the size of a jewelry box for a bracelet. I also emptied out a note. Paola touched the box and started sliding it towards her so she could look at it. "It's beautiful."

I snatched it back so I could be the first one to open it. "Hands off." I slowly opened the hinged lid. Both sides of the box were lined in lavender silk. A long thin glass vial was nestled in the cushioned bottom. I gently removed it and held it up. A blush-colored liquid twinkled inside.

Neither of us commented, probably out of fear of ruining the spell of the magic potion.

I carefully handed Paola the vial. She held it with both the care she'd have for an infant, and the fear she'd have of plutonium. I took a few moments to read the note from Jacques and then debriefed her. "According to this, Jacques says that he was upset that I was taken off the Parfum Aix account." Paola raised an eyebrow. "More importantly, though, he feels responsible."

Paola took her eyes off the vial for a moment. "Why? You told me that he wasn't there the day you threw up."

I put down the note. "He wasn't there in person. But his perfume was. And he's upset that any of Parfum Aix's fragrances could have caused such a reaction. He says he did some research, and he's developed a new perfume that should have limited negative side effects for pregnant women." I took a deep breath. "You're holding the prototype."

Paola froze. Slowly, I regained control of the glass tube.

"*Dios mio!* He made a perfume for you!? Are you kidding me? What's he going to call it, Eau de Maxine?"

"Stop it," I argued. "It's for all pregnant women, not just me." But of course I was immensely flattered. I was determined to wear the perfume even if it made me nauseous.

I opened the vial and took a brave, broad sniff. It was glorious. I started wafting the scent towards my face, afraid to waste any of it by actually putting it on.

"Let me smell it! Please!"

I handed it over so Paola could enjoy it, and then I took it back. Her face reflected my thoughts. I tried to describe the smell, just to make sure we were having the same experience. "I'm thinking citrus. Maybe grapefruit, right? But there's a hint of herbs. Maybe cilantro." I sniffed the air again. "I don't know—there's something earthy and sweet, but not cloying."

Paola nodded. "None of it's cloying. I think that's what I couldn't stand about perfume when I was pregnant."

"Totally! This is so fresh! There's definitely lemon. Yum!"

"You know, perfume smells differently when you put it on your own body. Do you want me to try it for you, in case you don't like it?" I contemplated the idea as she held out her wrist. But as the stainless steel of her TAG Heuer Link watch glistened, I realized that time was running short.

"No, no. Not now." I put the perfume vial back in its box and stashed it in a kitchen drawer. "Olga's going to be here any minute."

Speed-interviewing, NYC Baby Prep-style, had been a very effective mechanism for Dale and me to identify a nanny. After five-minute conversations with 15 different candidates, we had both independently selected Olga as our first choice. Interestingly, Olga had picked Dale as her first choice and me as her second, but I had to attribute that to the trace amount of high school Spanish Dale still remembered and had probably used during the interview.

I then conducted another fairly lengthy interview with Olga at the NYC Baby Prep offices. I learned about her family, with specific detail about her mother, brother and children. There was no mention of a husband, a fact that was corroborated by her application, which listed her as single. I knew I couldn't ask her why she would have had children without a partner to help, but Olga didn't seem the type to have a master plan for personal development. In the end, it was none of my business. Between my assessment, the input from her references and the background work done by NYC Baby Prep, Olga seemed to be a hard-working, experienced and trust-worthy caregiver.

All that remained was a final meeting to show Olga around our apartment and to review some paperwork. "So tell me about the nanny," said Paola. She was busy clacking on her phone while she talked. I wondered if she was going to do that the entire time.

"Well, her name is Olga."

Paola looked up from the device. "Yeah. I got that." She finished typing a message while asking, "Latina Olga or Eastern European Olga?"

"Central American Olga. Or Cuban Olga. Olga Ramirez. I think she's from Guatemala." I rummaged through some papers on the kitchen counter to validate Olga's country of origin.

"You *think* she's from Guatemala?" Paola was very proud of her Mexican heritage. Whenever anyone lumped all Latin cultures into one Spanish-speaking basket, which I had just inadvertently done, she became indignant.

"Thank God I didn't say she was from Mexico."

"Damn right."

"Not to worry," I confirmed. "She's from Guatemala."

"Not like it matters," she said flippantly, trying to downplay her reaction.

I calmly put the papers away. "Paola, I need your help as a mother. This person's going to be taking care of my child. I don't care where she came from, as long as she doesn't have a record, and she's good to my son."

"Right." Paola gave me a demonstrative hug. "*Lo siento.* I never had to hire an all-day nanny like this. My mother was around and Nelson was actually a huge help, so this kind of freaks me out."

I took a step back. "You're not helping."

"Yes I am! I will! Give me some information. How old is she?"

"22."

"And you said she has kids?"

"Yeah. One's three and the other one is about six months old." There was a moment of silence as we both contemplated the comment. "Yes, it's weird that she's going to leave her kids so she can watch my kid when I go to work."

"True that. I bet her mom's watching her kids."

"And her brother's kids. Apparently, the grandmother's got her hands full."

Paola sat down on a kitchen stool. "Maybe you should just hire the grandmother. She sounds more than qualified."

"NYC Baby Prep has assured me that Olga is qualified. But to be overly protective, we've installed two nanny cams in the apartment," I said as I pointed at a tiny dot hidden behind a bookcase in the living room, and another one in the nursery.

"Nanny cams?" asked Paola. "You think you're going to need them?"

"No. But NYC Baby Prep said that it's industry standard and completely precautionary."

Paola thought about it for a moment as the doorman buzzed up Olga. "Well, all these nannies probably know that they are being watched, so if that's a deterrent, I guess it's a good thing." It sounded like she was trying to convince herself, rather than me, that nanny cams were a good idea.

"Well, let's not bring it up, O.K.?" I heard a knock on the door. I opened it widely without checking the peephole to verify that it was Olga. *Hola!* I said, as I motioned for her to enter.

Olga smiled and laughed a bit nervously. "Hello," she said, her English as bad as my Spanish.

Paola vaulted in, immediately striking up a conversation with Olga that I did not understand. After a few exchanges, they both said *guera* at the same time and started to laugh. I guess Olga had passed whatever preliminary test Paola had devised.

"You ladies done?" I asked, my tightened tone aimed more towards Paola than Olga.

They both settled down. Now that Olga was in my apartment, rather than behind a desk in a nanny agency, she seemed different.

At 5'2" and approximately 100 pounds, she had the physique of a lithe teenage gymnast rather than that of a working mother of two. Fitness, or at least the absence of obesity, was a preferred characteristic for a nanny. A thinner caregiver gave the illusion that her charges would be well-exercised and not overfed. Both Paola and I could agree that Olga satisfied this tacit qualification.

Olga's attire was a different story. During the interviews, Olga's dress had been quite sharp. She had worn well-fitted, clean, respectable clothing. I had to imagine that she had borrowed those clothes from a stockpile at NYC Baby Prep, since today's outfit was truly baffling.

I couldn't decide which was worse: the skin tight elastic denim jeans, the hoodie, or the skate-rat sparkling Sketchers. Was I supposed to have designated a dress code? Maybe it didn't matter. From what I had heard, infants and toddlers had a wonderful way of leaving their mark, so to speak, on all clothing and any fabric-covered item with which they came into contact.

"Well, let me show you around the apartment, O.K.?"

There wasn't much to see, given the square footage of our co-op. When entering the apartment, Olga had already walked by the dining room, which took up about a quarter of our home. I indicated that the area was off limits for play-time. It was the home of my vodka cabinet, and even though the lower doors were locked, I didn't want anyone horsing around in there. For the time being, it didn't matter, as boxes and bags of unsorted baby supplies had amassed in the room. It was a visual to-do list, and I tried not to look in there every time I entered or exited the apartment.

Propped near the entrance to the room was an unopened Maclaren stroller. Olga looked at the pictures on the box. It was my shower gift from Paola; so naturally, Paola had to quiz Olga about it. "So, Olga, have you ever used this type of stroller before?"

"No." Even I was disappointed with her answer. Wasn't I going to be paying her because she had some level of experience with the latest infant gear on the market? But then she piped up. "At my last job, they had Maclaren Techno XLR. Very nice stroller."

Paola elbowed me and said, "I thought about buying that for you. It's got all the bells and whistles."

"Well, you know, I no have to buy it," said Olga, smiling. "But I have to use it. And dis one you have is much better."

Paola seemed quite impressed by Olga's comments. But I wanted the best for the baby, and sometimes that meant paying the most. "Why is this stroller better if it costs less money?"

"Techno XLR is very nice. Is big. But for me, is too . . ." Out came some words in Spanish as she motioned her arms like she was playing the accordion. At this rate, our baby would learn Spanish in about a week.

"The other stroller is too bulky and heavy," Paola translated.

Olga smile-nodded. "Yes. XLR is bulky. Dis. Dis one is better."

Now that we all agreed that the right stroller had been purchased, I tried to herd everyone to the nursery. Olga, however, was not done. "You know, Mrs. Pede . . ." her voice dropped off as though she couldn't pronounce or remember my name.

"Pedersen. Like the name 'Peter' and the word 'son'. Pedersen."

"Pedersen. I sorry," she apologized. "But that stroller too big for infant baby. You have another? Or you use sling? Or Baby Bjorn?" I had to laugh at the fact that she couldn't even remember my name, but she had nailed the pronunciation of "Baby Bjorn."

"I don't have another stroller yet. I have a Baby Bjorn." I was going to get the box, but obviously, she knew what it looked like. Hopefully, she could help me get it on someday because it seemed like a scramble of straps and hooks. Maybe a sling would be easier. "Do you like the sling or the Baby Bjorn better?"

Olga was able to comment informatively about almost every baby product that had been purchased. She was like a human instruction manual, albeit in Spanish, for every infant-related item in the house.

On our way out of the nursery, we passed the Medela breast pump, which was sitting on a side table next to the rocker. "You going to breast feed? Pump milk?"

Olga asked the question so clinically that I wasn't embarrassed to answer. "I am going to try. I hear it is very good for the baby."

"Yes, yes. Very good. You should try. At least first few months." I couldn't believe how enthusiastic she was on the topic. Maybe Olga would be my lactation consultant, too.

"Did you nurse your children?" I asked. Then I remembered— she had her own infant, somewhere in another borough. What if she was going to pump milk for her own baby while she was watching mine? What if her milk got mixed up with mine? None of this had been covered in our negotiations. My face flushed with panic.

Olga shrugged her shoulders to my question. "I try to nurse. I very small. I just no make enough milk." She said it like it was a failure. I was still grappling with the fact that this tiny woman had given birth, *twice*. But this new concept of not being able to produce enough milk. . . .Was that because she was petit, or genetically pre-disposed to that condition? "My mother watch my kids," she concluded. "Is easier for her to use formula."

"Oh. I see," I said, relieved. We gathered around the front door as Olga prepared to leave.

"But you have used frozen breast milk before, right?" inquired Paola. I listened intently as Olga and Paola spent a few moments discussing the logistics of using stored, pumped milk to feed the baby. Apparently, not only was I going to have to pump the milk, I was going to have to keep it from spoiling by storing it in specialty bags or bottles in the freezer. I decided that maybe the real reason Olga didn't nurse was because it seemed like such a royal pain in the booty.

18

Dale and I both agreed that scheduling an induction for the baby would be the best way to ensure that Future Daddy could be on-hand for the arrival of Little Pedersen. Tawny had informed me that inductions, and even scheduled caesarian sections, were the norm these days, as many couples were affected by circumstances similar to ours. My mother, however, voiced concerns about interfering with the natural course of childbirth. My response was that my delivery would be accompanied by the maximum pharmaceutical regimen allowable under law, so kick-starting the process with induction medication was a no-brainer.

My induction date was also on the radar of the Human Resources Department at McCale, Morgan & Black. They informed me that I could work from home starting the week before my scheduled due date. It was positioned as a major plus for me, given my commute in the unpredictable New York winter. Deep down, though, I knew that the real reason McCale wanted me out of the office was so that they could mitigate their risk. Heaven forbid I go into labor in the office and not get the proper medical treatment. I could sue them for Obstruction of Obstetrician.

While we on the outside of the uterus were actively awaiting his arrival, our little fetus showed no signs of leaving the nest. According to my recent visit to the obstetrician, there were no indications of labor whatsoever. No signs of dilating. Nothing, except excellent pre-natal vital signs. I was scheduled for another visit to the doctor the following week. It was supposed to be my last.

My work with HKI had tailed off significantly. I had successfully positioned Jeffry as my interim replacement. He seemed to be adapting well, as he never emailed me or contacted me for advice. I wondered how he was interacting with Nancy. No doubt she was tracking his every move, especially since I had delegated Jeffry's bar examination prep to her. All of my insights into the nuances of taking the exam would be complimented by Nancy's disciplined mandate to complete regular practice tests. Between the two of us, there was no way Jeffry could fail the bar for a third time.

Now that I had a few days to spare, Dale reminded me of the commitment I had made to Helen Macaluso; I had promised to help her with her fundraiser. I searched through my emails and found the ones from her that I had said I would review, but had completely ignored. Apparently, I had communicated that I would come up with three original cocktails, one for each course of a menu that Helen had forwarded.

While this seemed like an ideal job for me, there was a bit of a stickler in the execution: I was pregnant. I couldn't possibly sample the drinks I was designing, nor did I want to. I'd have to do my best at gutting my way through the recipes, have Dale test them out, and hope the palates of the Long Island Heritage Club would be coated with enough pre-dinner cocktails not to notice the difference.

There was a lot to learn about Long Island. Initially, I had viewed this outcropping as a 100-mile stretch of land with airports on one end, the Hamptons on the other, and a bunch of shopping malls in between. Helen's encyclopedic description of Long Island's agricultural history changed that perception.

Farmers had been raising crops on Long Island for over four hundred years. The agricultural community was experiencing a renaissance, given popular demand for locally grown, organic food. And of course, Long Island had its own wine region, located on the North Fork, or the northeastern extension of the island.

I consulted Helen's menu. Vichyssoise, or cold potato leek soup, was planned for the soup course. According to her information, the potato had been a primary Long Island crop. I needed a drink that was relatively strong, something to cut through the starchiness of the potatoes. But I had to pull back on the alcohol content, lest the partiers pass out at Course #1.

I wanted to make a drink with the consistency of a frozen margarita, but with gin as a base, not tequila. From a flavor profile perspective, it had to tie in with the soup, so I added some cocktail onions to the recipe. After all, gin and onions together comprised the Gibson; this would be a frappéed version. I'd have to fine tune it when Dale got home, but adding chopped chives as a garnish would be a fun dash of color for an unusual first cocktail.

My next order of business was to create a drink to complement the salad course. It was a pretty standard salad, something on every chop house menu in Manhattan: bleu cheese, apples and walnuts over organic greens. I flipped back through Helen's information for inspiration and found it: apples. New York was The Big Apple for a reason, and although upstate New York was home to the bulk of the apple agronomy, Long Island had some apple orchards of its own.

An apple liqueur would be a perfect anchor for the drink, but I didn't have any in the apartment. I hit the Sherry-Lehmann website and ordered up some Calvados for delivery later in the day. I learned that a good bottle retailed for at least $50, so serving a Calvados-based beverage to several hundred people might blow Helen's party budget. I figured I'd lighten it with local apple cider and sparkling water. That would make the flavor reminiscent of Martinelli's Sparkling Cider, a.k.a. the drink served to kids while their parents got smashed on Champagne on New Year's Eve.

In order to give it some backbone, I opted to add a splash of bourbon whiskey. I preferred Maker's Mark not only for the taste, but also for the fact that they owned a trademark on the red wax seal of their bottles. That was a stroke of marketing genius. I'd have to advise Jacques about some sort of packaging innovation for his *Créneau* gin.

In any case, Maker's was from Kentucky and I had to defer to Long Island sourcing whenever possible. Sherry-Lehmann was featuring the newly introduced Long Island Rough Rider whiskey, its name inspired by New Yorker Teddy Roosevelt and his rough-riding cavalry. I added that to my shopping cart, too.

The main course was farm-raised lamb. Red meat called for red wine, and the obvious thing would be to use one from a North Fork vineyard. I decided to concoct Sangria, with a Long Island merlot as a base. The pitchers were to be loaded with locally grown strawberries and apples, as well as lemons and soda water. To fortify the drink, I used Laird's Applejack. Unlike Calvados, which originated in France, Laird's is produced in New Jersey. (Not Long Island, but a lot closer than Brittany.) Importantly, Laird's

Applejack is a brandy that was favored by both George Washington and Abraham Lincoln. The distillery had been around since 1780. How was that for heritage?

I knew Helen would be excited about the drinks, and I couldn't wait to mix them for Dale when he arrived home from work. Happily, my order from Sherry Lehman arrived at the apartment just after lunch. It was an on-time delivery. I was hoping that mine would be the same.

19

I propped myself up on the stool next to the kitchen counter. I had to, because I couldn't breathe. I had slouched too long while sitting, so the bulge of baby mass in my lap had blocked the functionality of my diaphragm. Yes, I was now at the point where I had to assist my body with the involuntary act of breathing.

I got up and waddled around, trying to catch my breath, and wandered into the nursery. The curtains, recently installed by NYC Baby Prep, looked exactly as they had in that original photograph I had seen in Tawny's office—a blue and green gingham pattern with embroidered tennis racquets and lacrosse sticks. The baby's bookshelf was already filled with classics like *The Very Hungry*

Caterpillar, Barnyard Dance, and a vintage collection of Hardy Boys mysteries. Most of the books wouldn't be of interest for months but were necessary to create a scholarly environment for our son. I had even pre-washed all of the baby's clothes in allergy-free detergent and arranged them in the dresser.

I stepped around the box for the crib, which Dale had yet to assemble. He had promised to complete the task this weekend. As frustrating as it was not to have it in place, I could only manage so much of the prep work by myself. Besides, I could always call NYC Baby Prep and get an installer over to the apartment on demand.

Behind the crib box, on the far side of the room, was a large, framed poster available exclusively to NYC Baby Prep clients. It was a four foot by six foot bar chart delineating the developmental milestones of an infant's first year of life. The NYC Baby Prep designers had done a fantastic job with the graphics so the "Developmental Gantt Chart," as it was called, was easy to read. I knew I would be referencing this poster on a daily basis. It was going to be a great resource to track how my baby was doing against the typical norms.

I bent over to study what was supposed to happen during the early stages of the baby's life. The umbilical cord could fall off in the first week, responding to sounds would occur in the first month, and smiling was probable by month two. As I read about what was expected in the third month, the phone rang.

My back twinged as I stood upright. I didn't realize how long I had been hunched over, but the sensation of acid rain trickling down my lower back was disconcerting. I hoped I hadn't pulled a muscle. Maybe I had a hernia. Or worse—I could be in labor. I stopped short and realized that it was much too early for that. I shoved the idea out of my mind, focused on answering the phone, which was robotically emitting the words, "Nichols, Steven and Anna Marie."

"Hey, Mom." I squeezed the words out of my mouth.

"Maxine, how are you?" It wasn't a pleasantry. The closer I came to the due date, the more inquisitive Mom became about my physiological well-being.

"I'm O.K." I let out a groan as I bent backwards, trying to stretch out my back. I couldn't wait to see a chiropractor once this kid was out of me.

"You don't sound good. Is everything O.K.? Even though it's before the due date, the baby could come at any time. You know that, right?"

"Yes. And even though you have reminded me of that fact every day for the past two weeks, I am glad you've brought it up again." I lumbered my way over to the living room couch.

"What are you doing? Are you working out? Isn't it about time you stopped that sort of thing?"

"Mom, I just had to sit down. It takes effort at this point." I shoved a throw pillow behind my back, but that didn't seem to help.

"Are you in the living room?"

"Yes."

"On the upholstered couch?"

"Yes."

"Well, I hope you are sitting on a towel. If your water breaks, you will ruin the fabric on that piece of furniture."

She did have a point. I wanted to get up and get some towels, but another wave of pain shot through my back. I started to get concerned. If it was too early to have real contractions, maybe I was experiencing the false ones. As if I was supposed to know the difference.

I looked at the clock. 2:45 pm on a Thursday. Starting last week, Dale had agreed to check his phone for texts and calls during the day in case something like what I thought was happening occurred. But I had to get off the phone with my mother before I could call him. But I didn't want to call him unless I was sure of what was going on. "Mom, I think I had a contraction. I can't tell for sure."

"What?! Maxine, you get to the hospital right now! I will come and meet you there!" My mother flew into hysterics, which was not helping me at all.

"Mom!" I shouted back.

"Don't yell!" she screamed. "It'll only make it worse! And where is your husband?!"

I took a deep breath, per the instructions from my pre-natal classes. I went to that soothing place on the beach and tried to listen to the crashing of the waves. No contractions. Everything was under control.

"Mom," I said calmly. "Please chill out. I will hang up if you freak out on me." Whatever was happening had reduced my vocabulary to that of a spaced-out tween.

She apologized. "O.K. How often are the contractions coming?"

"We haven't established that they are contractions," I said in denial.

"Maxine!" I could feel her lips pursing. "Go get a watch with a sweep hand. Didn't they tell you anything in those pre-natal classes?"

"Sweep hand?"

"Just get a watch, Maxine. The two most important words when dealing with contractions are 'duration' and 'frequency.'"

Another shock blasted through my back. Now I had two words associated with contractions: "freakin' painful." I moaned pathetically as I shuffled to the kitchen counter. Slowly, the instructions from the classes were coming back. I wasn't supposed to go to the hospital until the contractions were less than five minutes apart. I still had time. Or at least I thought I did. "O.K. You're right. I remember. I'm writing it down."

"How many contractions have you had?"

"I think two." I hunched over the counter and decided I would wait for the next contraction before I started to record anything.

"What do they feel like?"

"What do they feel like? *Really?*" I couldn't believe she was asking me to describe the pain, when I was supposed to be focusing on anything else *but* the pain. "Well, Mom, it feels like someone has wedged their fingers into the blood vessels and nerves in my lower spine and then made a big fist and ripped everything out. Sound about right?"

"I'm coming down there." I could tell from her voice that she had made up her mind.

"You're going to hit a ton of traffic, Mom. How about I call you when I'm on my way to the hospital, all right?" Ironically, the last person I wanted around while I was trying to give birth was the person who had given birth to me.

"We're coming now. Why don't you start trying to get hold of your husband? He's the one who's going to have to deal with traffic."

I hadn't even thought about that. Dale's office was over half an hour by taxi from Lennox Hill without rush hour traffic. The longer it took for him to get out of the office, the longer his commute to the hospital would be. Ordinarily, I'd think the subway would be the fastest option, but the express trains on the Lexington Avenue line were closed for repair work. He'd have to do some cross-town subway-bus jig that could take well over an hour. What if Dale missed the delivery? What if I called him up to the hospital on a false alarm? And why wasn't this baby coming when it was supposed to—at the scheduled time next week?

I tried to reason with myself. Maybe I just had muscle spasms. I convinced my mother to at least pack her bags and make some overnight arrangements before she and my father came charging into the city. That would buy me some time to determine if I actually was in labor and, if so, to track down Dale.

My mother had just called again, this time to tell me that she and Dad were leaving. She had a semi-meltdown on the phone when she told me of a reported wreck on the Hutchison Parkway. They would have to detour, and blah, blah, blah, *contraction*. I had confirmed with myself that, indeed, I was in labor, and at this point, I didn't care how far apart the waves of pain were coming. I needed to get to the hospital immediately so I could get the proper medical attention, i.e. drugs. I told my mom I'd keep her posted and I hung up the phone.

I had already texted and called Dale a few times, but I hadn't heard anything. If he was actually on the trading floor, he'd never hear the phone ring or feel a vibration. That seemed like the only logical explanation for why he hadn't called me back, but it had been years since Dale had been down there, yelling like mad with the minions. He was too senior for that now. I knew his phone got reception all over the office at Worthington, so I was baffled as to why I hadn't heard from him. I picked up the phone and called his secretary directly.

"Worthington Investments, Mr. Dale Pedersen's office." Sabrina spoke with a lilted Dutch accent. I had only met her a few times, but she always looked like she had stepped out of a duty-free Bally store. She was overly protective of Dale's business calendar.

"Sabrina? This is Maxine, Dale's wife."

"Yes. How are you feeling, Mrs. Pedersen?"

"Sabrina, I am in labor. I have been trying to reach Dale for the past 15 minutes and he has not returned any of my texts or calls." I had to stop because I was out of breath.

"Yes, well, Mr. Pedersen is in a closed-door meeting with Mr. Macaluso until the trading day is over." She paused and then said, "He will not be available for another 58 minutes."

I pounded my fist on the counter. I would have used her jawbone as a cushion if I had been within striking distance. "I am certain that both Dale and Mr. Macaluso would understand if you interrupted the meeting. I am sure you can find a way to inform Mr. Pedersen of my condition."

"I am afraid I cannot do that. But I will let him know immediately when the meeting breaks up." That was even less helpful because there was no way the doors to Macaluso's office were going to magically open when the final trading bell rang at 4:00pm. Who knew how long the meeting would go on? Dale might not be available for an *hour* and 58 minutes!

"Look. Sabrina. I think you're being a little unreasonable."

"I think you're being unreasonable by asking me to violate the Worthington Code of Conduct."

Even in agonizing pain, I knew better than to threaten her with termination. I wasn't going to get anywhere with Sabrina, so I slammed the phone down. I texted Dale again. Nothing.

I gathered my belongings, pausing at the computer in the living room. It was the place where I worked, and now work was on my mind. I wrote a quick note to Deirdre and Caine, cc'ing Joy, Jeffry Hsu and Nancy Lallyberry, officially signing off. I congratulated myself for maintaining my professionalism in the face of excruciating pain.

While I endured another contraction, I considered other means of breaking Dale out of Bobbie's fortress of isolation. I could try to reason with Bobbie's secretary, but if Sabrina had stonewalled me, Sir Macaluso's secretary would be exponentially worse. I had to take this issue straight to the top. I dialed Helen Macaluso.

She answered the phone cordially. "Maxine! Good to hear from you! How are you doing?"

"Uh, well, I am heading to the hospital and I can't get in touch with Dale. I was wondering if you could help me."

Helen stammered. "Is everything O.K.? Are you all right? Do you need an ambulance?"

"Goodness, no. I'll be fine, but the contractions are heavy. Listen, Dale is in a closed-door meeting with Bobbie until the end of the day and his admin refuses to interrupt them. Dale won't return my texts. . . ."

She cut me off. "I am on it, Maxine. Don't you worry about a thing. I will take care of this. What hospital are you headed to?"

"I'm going to Lennox Hill. Dale knows where to go. I am leaving now."

"Good. Your safety is the number one priority. Get yourself over there immediately. Dale will be there. Good luck!"

20

The cab driver almost made a break for it when my doorman announced, "She's in labor!" He, like my mother, was in hysterics. I had to maintain my composure out of self-preservation. If I went bonkers, no cabbie in the Tri-State area would pick me up.

I quickly opened the taxi door and said, "Don't worry. Everything is fine. Just get me to the hospital. 77th between Park and Lex." Then I threw down a pile of towels on the backseat, a move that seemed to assuage the driver's fears. If I was going to make a mess, at least I had had the foresight to safeguard the sterility of his cab. The doorman threw my bags on top of a cigarette hole in the seat next to me, and we were off.

The cab jerked and lurched. Every sudden acceleration caused my heart to flutter. I clung to my phone for dear life. Instead of looking out the window at the continuous parade of accidents we were avoiding, I emailed, texted and called anyone who might communicate with me.

Finally, mercifully, I received a text from Dale. "Coming" was all it said, but that was good enough for me. I'd rather he hoof it pronto than stand around sending me a lengthy text. Helen called me to let me know that Dale had been pulled out of the meeting and that someone from Worthington had made arrangements for some sort of VIP transportation. I was going to ask for clarification, but the cab was approaching the hospital and I had to hang up.

Out of gratitude to me for not giving birth in his cab, I think, the cab driver helped me into a wheelchair at the emergency room of the hospital. I was grateful for his consideration, and since I couldn't speak Senegalese, I tipped him ten bucks.

The administrivia of the admissions process was expedited when my water broke in the wheelchair in the E.R. vestibule. I reminded myself that I was wearing black pants, so the fluid wouldn't be visible. But when the nurse helped me off with my clothes, I gasped in disbelief. Whoever had coined the term "water breaking" should be sued for fraud because whatever was all over my legs was far from a clear liquid. I sopped up what I could with my pants, which I then instructed the nurse to chuck into the medical waste bin because I never wanted to see them again.

My next emotion on the journey towards Delivery Acceptance was embarrassment. My initial physical exam, done by the on-call doctor, not my own physician, was interrupted when another doctor came in to consult about some lab work or x-rays or some such triviality that I didn't care about because all of my private parts were on display. That emotion turned to fear when I was informed that I had dilated to eight centimeters. It was almost time to start pushing.

Then there was panic when I demanded my epidural and the doctor said casually that he would, "See what he could do." I would have gotten up to poke his eyes out if not for the stirrups. The doc left, and in desperation I looked to Katie, my fresh-out-of-school nurse, for an explanation.

"I should still be able to get an epidural, right?"

Katie put an automatic blood pressure cuff on my arm. "This is going to go off every few minutes. Don't be alarmed when it does."

I jerked my arm back to my side. I had a new emotion: insolence. "I don't want to be inflammatory here, but I am a lawyer. If I do not get my questions answered in a satisfactory manner, I am going to bring the biggest, hairiest, ugliest. . ." I pulled my legs out of the stirrups as I paused to catch my breath, ". . . lawsuit against you, the doctors, the board and all the employees of this facility."

Katie pulled off a rubber glove and tried to stifle laughter.

"What?!" I yelled.

"Nothing," she said quickly, engaging herself in checking all the monitors in the room. "It's just that when you said, 'biggest, hairiest and ugliest,' well, I wasn't sure where you were going with that. Around here, that could mean a lot of things."

I grabbed the sheets with both hands, marking the arrival of another contraction. "Don't worry," she assured me, "You should get your epidural. In fact, I'll go check on it right now."

I heard my phone ringing across the room, but there was no chance of reaching it. I would have buzzed the nurse to help me, but if she was tracking down an anesthesiologist for me, I wasn't going to interrupt her. Drugs first, then cell phone.

The nurse came back with the anesthesiologist and someone else—I presume an assistant—to hold me down. He greeted me and then asked the nurse about the frequency of my contractions and reviewed my chart. I asked the nurse for my phone. Then the anesthesiologist asked her to contact my regular obstetrician.

"Why? Can't you just do what the on-call doctor says?" I demanded. "He said I could have an epidural!"

"Look, Mrs. Pedersen," he said calmly. "I know you're in a lot of pain." I gave him the look he received about ten times a day, the one where we women all called collective bunkum on his ability to even remotely understand our condition. But he was the holder of the needle, so I let him continue. "The good news is that it looks like you'll need to start pushing soon. This is going to be over with before you know it. I'm just concerned about administering the needle with your contractions coming at such a frequency."

I looked at the nurse. "What is the frequency?"

"Of your contractions?" She looked like a flustered witness as she reviewed the data on the monitor. "Every two minutes."

"Fine," I directed. "After my next contraction, you have over 90 seconds to get the needle in. I swear I will be perfectly still." My head dropped as I tried to bravely absorb another contraction as proof of my steely fortitude.

My phone rang again. The anesthesiologist looked horrified. "You must get rid of that." Then he glared at the nurse. "Clear the room of any noisy devices!" And then he ran off to answer his pager.

Katie handed me my phone, which bore the fantastic news that my husband was finally calling. "I just got here," he said. "What room are you in?" I told him where I was and that he should hurry. "Great," he said. "We're coming up."

"What?! Who is we?!" But the line went dead.

What a nightmare. Why were all these people parading through the room and no one was getting me what I needed? Another contraction signaled the painful realization that in the end, no matter who was around, or how many drugs I did or did not have, I, alone, had to birth the baby. I turned the phone off and handed it to the nurse. "Take it. I don't want it anymore."

Katie wiped off my forehead and offered me some ice chips. "Was that your husband on the phone?"

"Yeah."

"Well, you're lucky. He's just going to make the delivery. Do you know what you're having?"

"It's supposed to be a boy."

"Do you have a name picked out?" I was starting to understand her technique. Keep me talking so I could remain calm.

"My husband wants Hamilton. After Alexander Hamilton, the first Secretary of the Treasury." Katie nodded in oblique recognition. "My husband works on Wall Street."

"Oh, neat."

The blood pressure cuff went off. "And what name did you pick?"

"Henry. For Patrick Henry."

"Patrick Henry who?"

"Patrick Henry, the patriot," I stated, my frustration clearly audible. "You know, 'Give me liberty or give me death!' The Stamp Act? Sound familiar?"

She nodded and smiled, smartly taking the Fifth as she left the room to get more towels. That left me to listen to the woman across the hall. Even though her door was closed, the entire labor and delivery unit became painfully aware that she was in labor thanks to her deafening screams.

Katie came back in. I attempted to sit up to show my authority, even though I didn't have much of it. "Is that what's going to happen if I don't get my epidural?" Katie looked at me nervously, and without my saying so, ran off to find the doctors.

She went out, and Dale came busting into the room. His face was bright red, his hair was a mess and his pants were filthy. He rushed over to me. "Oh, my God! Are you all right?" He gave me a kiss and then took a step back. "Man, what's with all these cords and shit?"

"Can I come in?" asked someone from the hallway. It obviously wasn't one of the hospital employees, because they barged in whenever they felt like it.

"Who is that?" I whispered.

Dale quickly scanned me, I presumed to make sure I was decent. "Check it out. This is my escort!" Dale took a step back and motioned at the doorway. In strode a stocky N.Y.P.D. officer, sporting a leather jacket, knee high black boots and Ray-Bans. He took the sunglasses off and introduced himself.

"Thomas O'Shaughnessy, ma'am." And then he slapped Dale on the back like he had just done a beer bong.

It was unmistakable. With the glasses off, Thomas had the same bloated, freckled face as Patrick. Nature had selected practically the same chromosomes from the O'Shaughnessy Family DNA to make a virtual replica of Patrick. And here he was, in my delivery room.

"Patrick got his brother to give me a police escort from downtown. It was so awesome! And we got here in no time. Man, thank you so much!" Dale and Thomas exchanged a bear hug.

As if the room wasn't crowded enough with those two, a pair of doctors, my nurse and a couple of other tourists stuffed themselves inside. Then Dale got serious. "Who's the doctor here? How is my wife doing?"

"Mr. Pedersen," piped up the on-call physician, "I'd love to be able to check on your wife, but we've got a bit of a full house. Only immediate family is permitted in the L.D.R.s."

I winced in pain as I said, "Thomas, thanks a lot for getting Dale up here so quickly. See you soon, I hope."

But he didn't leave. "Maxine, don't you want an epidural?" Then he looked at the medical crew and said, "Is one of you going to get her an epidural?"

Meanwhile, Dale's phone started to ring. He put it on his chest when he said, "It's your parents. They just got here. Should I send them up, or what?"

"ENOUGH!!!" I shouted so loudly, the woman across the hall momentarily stopped screaming. Then I regained control of my voice. "Thomas, you take Dale's phone and find my parents. Go to a waiting room somewhere." Thomas did as instructed. "Dale, all I want you to do is hold my hand and help me. O.K.?"

"Got it." He placed himself on my left side and held my hand tightly. He looked at me, smiling, his eyes glazed over with moisture. "I love you," he said.

"I love you, too," I replied. My eyes welled up with tears— tears of joy, pain and relief. Through the bustle of the doctors and nurses around us, Dale and I both realized how close he had come to missing the birth of our son. I never thought I would have said it, but thank goodness for Patrick O'Shaughnessy.

21

I never got my epidural.

Dale got a bruised hand, an earful of profanity, and an eye-full of afterbirth.

We got a baby boy. Henry Hamilton Pedersen.

With Dale's arrival, I went into full-on labor. There had been no time to administer an epidural without the risk of spinal paralysis. At the time, that seemed like a good trade-off. Through the pain, I wondered why I had waited so long in the apartment before I had left for the hospital. But I was assured that I had followed protocol. Nothing I could have done would have controlled what the baby was going to do. It was a rude initiation to a phenomenon I was sure to experience again and again over the course of Henry's life.

Once Henry had passed into our world, I asked Dale to fish the camera from my tote. That brought him in plain view of the birthing site. He looked like someone who had just witnessed a gruesome car accident and couldn't stop staring at the convoluted mess of the remains. His mouth started to move and he began to stammer about hospital infection rates and patient privacy. I just shook my head, since at this point, the worst had to be over.

One of the nurses, probably familiar with his expression, guided Dale and the camera out of the room. I remember hearing the nurse tell Dale that his responsibility was to follow her around with the camera and document everything for me to see later. Mechanically, he nodded his head in compliance.

Katie and a few other saints helped clean me and the room up. "We'll be moving you to a postpartum room pretty soon. You'll be able to see your parents and any other visitors," she informed me.

"So where's the baby?" I knew the answer, but couldn't articulate a better question at the time.

Katie tied up a big trash bag of debris. "The nurse will bring him to you. You're going to nurse him, right?"

"Yeah, but I mean, already?" When I had mentally committed to nursing, I hadn't realized that it was going to happen almost immediately after the arduous delivery process. I could barely sit up, I was connected to a million tubes and, oh, yeah, I had just endured more pain than I thought humanly possible. "How am I supposed to start nursing? I don't even know what I'm supposed to do."

With a loud smacking sound, Katie filled a new garbage bag full of air. "I'm sure you'll figure it out. And there are plenty of lactation coaches here to help." She handed the bag over to somebody else. "I've got to go check on some other patients. Good luck with the baby!" She darted out of the room, and in a few minutes, I was rolled to my next destination.

Dale helped move me to the postpartum room, my home for the next day or so. Henry was in tow, in a rolling bassinet. He was crying. It was such a hopeless feeling to hear him upset, and to know that there was nothing I could do to help.

My husband was oblivious. In the elevator, Dale tried to show me pictures he had taken of Henry's first minutes outside the womb. He had one of Henry being weighed, one of Henry being measured, a few of Henry making his first footprint and even a video of Henry being cleaned. I couldn't concentrate on any of it due to the wailing.

As we proceeded to the room, I felt embarrassed by Henry's behavior. People were staring at me and then the rolling bassinet. The baby was barely one hour out of the chute and already, I was being condemned as a bad mother.

The nurse wasted no time in re-hooking me up to whatever monitoring equipment was in the new room. She instructed me to lie down so I could breast feed the baby. I shimmied as best I could, and then, per her instructions, I shoved myself back towards the side of the bed to make room for Henry. She told me where to put my arm, moved a few pillows around and then positioned him right next to me. But all he did was cry.

Even the nurse seemed frustrated with poor Henry. I was trying to feel empathetic, but I was so exhausted myself that I wanted her to just take him out of the room. And then my mother came in.

She was fully made up, wearing a black knit pants suit and dress pumps. The nurse stood up, presumably to allow my mother to give me a hug. But Mom went straight for Henry. She scooped him up and the crying stopped. I hoped that I, too, would inherit this magical gift of motherhood. Maybe I had to earn it first, through years of body deformation and mental anguish.

Mom handed Henry back to the nurse, who was successfully

able to get him to "latch." I was not happy that a term synonymous with a piece of hardware was being used to describe the intimate bond between mother and child. On the one hand, nursing was natural, peaceful and calming. But if I thought about it too hard, I felt like I was the featured gorilla on Animal Planet.

And then I considered what a joy it must be to be a man. Dale's greatest physical transformation was the grin pasted on his face. I'd never seen him so happy, texting pictures of Henry to the team at Worthington, bragging to O'Shaughnessy over Henry's bright eyes and burgeoning intelligence. For nine months, as my body morphed and Henry grew inside it, Dale hadn't changed. And for some naïve reason, I thought that once the baby was born, I'd be back to normal, just like Dale. Now, as the primary food source for our baby with about 15 pounds to lose, I had no idea what "normal" was anymore.

The 36 hours following my arrival on the postpartum ward can only be described as agitated relaxation. Almost all the concerns that would normally occupy my mind—work deadlines, social commitments, working out, foraging for meals—were either addressed or temporarily put on hold. I was officially on maternity leave, everyone came to visit me, labor was a monster work out, and all of my meals were brought to me on a hospital platter.

The vacant spots on my mental to-do list were more than occupied by the new activities of motherhood. I could have taken a month-long seminar on nursing alone, what with all the positions, the side-switching, and that ridiculous apparatus known as the nursing bra. And once I got Henry latched on, I had to record the duration and frequency of the feedings. The self-calibration and monitoring was eerily similar to recording my contractions. What was next—monitoring bowel movements? I didn't want to think about that since I hadn't even changed a diaper yet.

When I was told I would be discharged come Saturday morning, I couldn't get out of the hospital fast enough. I was anxious to enjoy the serenity and privacy of home with my husband and new son.

22

I carried Henry down the hallway to our apartment, snuggled in a thick blanket. Dale struggled behind, carrying everything else. Aside from the tote I had packed for the hospital, Dale was now juggling a bag of supplies from the postpartum room, assorted presents, and a vase of flowers.

We stared at each other when we got to the doorway, each of us laden with cargo and unable to open the door. At some point soon, I'd have to learn how to hold the baby and unlock the apartment. But since my keys were in my tote, attempting that feat would have to wait until later.

Dale awkwardly placed the vase of flowers on the floor and then dumped everything else. A couple of roses had been bent in transit, which I could remove once I got settled inside. "Good thing my parents brought the rest of the flowers home with you last night," I said. The arrangement from Worthington, I had to imagine, must have required its own seat in the cab. Knowing my mother, she probably artfully arranged everything around the apartment before returning to Westchester to take a Xanax.

Dale unlocked the door and rushed inside with the bags. The door closed in front of me, which gave me a moment to consider if what I had just seen was a figment of my imagination.

"Oh, my God! I'm so sorry!" said Dale as he opened the door again. I walked into the vestibule and froze. The apartment, which I had tidied up so neatly in between contractions just a few days before, was in shambles.

Navigating the cardboard boxes that once contained the crib was like stepping through an obstacle course. It would take an hour just to break them down and neatly tie everything up for recycling. Then the Royal We (i.e. Maxine) would need another hour to pick up the packing debris, which had managed to wedge itself into every crevice of the apartment. Lord knows what I would find if I looked in the kitchen sink.

"Jesus Christ, Dale! What happened?" I pulled Henry closer to me so he wouldn't have to see the chaos of his new home. It was pointless, since, from what I had read, he couldn't see farther than the distance to his own hand. I kicked a pizza box out of the way as I walked further into the apartment.

All the vases were grouped together on the kitchen counter. "What went on in here? My mom dropped off the flowers and you had a kegger? I thought you said you were coming home to assemble the crib last night."

Dale grabbed a garbage bag and started to clean up the mess. "Look, I'm sorry. Mike came over to help me put together the crib—which we did do, by the way—and then I just got distracted. You know, last night of freedom." He picked up a crinkled beer can near my foot and then wiped off some mysterious goo from the floor with a soiled napkin.

"Well done," I said, looking at the array of dirty glasses on the coffee table. "It looks like the kitchen threw up into the living room." Henry started wriggling in his blanket. His little hands, covered with mittens, grabbed at his face as he started to cry.

Dale stopped and peeked into the blanket. "What's wrong with him? Is he O.K.?"

"I'd like to put him down somewhere. He's kind of heavy." It was odd to think that a 7 pound, 14 ounce infant could cause so much muscle strain, but my back was killing me. "If I put him on that spot on the couch," I swung my elbow towards the one clear spot on the couch, probably where Dale had been overseeing the destruction of the Pedersen household, "he could fall off."

"He's not going to fall off the couch, Maxine," said Dale, as he rushed to that location to tidy it up.

I didn't want to argue. Not knowing which way to go, I started to swivel Henry in my arms. "You know," I said, "we do have a maid. You could have arranged for emergency service this morning."

"Well, you always take care of that, and I don't have her number, and I didn't want to bother you."

"Bother me? Wow. How considerate! Because let me tell you, bringing our son home to a pig pen doesn't bother me at all!" I started walking towards the nursery, when I almost slid on something underneath a McDonald's bag. "No wonder you didn't want my parents to come home with us this morning. If my mother had seen this place, she would have jabbed you in the eye with the Wii console."

"If she could find one," said Dale, sarcastically. "Besides, I thought we should have this time together. . . ."

"Whatever." I safely made it to Henry's room to see that, as Dale had claimed, the crib had been assembled. And that was it. "Where's the mattress? And what about the sheets and the bumper?" Henry was picking up on my agitation, his crying intensifying. "I gotta put this kid down, Dale."

"Try the changing table. There's a mat thing on there."

There was a mat thing on there, but the fabric cover was soiled with grease. Dale and Mike must have put their tools on it while they were assembling the crib. I'd have to baby proof the entire room again, scouring for hidden bolts, washers and, potentially, an abandoned power drill.

"O.K., I am going to the bedroom," I declared, it being my final option aside from depositing Henry into the bathtub.

"You sure you want to do that?"

"Don't have a choice Dale," I said, my voice cracking. My back hurt. Henry was crying. The apartment was a pit. Why had I been in such a rush to leave the hospital? I carefully stepped through the wreckage and opened the door to our bedroom.

Dale dropped his collection bag, and in two long leaps jumped over to my side. "So, what do you think?" he asked, grinning.

The room was immaculate. Not only was the bed made, but the duvet was cleaned and pressed. Shams were seeing the light of day for the first time in months. Bedside table drawers and armoire doors were closed. Even the rugs on the floor were plainly visible.

"Well, now I know how you cleaned this place up. You just threw everything into the living room," I joked, a tear running down my face. "I am impressed Dale. I didn't know you had it in you."

"I hate to burst the bubble here, but there's no way I could—or would want to—do this. Not that I don't love you." He kissed the tear off my cheek.

I laid Henry down in the middle of the fluffy bed and flopped down next to him. I pulled over a pillow for my head. The end of the pillowcase was stuffed inside the pillow, just like my mother used to do it. "So, I guess my mother was here."

"Yes, she was," said Dale from inside the closet. "I thought it was a master stroke to get her over here and away from you in the hospital. Killed two birds with one stone, eh?"

Henry's cries were fitful and constant. I checked my watch. "Maybe he's hungry again. I fed him about two hours ago, but the pediatrician said I should feed him as often as possible."

I sat up, considering what position to use. I was too tired to hold him anymore, so I lay down for the side-lying position. Henry just sat there crying while I frantically removed my sweater and then my shirt. I couldn't help but think that things might have been a lot easier if Henry had been born in July. But when I got down to the nursing bra, which was damp with milk, I began to appreciate the concealment benefits of winter layers.

Stripped down to just my motherhood, I tried to engage Henry in nursing. He wanted nothing to do with it and showed his frustration by punching me in the chest. I told myself to be patient. Nursing was hard. "Come on. Come on," I pleaded. But the punching and crying continued. Dale waited near the doorway, ready to bolt right out of the room once Henry latched on. I tried changing sides, and even positions, but nothing worked.

"Maybe he doesn't want to eat," offered Dale. "Maybe he's tired." I grabbed my sweater and put it back on, leaving the front unbuttoned in case I wanted to try nursing again. Dale pointed to a circular wet spot on the duvet. "Is that drool or milk?"

I just collapsed in a pile at the end of the bed, with Henry crying helplessly behind me. Through the fingertips that covered my face, I pleaded with my husband. "Dale, can't you pick him up and walk around with him or something? Please try to calm him down! I have been dealing with him non-stop! I need a break! Please!"

"I don't know what to do for him." Dale backed into the doorway, his face blank. "Uh . . . I'm going to finish cleaning up and I'll leave you alone. Maybe you just need some privacy."

"I don't need privacy! I need help!" Raising my voice only irritated Henry more. Nevertheless, I kept talking to try to keep Dale in the room, since I didn't know what to do either. "Maybe we should call a lactation consultant."

"Now? Are you crazy? And what are we supposed to do until she gets here?"

"I don't know. Maybe Henry will cry himself to sleep." It was a completely irresponsible comment which seemed rational when I said it.

Dale put his hands on the door jamb. He let his head fall forward through his arms, where it hung for a few drawn-out seconds. Mercifully, he picked Henry up off the bed. He started walking around the room, coddling his son. I was going to ask him to wash his hands since they had to be filthy from the garbage he had been handling, but Henry stopped crying. Too bad Dale couldn't lactate. He seemed to be a better parent than I was.

"Is he sleeping?" I whispered.

"No. I think he's just getting used to the place." I lay down again, the smell of fresh linens lulling me to sleep land. "Come on, little guy," whispered Dale, as he carefully laid Henry down next to me. He gave me a kiss on the cheek and walked out the door.

With no distractions, Henry and I were able to tackle the

latch-on problem in quiet solitude. It was a short meal, though, as Henry fell asleep. I had already learned that short meals meant shorter breaks between feedings. If I had any shot at a nap, I'd need to get him into the bassinet, pronto.

I laid out a blanket and made a several attempts to swaddle him. For all the folding and unfolding I was doing, I probably should have supplemented my pre-natal classes with a course in origami.

Dale came in right when I had perfected the swaddle wrap. "Well, that seemed easy enough," he said with a smile. Joking aside, his expression was full of relief. We both knew that despite our collective years of education, neither one of us had any practical experience in being a parent. Trial by fire never seemed so sweet.

23

The holidays were an absolute blur. I remember that before Christmas, Dale's parents came for a visit. We had ventured to the David Burke Townhouse for brunch. I didn't eat much of my meal, since I kept leaving the dining room when Henry got fussy. I was told I was being over-sensitive; I just wanted to crawl into a ball and sleep for a month.

Christmas itself was less stressful than usual. Because of my overwhelming maternal obligations, I was able to recuse myself of all holiday responsibilities. We spent the day at my parents' house and enjoyed an excellent crown roast of pork, prepared by my mother. Dale watched Henry while I helped my mom tidy up, which may or may not have been an even trade, since I had to use a Brillo pad to clean out the roasting pan.

Once New Year's rolled around, all of my sleep reserves had been depleted. The last thing I wanted to do was tart myself up for a New Year's Eve party. Nothing fit anyway. Nursing was supposed to help me lose weight, but I wasn't sure what could be done for my newly splayed hips. Pelvic reconstructive surgery with a bonus tummy tuck seemed more appealing by the day.

Even though I didn't feel like socializing, I knew it wasn't fair to deprive Dale of the opportunity. He went to Mike Simonson's annual New Year's Eve party alone. It was just as well since Henry and I were asleep by 10:00 pm. At 2:00 am, Dale stumbled through the doorway, totally smashed. Ordinarily, I would have been angry with him for disrupting my slumber, but Henry had already beaten him to the punch. While Dale pounded water to hydrate before passing out, I carried out my function as resident milk maid. Happy New Year to me.

I soon came to realize that my life existed at the pleasure of the infant. If he was hungry, I fed him. If his diaper was dirty, I changed him. If he cried, I picked him up. I couldn't even go to the bathroom without validating his well-being first.

As a rational person, I reminded myself that the rest of my life would not be this inhibited. I discussed this issue at length with the only other mothers I trusted, my own and Paola. Both encouraged me to try to venture out of the apartment with Henry. The entire island of Manhattan was at my disposal; all I had to do was figure out how to navigate it and its almost two million inhabitants, with an infant.

When I considered the myriad issues to be tackled just to leave the apartment, I began to realize why people had live-in nannies. I had to take pen to paper to map out all the factors impeding my freedom. The nursing schedule. Henry's burgeoning nap schedule. Rush hour traffic and the associated frenzy of pedestrians crowding the sidewalks. By the time I was done, I had identified only two twenty minute windows during which Henry and I could leave the apartment without potentially being trampled.

So, as I had been trained by NYC Baby Prep, I followed this schedule faithfully. For a while, it worked perfectly. But I knew it wouldn't last. Something would alter the plan; I just lay in wait, wondering what it might be. A power outage or a fire alarm in our building would do it. Or maybe Paola would have some sort of childcare emergency that I could actually handle, now that I was at home. But alas, the source of the first major schedule disruption was far more mundane than a building malfunction or a desperate friend. And it was far more disgusting, too. It was poop. Baby poop.

Henry had a bowel movement that could only be described as epic. Inexplicably, I had used the last baby wipe to clean off his face. No back-up wipes were in the changing table. I tried toilet paper to clean him up, but the soft tissue disintegrated upon contact with the poop. I moved to the next paper product, aptly called "Bounty." After an aggressive wipe with one of those quilted sheets, Henry let out a wail unlike anything I had heard before. For a moment, I wondered if he had been permanently scarred by the shrieking lady in the L.D.R. across the hall from me at Lenox Hill.

It was 5:30, in the thick of rush hour, but all I had to do was get across the street to Duane Reade so I could buy more wipes. The first order of business was to unshackle the accordion-like apparatus known as the stroller. Forget saving a few square feet of floor space in the co-op; I was never closing that thing again. I got Henry all situated, threw on my coat, and made a break for it.

Half way to the elevator, I realized I had forgotten my purse. I attempted to turn the stroller around but wound up banging on the walls, scuffing the hallway drywall. The co-op board was going to love that. Somewhere there was probably a camera that had recorded my inadvertent act of vandalism. I didn't care. The board could bill me.

I ran around my apartment frantically looking for my purse. It wasn't on the kitchen counter, where I usually left it. I ran to my bedroom, threw around some of Dale's laundry, but found nothing except a shoe that had been missing for a week. I ran into Henry's room and from there, I saw my purse on the couch in the living room.

Relieved, I set out to depart again. Henry's face was red with hysterics, so I picked him up to try and calm him down. As I put my hand on his bottom, his blanket felt soggy. I looked at the stroller, and to my horror, a light brown stain covered the seat. I ran as quickly as I could to the changing table to survey the damage.

I opened the blanket. There was poop everywhere. Henry's cute little outfit was officially broken in with markers on every layer. As I unwrapped him, I started to stress about the need to switch diaper brands, because whatever I was using had failed miserably. Or maybe I had the wrong size. When I finally uncovered him, I found the real source of the problem: I hadn't put a diaper on him at all.

Since I didn't have any wipes to clean him, I wound up giving him a bath. And when I finished that, I made sure I put a diaper on and dressed him again. This time, I put him in his crib while I cleaned up all the soiled clothing. Amazingly, I was able to detach the messy pad from the stroller. I stain-treated everything and put it all in the washing machine on the sterilize cycle. Then I sprayed air freshener in the entire apartment, in the hopes of getting rid of the stink.

With the stroller inoperable, I wound up lugging the car seat to Duane Reade. I made it in and out without incident. I felt like I had just passed some hazing exercise for new mothers. With the episode behind me, things had to get easier.

But when I opened the door to my apartment, it still smelled like poop.

By mid-January, New Yorkers had just about recovered from their holiday season hangover. Those in Hong Kong, many of whom had not been pre-occupied with celebrating the birth of Jesus Christ, had been working steadily over the past few weeks. Which meant that the McCale HKI team, with the exception of me, had been working steadily over the holidays, too. I started checking my work emails and voicemails every day so I could find out just what was going on.

Most of my inbox was filled with Nancy Lallyberry call-to-action emails, all of which I deleted. I had to balance the opportunity for sleep with the need to chime in about what fonts Nancy thought the team should use for the international briefs. I was pretty confident that she could handle that one on her own.

Occasionally, I'd receive a draft or final document for HKI, but that was only when the entire team was copied on the email; none of my input was requested and more disappointingly, required. I considered contacting Deirdre Morgan directly to glean some more information, but she had encouraged me to stay off email and voice mail and to, "Enjoy whatever maternity leave you may need."

Still, as the days dripped by, I felt like I was falling farther and farther behind. I was too exhausted to return to work, but I did have some pockets of free time while Henry was napping. I opened a container of Nutella and re-evaluated the term "free."

Whenever Henry took a nap, I was either napping myself or doing chores around the apartment. Most days, I could barely get myself dressed. I felt like I had free time, but that was because the majority of my day (and night) was spent on borderline menial tasks which required a bare modicum of intellectual capability. Yet for some unknown reason, I spent whatever free time I did have on mindless activities like sleeping, tidying up, or watching the Discovery Channel.

Paola had warned me about this syndrome. She called it "motherhood." She had coped with it by attending a peer group called "Even Moms Can Learn." The group held regular meetings in the basement of a nearby public school. It was run by Blythe Kasselbaum, an acquaintance of Paola's from Penn. Blythe also wrote a popular blog about parenting, which obviously gave her all the qualifications she needed to lead a monthly meeting on the topic. Paola encouraged me to attend.

Initially, the thought of sequestering myself in an underground space with a bunch of griping mothers sounded like a horrible idea. It was at this point that I wished I had joined a book club, or some other social outlet at which I could discuss something other than my child. But then I remembered my calamitous trip to Duane Reade, and I realized that maybe I could benefit from the years of experience of other, more seasoned mothers.

I went to Blythe's blog and checked the meeting schedule. The next session was set for mid-morning, this Saturday. I described the group to Dale, and he thought it sounded like a bunch of griping mothers in a basement. Then I told him that I was planning to take Henry with me. Suddenly, my attendance seemed like the greatest idea since the launch of Inter-Tech.

By the time Saturday morning rolled around, I was a basket of nerves. I still hadn't mastered the art of leaving the apartment with Henry, and I was running way behind schedule. I had to ask Dale for help. It was risky, since more often than not I had to help him with whatever I needed him to do, thereby negating the value of his contribution. It was frustrating for the both of us, since I think Dale would have liked to help more with the baby. Unfortunately, Beat the Boss was more important than *Pat the Bunny*.

"Hey, I'm running late," I declared, an explanation of why I needed help. "Do you think you could dress Henry?" I lifted my elbow and released some of the clothes I had collected for Henry from my armpit.

"Yeah. Just let me watch this segment." Dale was lying in a half propped up position on the bed, his eyes locked on the TV. He was wearing a workout t-shirt, which was caked with dried sweat from a morning basketball game. He had made the monumental effort to "change" by replacing his gym shorts with clean boxers.

"Can you just do it?" I put Henry on his back in the middle of the bed. His head was right near the remote, which I snatched up and used to put the TV on pause.

"Hey! What are you doing?!"

Henry lay there gurgling on the bed. I pointed to him and then ran off to dress myself in the bathroom. I heard Dale get off the bed and go into the living room. When I heard the TV go on in there, my heart started pounding.

"Are you just going to leave him there on the bed?" I demanded, pulling a shirt over my nursing bra.

I could hear Dale crack open a soda as he sauntered back to the bedroom. "I'm here, right? Chill out. The kid's not going to roll off the bed." Dale put his drink down on a newspaper that was hanging off the bedside table. It looked perilous up there, but I didn't have time to move it. He rubbed his hands together and smiled at Henry. "O.K. So what am I supposed to do here?"

I couldn't believe what I was seeing. Dale couldn't even dress himself. No wonder he was struggling with Henry. I slipped on a pair of stretchy pants and some socks, surveying the situation from the safety of the bathroom.

Dale picked up the onesie I had laid out. He had the sense at least to unzip it, but it was downhill from there. First, he made the mistake of putting Henry's arms in first. I think he realized the foolishness of this approach when he tried to get Henry's legs into the outfit. Henry kept kicking, his legs eluding Dale's grasp. That, coupled with the flailing arms, led both parties to extreme frustration. Henry cried. Dale gulped his Coke.

I grabbed some boots and took them into the bedroom. Dale put his arm up. "Don't say anything."

I really wanted to give him some advice, but I resigned myself to let him deal with Henry. He'd have to learn how to dress his son sometime. I put on my boots and wondered whether Blythe Kasselbaum ran a class called "Even Dads Can Learn."

24

"Your first time here?" The words came from a woman wearing a gold track suit with running shoes too clean to ever have been used for jogging. Two inch gold hoop earrings hung from her ears. Three gold necklaces hugged her collarbone. Her brown hair was wavy, cut in layers from her bangs to her shoulders, and heavily but professionally highlighted. Like me, she was holding a car seat with a baby. I looked down at the one thing we seemed to have in common.

"Yes, it's my first time here." She was staring at me. "Is something wrong?"

The woman tapped her head above her right ear, just where my Blue Tooth earpiece was propped. "You'd better take that freakin' thing off before the mommy police tackle you." I immediately removed the device, wondering if I had missed the memo about over-exposing infants to toxic radio waves.

"Thanks for the tip," I said.

She smiled cordially. Her teeth were bright white and perfectly straight. Maybe she was a dental hygienist. "Angela Perretti." She reached out to shake my hand.

I shook back. "Maxine Pedersen."

We both took a few steps down into what must have been a shared classroom space during the school day. Faux wood paneling covered the lower half of the walls, the remainder of which was painted a municipal gray-green. On the floor was a matted brown carpet so filthy I was grateful that Henry didn't crawl yet.

Then I realized that if I didn't start planning, he might very well wind up in a school like this. I had no idea how good the schools were near the co-op Dale and I had just bought. Why hadn't we looked into that? "Are you O.K.?" Angela asked. "You gonna hurl or something?"

"Maybe."

Angela winced.

"Figuratively."

Angela looked perplexed.

"No," I confirmed. "But is there an Even Moms Can Learn session about schools for kids?"

"Oh, my God," she laughed. "That's a totally different group. Most people join when they're pregnant." She looked at my belly, still distended, but with fat, not another baby. "You're probably not too late though. I'll hook you up after class."

I could tell that Angela was totally wired into the Manhattan baby scene. A friend like that would be priceless. I followed her into the room and sat down next to her.

"O.K., everyone! Please find your seats. We'd like to begin this month's session of Even Moms Can Learn!" The rest of the moms sat down, slowly revealing a heavy-set, white-skinned woman with jet black, shoulder length hair, squinty eyes and a thin-lipped perma-smile.

"That's Blythe Kasselbaum. She's organized this whole operation," shared Angela. She sat transfixed, admiring Blythe's every move, listening intently to every word. I couldn't tell what all the fuss was about. And whatever esteem I should have had for Blythe dropped about two notches when I saw the typo in her PowerPoint presentation. The title on the slide master, which was highly embellished with frills and sundry baby motifs, read "Even Mom's Can Learn."

I leaned over to Angela. "Mom's?" I asked, drawing out the word and furrowing my eyebrows. "With an apostrophe? Come on."

She looked at the overhead and then gave a revelatory smile, leading me to assume that she had never noticed the error. "Are you an editor?"

"No."

"Writer?"

"Nope."

"Lawyer?"

I nodded.

She looked at Henry. She looked back at me. "How old is he?"

"About eight weeks."

"So you're still on maternity leave?"

"Yeah. I head back in a couple of weeks."

"Well, good luck with that. Working with a baby is a bitch."

Terrific. That's just what I wanted to hear. "And what do you do?" Maybe she was in one of those pyramid-scheme sales groups where all the members were coerced into selling products that they all reluctantly bought from each other. And this "other group" about finding schools for kids was just an excuse to get me to come to one of her new-member hazing meetings.

"I'm in H.R." She paused, and for clarification she said, "Human Resources. I do part-time staffing." I knew what H.R. meant. I just couldn't believe that any company would hire her to manage its staff. Angela was just full of surprises.

Blythe pushed a clicker in her hand which magically started her presentation. "This week's topic is 'Getting Our Kids to Sleep through the Night.' But before we begin, I'd like to go around the room and have each of us quickly introduce ourselves and tell everyone the names and ages of our children. I'll start. As you know," she chuckle-snorted, "I am Blythe Kasselbaum . . ."

As the introductions progressed, I learned that about half of the women had at least two kids, and that, along with Angela's daughter, Gina, Angela also had a three-year-old son. With the introductions complete, Blythe began the presentation.

She started out by giving us some high-level pediatric health information, the sources of which were sketchy and very well could have been her imagination. According to her, infants should be able to sleep through the night at approximately four months old. Given her timetable, I would have to endure another two months of Henry disrupting my nights. How was I going to work in such a sleep-deprived state? If there was any way to get him to start sleeping longer, sooner, I needed to know.

"Would anyone like to share a success story about your child and his or her sleeping habits?" asked Blythe. Several mothers—the ones with more than one child—offered their opinions immediately.

"Well, I found that if I kept Marcie up super late—like 'til about midnight—she'd sleep until at least six in the morning," said

Mom #1. The majority of the circle nodded in respect for the idea. Encouraged, she continued, "Then, each week, I'd put her to bed earlier by fifteen minute intervals. I'm a really anal person, so for me, I really needed the structure."

This woman sounded like a total control freak. Then I remembered that I had been a slave to the NYC Baby Prep Schedule of Activities binder, to my own nursing schedule, to Henry's sleeping schedule. Wait a second . . . what had happened to me?

"Well, we know that children—and parents—thrive on structure," observed Blythe, as if she had read my mind. "What are some other ideas?"

"My son has been huge since he was a baby," offered Mom #2. "He was over ten and a half pounds at birth, so he eats a lot. We'd do what you did," and she gestured to the first mom, "but it just didn't work. Barry would wake up screaming about four hours in. He was starving. So, we decided to be proactive and wake him up right before we went to bed for a big feeding. That seemed to work for us."

"So does he sleep through the night now?" asked Blythe.

"Sometimes. He still wakes up about half the time for a feeding."

"And how old is he?" asked another woman.

Mom #2 hesitated. "He's 18 months old." The room fell silent. Blythe, without a suggestion of her own, shifted around in her chair probably hoping that someone would come forward with a solution. Nobody did.

"Well," concluded Blythe. "Would anyone else like to share an experience?"

Angela raised her hand and blurted out, "How long is his nap?"

"Me?" asked Mom #2, surprised.

"Yeah. Your kid's nap. How long is it?"

"He sleeps between three and four hours." Considerable

murmuring arose. Mom #2 looked around the circle feverishly. "Is that a long time?"

Several ladies spiritedly concluded that transferring Baby #2's napping hours to nighttime sleeping hours would result in improved relaxation for the entire #2 Family.

"That was very insightful," complimented Blythe as she smiled at Angela. Angela blushed with pride.

The scenarios continued at a dizzying pace. Henry, too, seemed overwhelmed by the stimulation, and he started to cry in his car seat. I rocked him aggressively, which did nothing except make my wrist sore.

Angela whispered, "Why don't you pick him up?" I looked around and realized that half the moms were out of their chairs, doing exactly what I should be doing with Henry. And some of the children were actually *walking around*. No one seemed to care. Even more astonishing was the fact that I hadn't even noticed.

I removed Henry from his car seat, plunked him on my shoulder and shimmied around the room. Apart from Henry's continuous need to grab my hair, it was actually very sweet to have him up and about. Social interaction had to be good for him, even if he couldn't understand the significance of the noises around him.

One mother was verbally flogged for habitually using Benadryl to get her child to sleep. Another was exalted for bringing her child into her and her husband's bed for the same purpose. That concept seemed totally contradictory to the point of the discussion; maybe the baby would sleep, but what about the parents? My perspective was shared by Angela, whose eyes bulged out of her head as she mouthed the words, "Never do that."

Blythe raised her hands and flapped them a few times excitedly. "Does anyone know about the Ferber Method?" She said it like a fifth grader who had just found out that one of the girls in her class had started her period.

The room fell silent. The word "ferber" sounded like a weird stuffed toy. Maybe Blythe used a "ferber" for bedtime role play and puppet shows?

Angela broke the silence. "I used the Ferber Method with my first born and I'll swear by it."

"You did?" gushed one of the moms. "Isn't it cruel? How could you do it?"

"It's all about short-term pain for long-term gain," said Angela.

"What is the Ferber Method?" I asked, this being my first contribution to the group.

Blythe responded. "It takes a lot of will power, but you basically let your child cry him- or herself to sleep." The words sunk in. That did seem cruel.

"But how do you know that there's not something wrong? Maybe the baby's hungry or has a dirty diaper," I said, much to the concurrence of the group.

"You only do it after your child has actually slept for six or seven hours straight through the night," said Angela. "That way you know they can do it. And you should be able to tell a difference in your child's cries—the dirty diaper one sounds different than the tired cry, which is different than the hungry cry."

Really? Was there an app for that? Because I had never heard of such a thing.

"How long did you let your son cry?" asked another mom.

"The first night was about three hours." There was a collective gasp in the room, but Angela and Blythe shared a simpatico glance. "The second night was about the same amount of time. But by the third night, he only cried for 30 minutes. And that was it."

And with a few more exchanges in the group, that was it for the meeting, too. Everyone seemed dutifully edified, and Blythe wrapped up the session to a round of applause. I made my way over to her and introduced myself as Paola's friend. I then asked her for some advice about finding schools for kids. She referred me to her blog.

Fortunately, Angela was waiting for me near the exit of the basement. She adjusted the faux fur collar on her gold-toned quilted down coat and said, "So, d' you ask her out on a date?"

"How very P.C. of you," I said, "especially for an H.R. rep." I smiled as I slid my trench coat over my arms.

She gave me a wry smile back and said, "Oh, please. You should hear the crap I have to listen to. I work in the construction industry for God's sake."

"Really?" I said, not surprised.

Angela picked up her car seat. "It's practically a friggin' miracle if I can get one of those bozos to sign their name on a piece of paper. Half of 'em call their union rep to see if it's O.K. just to go to the bathroom. And it's holy hell if I have to terminate one of 'em." Angela's tough pragmatism seemed perfectly suited to performing such a miserable function. I guess everyone had their calling.

I held the door open for her as we walked out of the school. "Well, I gotta head back to start dinner." She smiled approvingly at me. "You should come to the next meeting."

"Yeah, well, I'll probably be back at work by then. I don't know if I'll have time on the weekends to break away."

"You will if you want to," she advised. "It's all about choices."

25

There was no doubt that Nancy Lallyberry was annoying. But her role as office sycophant did make her knowledgeable on the status of everything in the office, from the number of times her admin returned late from lunch (an average of 2.1 times a week) to the partner with the highest number of frequent flier miles (Harry McCale). Since I hadn't received any major updates about HKI in weeks, she was my most dependable resource to find out what had unfolded during my absence.

If I hadn't known her so well, I would have thought she was the nicest, most considerate person. She was curious about the baby, wondering why I was bothering to check email at all, and confident that I would get right back into the swing of things. She was like my own little cheerleader.

Nancy was kind enough to communicate that HKI had expanded in scope. Not only were Deirdre Morgan and Paul Black on the team, but Harry McCale had also joined. My initial reaction was excitement; I could get great exposure as a team lead working for the three key partners of the firm. But the more Nancy and I communicated, the more concerned I became. From what I could surmise, she had somehow elevated herself from her former role as a team lead to, basically, Deirdre's deputy.

This was bad in so many dimensions.

The entire organizational structure of the project must have changed. Had Jeffry Hsu magically developed amazing writing skills and taken over my role on a permanent basis? Had Nancy assumed my title as *Most Likely to Make Partner*? It was excruciating to sit at home, knowing that while I was gone, my role on HKI, and potentially at McCale altogether, was fading. I had to get back to work soon.

And so, at the height of panic, my mother called. She and my dad had agreed to stay late after a matinée of *Der Rosenkavalier* to watch Henry so Dale and I could go on a date. I said a quick prayer that she wasn't going to cancel on me and answered the phone. "Hi, Mom."

"How's Henry?" I was used to this; I may have been the one talking, but I was just a surrogate to provide updates about my mother's grandson.

I looked over at Henry, who was examining a stuffed black cat in his playpen. He smiled at me and I reached to pick him up. I did so without dropping the phone, a skill I had mastered while home over the past few weeks. "He is excellent." He gurgled in response, punching me in the shoulder.

"Oh, I can hear him! I can't wait to see him! I'm telling you, if this opera is a bust I am leaving at intermission to come over there so I can see more of that beautiful little boy."

"You're more than welcome to come whenever you want, Mom." But that would never happen. As the crow flies, my parents only lived 20 miles away, but the commute made an impromptu visit to Manhattan prohibitive. The next time Paola complained that her mother was five minutes late to watch her kids because she got stuck in midtown traffic, I'd have to stop myself from gagging.

I then provided my mother with what she really wanted: an update on Henry's two-month pediatric exam. Henry was trending well and had grown and gained weight to keep him in the 85th percentile of national infant height and weight metrics. He was ahead of selected milestones. I was able to track his progress against the handy NYC Baby Prep Developmental Gantt Chart poster in Henry's room; the pediatrician provided confirmation.

Regardless of the chart or the doctor, I knew that Henry was doing great because he was happy, responsive and engaging. Truth be told, I had expected that by now, I would have morphed into a hyper-competitive mother, comparing Henry's attributes to those of every other infant. That, in turn, would validate Henry's position as an exceptional child, and mine as a superlative mother.

Instead, I got my validation from my one-on-one interactions with Henry. Since I hung out with him practically 24/7, I observed the minute changes in his behavior that collectively indicated great health. I didn't need a medical degree to notice that Henry could raise his head a bit higher, or tug on my hair a bit harder with each passing day. And I could certainly tell he was gaining weight as he had already moved into an entirely new set of clothes.

Dale noticed none of this. I chalked it up to his Y chromosome. In reality, I knew that his work schedule precluded him from collecting all the data that I could; he just wasn't around. And very soon, I would become as ignorant as my husband was about the intimate developmental progress of our son.

Paola had tried to assuage my growing guilt on this issue. She had informed me that the pace of Henry's infantile development would slow considerably over the next year. In lockstep, my heavy conscience would become progressively unburdened. Even better, as Henry approached 18 months, I would welcome the chance to spend a good portion of my day away from him. Paola's daughter was around that age, and she described Amanda as something akin to a one-woman wrecking crew with spontaneous bouts of tearful hysteria. But Henry couldn't even sit up; what if I missed him achieve this feat because I was at work taking orders from Deirdre?

I wasn't the first one to deal with this situation, and I wouldn't be the last. I'd have to follow Henry's lead and make a little progress each day, while trying to figure out how to incorporate him into my life. He'd grow into a toddler, and I would perfect professional motherhood. Hopefully, by the time he turned 18, I'd have the whole work-life balance thing figured out.

With my maternity leave almost up, I decided to visit the office. I needed to prep it for my return, and that meant dropping off the duplicate breast pump, shields and bottles that had been purchased specifically for office use. I could only imagine Caine's reaction if we were to share an elevator ride on my first day back to work, and I had the pump strapped to my shoulder. He'd probably think it was a bomb.

When I stepped off the elevator, I was surprised that the first thing I noticed was the smell. It was a combination odor of industrialized floor tile carpet and reams of copy paper. I had an impulse to sit at my desk and start working. But when I got to my office, it became clear that I'd have no chance to satisfy that urge.

I didn't even have to open the door; standing in the hallway, looking through the glass walls, the space was unrecognizable. Boxes were piled from floor to ceiling covering practically every inch of the floor. I couldn't even see the back wall. Upon closer inspection, it seemed as if my office was being used as some sort of staging area for the mailroom.

I went in. I discovered that all of my personal items had been removed and neatly stored in a box under my desk. The box was taped and labeled, "Maxine Pedersen. Maternity Leave." At least it didn't say, "Maxine Pedersen. Staff Reduction Candidate." Was office space really that tight? Or was this supposed to be some subtle message about my future at the firm?

I allowed my blood pressure to subside before taking action. I left a friendly but direct message with the office manager requesting that my office be emptied and professionally cleaned within 48 hours. I also updated Joy on the situation, letting her know that I would be making periodic trips to the office in preparation for my return. Then I went home and had a vodka tonic.

Timing for the cocktail was excellent. I had instructed Dale to bottle feed Henry while I was gone. Dale had done a pretty good job, I had to believe, since both father and son seemed content, sitting on the couch watching golf on TV. I pumped the milk I would have used for Henry's feeding. I did a Milkscreen test on it, which it failed, so I chucked the freshly squeezed beverage. No loss, though; I had about 100 ounces of it stored in the freezer already.

During my last week home, I enlisted Olga to work half-time. This worked out great for her, since she started to earn money sooner. It was also a perfect transition for me and Henry. I was able to share Henry's likes and dislikes, and he was able to get acquainted with Olga in an unstressed environment. After some initial protests, which were heart-breaking to hear, Henry seemed to take a liking to his new companion. She seemed adequately relaxed and competent.

With the nanny on board, I had to make sure the nanny monitoring system was functioning. Up until this point, all I had done to get it up and running was to take possession of the system's instructional binder, which I had ignored.

Reading through a bunch of blathery jargon was the last thing I wanted to do. But I told myself to pretend it was legal research and that reviewing it would be a good refresher for my seamless transition back to McCale. I had to tell myself something. Nobody likes reading instructional manuals.

After pouring over the book for about an hour, I learned how the surveillance data was stored. I set up passcodes so I could review all the historical files at my leisure. Alternatively, I could log in and view the apartment live, through either camera.

I decided I should put the latter capability to the test while Olga was watching Henry. I took my laptop to the neighborhood Starbuck's and logged in to the system. As the image of my apartment filled the screen, my hands started to sweat. It was absolutely surreal to watch my son being handled by another person. Henry and Olga looked like they were starring in some sort of B-movie horror film, given the lack of sound and the hazy picture quality.

The very nature of this voyeuristic act implied that I did not trust Olga. But I was less concerned about what she thought about me than I was about the safety of Henry. I assured myself that with all of Olga's nanny experience, she was probably used to the situation. In fact, she had probably already identified the location of the cameras in the apartment.

All I needed to see, though, was Henry's smiling face. It was such a relief to see him content and happy. I watched as Olga put him on the floor with his back facing the camera. I couldn't see his face anymore, but I could see his arms jerking up and down. That usually meant he was smiling. Olga's face lit up as he flailed around, and she handed him his plastic keys. He handed them back to her and I could tell that she laughed. I smiled, too.

I shut my laptop. Henry was in good hands. I sipped my decaf Chai tea and felt confident that everything was in place for my resumption of activities as a senior associate at McCale, Morgan & Black.

26

I woke up. I checked on Henry. I showered. I brushed my hair. I applied my make-up. I put on the clothes I had laid out the night before. I grabbed my phone, the Baby Boppy and Henry, and did my motherly duty while checking email and voice mail. I burped Henry, answered the door, let Olga in, and handed him over.

I looked at my watch. Only 49 minutes. Under an hour. Good.

It was a crisp, clear February morning. Without a diaper bag, stroller and baby, I felt unusually spry, darting through the rush hour crowd in Grand Central Station. Nonetheless, I didn't stop to get coffee; I'd drink whatever was in the break room. I had a

Clif Bar and a banana in my bag, and I would eat breakfast at my desk.

I cruised into the McCale office. To my disappointment, there was a surprising lack of fanfare over my return. One or two admins hugged me in the lobby, but otherwise, I just received a few smiles from the staff. My life-changing event hadn't changed anything inside the walls of McCale, Morgan & Black. Maybe that was a good thing.

Joy was the one exception. She was particularly interested in the story about Dale and the police escort and gushed over the pictures of Henry. I think she could have listened to me talk for the entire day. By 11:30, all of the chit-chat and return to the office administrivia had limited my billable hours to a mere 90 minutes.

I had been at the office over three hours. My calendar was open, so it seemed like a good time to pump. I grabbed the machine and scooted to the bathroom just a few yards from my office. I zipped by Joy too quickly for her to ask where I was going. Given the conspicuous, clunky pleather box attached to my shoulder, she had to have known exactly what I was doing.

I set up shop at the bathroom sink, as far away from the door as possible. I was prepared to employ my blazer as a privacy shield if someone came in, but nobody did. I wished there had been outlets in the stalls so I could have done my pumping duty in privacy. It was a mathematical certainty that, at some point, someone would enter the bathroom while I was pumping, and I would get busted. Although "busted" wasn't the right word since I wasn't doing anything wrong. In any case, when I was finished, I put the pumped milk in a brown paper bag with my name on it, and shoved it in the back of the freezer in the break room.

Back at my desk, I checked my watch. 12:13 pm. I had pumped ten minutes on each side, so twenty minutes was accounted for.

Between the set-up/clean-up time and the few minutes to package and store the milk, I was looking at at least another five to ten minutes for each session.

Disappearing for half an hour at a time was going to take some maneuvering. Next time, I would definitely bring my phone so I could check email while pumping. Perhaps I could even send messages from the bathroom to waylay certain people, like Nancy or Deirdre. I'd have to stockpile a list of reasons for Nancy to charge over to Deirdre's office so I wouldn't be bothered: *Nancy, Deirdre needs you to install that new valet parking app on her phone ASAP! Deirdre needs the memo reprinted in 12 point font, not 11, pronto!*

As I got back to work, I noticed a marked increase in hallway noise. Then I realized why the bathroom had been empty. Monday at 11:00 was Deirdre's high-level staffing meeting. It explained Deirdre's absence from the bathroom, as well as Nancy's. Lallyberry had probably been at her desk on stand-by, waiting for some scrap assignment to fall off the conference room table and into her inbox.

Realizing this, I immediately blocked off 11:30 on Mondays as an ideal time for pumping. I decided that any time there was a scheduled meeting involving Deirdre and/or Caine, I should be pumping. I poked my head out of my office door and said, "Hey, Joy? Can you come in here for a minute?" I sat back down at my desk and tried to feel authoritative, despite my impending, totally personal request.

"Do I need to take notes?" she asked as she stood in my doorway with a notepad.

I waved her in. "Not now. I sort of need a favor."

"Does this have anything to do with. . . ?" She raised her eyebrows as she stared at me. To the average onlooker, her gaze might have seemed indiscriminate, but I knew that she was staring directly at my chest.

"As you've probably figured out, I am going to try to pump at work."

Joy gave me a big grin. "I nursed both my kids for a year. I think it's fantastic that you're doing it!"

"Yes. Well, it seemed like a great idea when I was in the privacy of my own home. Here at work . . . that's a different story."

"Oh. Do you want me to keep watch while you do it in your office?" she offered. I looked at the glass wall of my office. I really liked Joy, but if she could only sit where I was sitting, she would have realized the absurdity of her suggestion.

"No. There's no privacy in here. And even if there were, it's not your responsibility to act as a look-out for me while I am participating in non-billable activities."

Joy sat upright in her chair. I slouched over in an effort to seem more informal.

"You understand the benefits of nursing. It's the logistics of pumping that is the problem. I'd like to mitigate the chances of an encounter in the restroom by being a little more educated about partner meetings, client presentations, and things like that."

Joy nodded her head knowingly. "I get it. You want to pump while everyone else is at a meeting so they don't walk in on you in the bathroom."

"Exactly!" It did sound a lot simpler when she said it. Joy agreed to monitor the company calendar for regular meetings, and she would alert me of any client visits. Joy was excused, and I checked my desk clock. The last 15 minutes, like the 30 before it, had been totally off the grid. To what code could I charge "Pumping in Bathroom" or "Scheming with Administrative Assistant"? By the time 6:00 pm rolled around, I would have to take at least one, maybe two more trips to the bathroom. That was going to put my daily un-billable total to well over an hour.

Somehow I had to make up the time, by either coming to work early, staying late, or working from home. Olga had reminded me that morning that she had to leave promptly at 6:30 pm that day and every day. I'd have to do my best to accommodate her schedule, so working from home after work was going to have to be the solution, at least for the short term. I hadn't even made it through my first day at work, and already I felt like quitting the pump.

"Maxine! It's good to have you back." Deirdre Morgan strode into my office and shook my hand.

"It is good to be back." I said as my eyes darted wildly around the office, checking for any stray nursing paraphernalia.

We exchanged a few pleasantries about Henry and parenting foibles. Deirdre shared her own story about how alarmed her husband had become when the remnants of their child's umbilical cord had come off. From her vague description, I couldn't tell if Deirdre had been home for this momentous occasion or not. Which would have been weird, since it had happened to Henry within the first week of his life. And then I wondered if Deirdre had taken any maternity leave at all.

"Well, Henry sounds delightful," she concluded the second I took a breath. "Shall we go to the meeting?"

"Meeting?" I asked. The word slid out of my mouth before my brain had time to stop it. It was too late to scan the emails I should have been reviewing over the last half an hour. I didn't have the energy to pretend I knew about any meeting, and Deirdre didn't have the time for me to fake it. I just grabbed a pen and pad followed her down the hall.

I composed myself. I didn't get one-on-one time with Deirdre too often, so I plowed headlong into issues pertaining to HKI. "We haven't heard back from the local office of the F.T.C. yet, have we?"

Deirdre smiled as she opened the conference door for me. "No, but I am impressed that you're so up to speed with the account." I sighed with relief, since apparently nothing had happened since the last status report had gone out.

Deirdre glided right by me to the head of the table in the conference room. Her presence cast a pall over the characters assembled inside, which included Jeffry Hsu, Nancy Lallyberry, and a handful of eager-looking junior associates rummaging through accordion file folders, trying to look worried. A red light blinked on a speaker phone at the center of the table, indicating that someone else would be joining the meeting. Since McCale and Black were not in the conference room, I wondered if either one of them would be at the other end of the telephone line.

I sat down in an empty chair between Jeffry and Nancy. This forced Nancy to move the gigantic mound of paper that she had managed to transport from her office to the conference room, ostensibly to have the entire case at her fingertips. When people described Nancy as "green," it wasn't a reference to her ecologically friendly work habits.

"Welcome back," she whispered.

"Thanks."

As Nancy reorganized some papers, I noticed the tinkle of the charms on her bracelet. The usual suspects were present: a heart engraved with some important date; a modified symbol for the scales of justice; a flower; and a small picture of a baby, probably Troy. Nancy didn't even have pictures in her office, so I was surprised to see one on her wrist. Had she worn the bracelet today as a tacit act of motherly solidarity, or had I just never noticed it before?

Deirdre took command of the meeting. "Harry McCale will be joining us from Hong Kong momentarily." She gestured at the speaker phone. I squeezed my pen. So much for an easy transition back to work. "While we wait for him to dial in, could someone give Maxine an update on the account?"

Before Nancy's hand shot up in the air, Deirdre honed in on Jeffry. I stopped staring at Nancy's bracelet and faced the junior associate, who looked miserable. His suit was crumpled, his face was sallow and from up close, it seemed as if he hadn't shaved in a few days. He was lucky that he didn't have a heavy beard, because that might have been the hygienic faux pas to get him kicked out of the office for a day of unpaid leave.

He stammered through a synopsis. Through his brief explanation, it was clear that Jeffry had a solid understanding of the situation. I could only assume that his shoddy appearance was some sort of pathetic badge of honor, a reflection of the long after-hours he had spent studying for the bar exam. I wondered if I could use my extra-curricular activities, i.e. parenting, as an excuse to a eliminate showering from my daily routine.

"Thanks for the synopsis, Jeffry. I read all of Nancy's emails while I was on leave, so I should be fairly up to speed."

Deirdre pulled her glasses down to the end of her nose and raised her eyebrows in my direction. Then I heard Nancy thank me. I realized that the first thing I had done in a group professional environment since my return to the workplace was to praise Nancy Lallyberry. My professional moxie had just been stunted by maternal empathy. What was going on here?

After a few productive hours of work and another successful—or rather, uninterrupted—pumping session in the bathroom, I was ready for a nap. I had forgotten how mentally exhausting the

McCale, Morgan & Black atmosphere could be. But rather than crawl up in my bed, I had to power through a team meeting. I had just called for a breather, as we had been hacking through the to-dos from the conference call for over an hour.

I settled behind my desk, admiring the one picture of Henry I had brought to the office. I checked the clock. Henry was probably napping right now. At least he was supposed to be napping. I wondered if Olga was sticking to the schedule I had prescribed. I thought for a moment about calling her to check in; but if Henry was, in fact, sleeping, then a phone call would wake him up.

This was ridiculous. I had given the team a ten minute break, and I had blown half of it contemplating something over which I had no control. I now realized why Nancy Lallyberry had no pictures of her son in her office. They were too distracting.

Thoughts of Nancy, this time anyway, helped me to calm down. Judging from the delegation of work so far, it was clear that Nancy had not re-organized the entire HKI team under her domain. I still had my team and she had hers. Maybe things weren't so bad.

I looked up, and there was one of my team members, Horace Blankenfield, gesticulating wildly right outside my door. I calmly waved him in.

"Horace. Chill out. What's up?"

Horace shifted his weight from side to side, like a toddler trying not to wet himself. His face was red. I stared at him until he squeezed out the words, "You gotta come now. To the conference room. Everyone's in there. Emergency."

It felt like a foghorn had gone off in my office. Urgent emails had piled up in my inbox, and I hadn't even noticed. Then Joy came in to find out what was happening.

"Is everything O.K.?" she asked, probably hoping it wasn't so there would be some excitement in the office. Which was the last thing I wanted, especially at this hour. Any emergency that cropped up after 3:00 undoubtedly meant that the entire team would be staying late to resolve it. But I had to leave at 6:00 so I could get back to relieve Olga. I couldn't be late relieving the nanny on my first day back to work!

More people charged towards the conference room. "Nothing's wrong," I lied, as I picked up a pad and darted out of my office. When I got to the conference room, it was standing room only. Paul Black had joined Deirdre Morgan at the head of the conference table. The two of them were hunched together in a mini-conference. The rest of us waited to learn our fate.

A few minutes went by. I could tell from the smiles and nervous glances that people were texting each other. That was a great idea, I thought. I could text Dale and see if he could get home tonight to relieve Olga. Then I realized that I had left my phone in my office. I started squeezing my way through the crowd towards the door so I could snag it when Deirdre started to speak. Someone shut the conference room door. No one walked out on Deirdre Morgan.

We all listened intently as Deirdre described a grand theft had occurred at the main warehouse of Hong Kong Industries. The target of the theft had been the products that our company, McCale, Morgan & Black, had been hired to patent. The HKI Board was in a panic over the loss of their intellectual and physical property.

Although it wasn't the best news, there were ways to accelerate the patent process, and HKI's paperwork with the Patent Office was fairly far along anyway. The loss of the inventory was a problem, but that seemed like an issue for the local police.

But it was the police, according to Deirdre, which were our biggest source of concern. The Chinese authorities had detained anyone with information pertaining to the case. Unfortunately, that included Harry McCale, who was supposed to have been on a flight home from Asia at this very moment.

Immediately, I knew that I had to find someone to get to the apartment by 6:30. I was tempted to ask Horace, who was shuddering next to me, if I could borrow his phone. But then Paul Black took over.

With a commanding tone, Paul described a high-level action plan. He was heading to Hong Kong by private jet as soon as Jeffry Hsu finished taking the bar exam. I jerked to attention. The bar exam was supposed to be on a Tuesday, not a Monday. It had been a long day, but not *that* long. Something was amiss.

Apparently, Black had secured a waiver not only for Jeffry to take the test early, but also for Jeffry to be given a compressed exam. He had somehow convinced the Bar Association that Jeffry's fluency in Cantonese, and his leadership on the team, were critical in extricating fellow bar member and Section Chair Harry McCale from the Big Brother claws of Communist China.

I knew that Paul was a brilliant attorney, but I was stunned by the direction in which he chose to wield his power. With Black's connections, I would have expected him to start working over some contacts at the State Department. He probably could have borrowed a top translator from the United Nations, rather than deprive Jeffry of one more night's worth of studying for the bar exam. And given Jeffry's past failures on the test, he needed all the help he could get.

Paul mercifully gave us a few minutes' break. That was code for, "Call the spouse and kids and let them know you're not coming home." I texted Dale as I walked back to the office. I wasn't sure why; even if he dropped what he was doing at that very moment, he'd never make it back up to our apartment in time to relieve Olga.

I shut my office door and called our nanny.

"Meezuz Peedairsen," she articulated. I only had to tell her one time not to call me by my first name, and the fact that she had remembered made me hopeful that she might be amenable to working with me around this professional crisis.

"How is your first day going? Henry's O.K.?"

"Henry is fine." I could hear him cooing in the background. "But my mother call to tell me that my son has a fever. Do you think you could come home early, Meezuz Peedairsen?"

Early? *Really?* It was her first day on the job and she was already unreliable. Was she going to make this a habit? Leaving early? And as everyone scurried around outside my office, I realized that my only option on my first day back at work was to do the same thing.

I looked out of the window of my office. Joy was packing up her things, getting ready to go home for the day. I waved hysterically to get her attention. I couldn't have her leaving early now, too.

I hung up with Olga and hauled Joy into my office. I explained the emergency meeting situation and the fact that I was about to blow it off so I could go relieve my nanny.

Joy had it under control. She said she'd explain everything to the powers that be, patch me through to the conference call and make sure all the proper documentation was forwarded on to me. Then she practically kicked me out of the office.

I wasn't quite sure who the one true professional was at McCale, Morgan and Black. Joy? Deirdre? Nancy? At this point, I just knew it wasn't me.

27

Jeffry Hsu had exceeded everyone's expectations with his mastery of the language, culture, and most importantly, the "legal" system in China. It took him less than four hours to negotiate the release of Harry McCale. For all I knew, the Hong Kong police commissioner was Jeffry's uncle, and he had created this whole fiasco just to make himself look good. Now the guy was a downright hero.

And as a reward, McCale, Black and Hsu took a day at the luxurious Peninsula Hotel to decompress before taking a chartered flight home. I couldn't even fathom what it might be like to suddenly desert my family at this juncture of my life. But for an unattached up-and-comer like Jeffry, it must have been heavenly.

I wasn't that young associate anymore. I was sleep-deprived and hormonally amped. Short-term as my situation was supposed to be, I had real issues with physical stamina. Since I was operating at full capacity before Henry's arrival, I had to modify my workload to accommodate the responsibilities of motherhood. Something had to give.

Lunch was now always at my desk, sometimes during a meeting. Pumping sessions were done in the bathroom with my phone. Team meetings were scheduled to accommodate my pumping sessions. Non-work communication was ignored until the subway ride home. And after work happy hours? I had to unsubscribe from about 15 lists just so I could stop receiving notifications of events I'd never attend.

My happy hour was arriving home after work to see Henry. He was usually in his playpen. Olga would be at the door, wearing her coat. She had no interest in dilly-dallying with her boss. I could sort of empathize with her; I couldn't stand it when I was way-laid at the office right when I was supposed to be heading home.

Nonetheless, each day I would body-block the door until she gave me a status report. Inevitably, it started with the comment, "Henry was good baby." That was followed up with an account of how much milk Henry had consumed and how long he had napped. Boring. I didn't want facts. I wanted charming tales about my amazingly gifted child.

Knowing that her timely exit required a more robust summary of the day's events, Olga and I instituted a change. We agreed that she would fill out a chart that included information about Henry's nap and eating schedule so she wouldn't have to review it orally with me. That way, she could use the time to describe some anecdote from the day. Sometimes it would be a mundane report about whom they saw at the park or a summary of comments people had made about how cute Henry was in his stroller.

Other times, I would hear about Henry's developmental progress. These updates were both exciting and bittersweet. I was thrilled
when Olga told me that Henry had sat up on his own, but also
saddened to have missed it. The same was true when Henry rolled
over for the first time. Dale consoled me, however, by reminding
me that we had made a heavy investment in a two-pronged surveillance system. With all probability, the nanny cams had captured
some of these landmark moments. That possibility was enough to
motivate me to spend some time scanning through the recordings
after I came home from work each day.

More often than not, I never found anything. Wasting 15 to 30
minutes of time on the footage was becoming increasingly tedious,
and I had to admit that I quickly lost interest in looking at the data
with any regularity. A spare half an hour could be used for more
important things, like billing clients or sleeping.

I kissed Henry on his head as I handed him off to Olga. "I will
see you later today. All right, little guy?" I patted him one more
time, eyeballing the nagging, flaky cradle cap on his head. I was
supposed to have scrubbed it off with a brush. Every time I had tried
to do it, Henry had wailed and wailed. Dale, in helpful daddy-o
mode, would remind me that Henry's cranium hadn't fused yet, so I
should probably lighten up on the scrubbing. This was something I
had to remember to get the pediatrician to handle. I reminded Olga
of the appointment with the doctor, which was scheduled for later
in the morning.

"There is appointment today?" asked Olga.

"Yeah. We talked about it yesterday." I strapped on my tote and slid on my walking shoes. "11:00—remember? Just bring Henry to the doctor's."

Olga bounced Henry on her hip. "You no need me for that. If you come back here and get Henry, I run errands for you while you're at doctor."

"What?"

"Uh. . ." she stammered. "I get more diapers."

"I just bought diapers this weekend." I pointed to the huge Costco box of Huggies in Henry's room. "Olga, I have to get to work and I don't have time to get back up here before the appointment."

She grabbed my arm as I made a run for the door. "You know, I just remember. I made play date for Henry at 11. The nanny's cell phone no work so I no can call her."

Exasperated, I said, "So? Don't go. You'll see her tomorrow."

"Well, she very popular. I no want to make her mad."

"Really? Well, I don't care about some random nanny. I gotta go. We talked about this. I'll see you at 11. Have a good day."

I bustled out before she could find another excuse not to go to the pediatrician's office. It was for Henry's four-month check-up. His appointments had all been sources of pride and delight, so I couldn't imagine why she wouldn't want to attend this one. As I took the elevator down to the lobby, I wondered how many times she had taken her son to a pediatrician. Maybe once, after birth? Did she have health insurance? Or go to a clinic? I had no idea. I just knew that since she had been watching Henry for the majority of the time over the last month, she needed to be at the appointment, not running around Manhattan looking for teething toys.

When I arrived at the doctor's office, Olga and Henry were there, but Henry was hysterical. Olga was sitting on the waiting room couch, barely pushing the stroller back and forth. "Is he O.K.? What's wrong?" I scooped Henry out of infant captivity and tried to console him. He looked exhausted, bags under his eyes. He was fitfully scratching his skin. "Is he hungry? Did you bring a bottle?"

"I no bring bottle," she said, skittishly. "I feed Henry before I come here." As evidence to her claim, Henry spit up on the shoulder of my suit jacket.

We were escorted into an examination room. Henry was still crying. The nurse encouraged me to try to nurse him, claiming that even if he wasn't hungry, he might find it comforting. Feeding Henry was only going to extend the duration of the appointment, so I was agitated. Plus, I wasn't used to nursing Henry without a pillow, so the entire experience was awkward. And then Olga was staring at me, probably hoping that I would tell her to leave, which I really wanted to do but was too stubborn to admit. All Henry did was wriggle, punch and cry.

Finally, the doctor came breezing into the room. "Hello, Mrs. Pedersen!" She took one look at Henry, and her cheerful demeanor vanished. In a low voice she said to the nurse, "Let's get him on the scale." The pediatrician smiled at Olga and asked me if she was the nanny.

"Yes, this is Olga Ramirez. She's been watching Henry since I got off maternity leave."

"So about 5 weeks?" asked the doc.

"Yup."

The doctor unemotionally acknowledged the nurse's recording of Henry's vitals. "Have you noticed any problems?"

"You mean, besides the hysterics?" I tried to make light of the situation, but I, too, was out of sorts. The nurse handed Henry back to me, and he seemed to calm down a bit.

The doc looked at her chart. "Henry has only gained a few ounces since your last appointment. He should have gained a few pounds, by this point." She looked squarely at Olga. "Has he been eating?"

Olga was staring at a poster of the alphabet that was pasted to the wall of the office. "Olga!" I snapped. "Are you paying attention?" I felt like I was talking to Jeffry Hsu. I never spoke to Olga in such a harsh tone, which I was sure the doctor wouldn't believe, even if I tried to explain myself. But then again, Olga had never been so disconnected and insubordinate.

"I sorry," she said. "Did you have question?"

The pediatrician asked slowly. "Have you had any trouble getting Henry to eat? He is not gaining weight like he should."

"He eat fine. I write everything down on chart for Meezuz Peedairsen. No problem," replied Olga.

"That's right," I said, relieved. I explained that Olga documented Henry's eating and napping schedule every day. I was pumping milk at work, and Olga was using the supply in the freezer. All seemed fine.

"Well, typically, without singularity in the caregiver role, the child can become confused," said the doctor. "The emotions of dealing with two individuals can affect appetite. And of course, switching between the bottle and the breast can reduce his overall consumption of calories."

It sounded like she was saying that it would have been better for Henry if I had been at home, breast feeding all the time. Even though her tone was not judgmental, I still felt guilty. "So, should we just expect this situation to correct itself? I mean, what can we do to try to get Henry to eat more?"

She reached out for Henry so she could do her physical exam of my son. "He should get used to the schedule. But the absolute best thing is going to be the breast milk. I know it's hard to pump at work, but for the health of your son, you have to do your best to keep up with it."

I chewed on my fingernails as the pediatrician performed the rest of the exam. She assured me that I wouldn't hurt Henry's brain by cleaning his scalp, and she gave me a specialty brush for the job. Everything else seemed normal, which was a tremendous relief.

Once the exam was completed, the pediatrician handed Henry back to me. "So keep on with the nursing. And I think you should try some solid food. Rice cereal. See if he takes to that. And I want to see you back here in a month to check on his progress, O.K.?" I agreed, and set something up with the receptionist.

All in all I thought the appointment was an unmitigated disaster. The last thing I wanted to do was head back to work, especially with baby barf on my shoulder. But I didn't have a choice. I handed Henry off to Olga, and we went our separate ways.

I decided to walk the ten blocks back to McCale. I was about to text Dale the news of the appointment when my mother called.

"Maxine? What's all that noise?"

"I'm walking back to the office, Mom."

"Is Henry with you? Did you have the appointment? How's he doing?"

I wanted to tell her everything, but I didn't want to alarm her. I wasn't sure how concerned I needed to be. I did know that I was confused, and I was planning on using the walk to clear my head. Talking to my mother, despite her legitimate interest, was not what I needed at the moment.

I decided to tell her about an issue that had been positively resolved by the doctor, rather than any negative news about Henry's weight. "Well, you remember that I was having trouble with the cradle cap? The rash on Henry's head?"

She, too, seemed relieved that the issue had been addressed. I filled her in with some other details, and then she courteously wrapped up the conversation by saying, "Well, I'm sure you and Dale are very proud of Henry. You're a wonderful mother, Maxine."

I sure didn't feel like it.

28

When I got back to the apartment that night, Olga and I exchanged a few words. Pleasant words, actually. She apologized for her behavior. She confessed that the reason she did not want to go to the doctor's office was that she had suspected that something was wrong with Henry, but she didn't know how to tell me. She had chalked his discomfort up to teething or to missing me. In any case, she was worried that she might get blamed if, in fact, there had been something seriously wrong.

I appreciated her sincerity. I told her that it was imperative that she tell me about any health concerns, even if she couldn't explain what the source might be. And I shared responsibility since, as Henry's mother, I should have noticed any changes in behavior, too. I think we both felt better about the situation.

By the time she left, I was exhausted. Maternal Guilt had beaten Client Billing in the battle for my attention, so I blew off everything work-related that I was supposed to do. I threw on some sweats, ready to spend some quality time with Henry.

My first order of business was going to be serving Henry his first bowl of solid food. I had picked up a box of rice cereal on the way back from the office, thinking that this could be a fun new activity that we could try together. And it was one "first" that Olga was not going to have for herself.

As I searched around for a proper, i.e. unbreakable bowl, I wondered if Daddy might be interested in participating. I texted Dale. He texted me back letting me know that he was headed out with Mike for a quick drink, but that he'd be back in about an hour and a half. He asked me to wait. I texted back describing Henry's eating and sleeping schedule, which allowed me to wait about another half an hour, tops. So he told me to just go ahead with it and take a picture. I guess Dale was going to drink away whatever paternal guilt was building up inside of him.

I pulled over the high chair that Olga had assembled. Since Henry had sat up on his own, Olga had advised that the high chair would be a good physical training tool to help build stabilizing muscles. Plus, he could play with blocks and other toys on the tray to help strengthen his gross motor skills.

That was Olga's plan, and I'm sure that during the day, some time in the chair was good for Henry. But every time I put him in there, the racket was unbearable. Anything that was put on the tray was immediately cast off. Inevitably, all would devolve to a mother-son game of Fetch, with me doing the grunt work and Henry laughing. The laughing part made the game somewhat tolerable, but tedium set in quickly thereafter. Sometimes, it seemed, I had a shorter attention span than my son.

I picked Henry up from the floor. He looked tired. His face was sallow, like he needed more sun. I made a mental note to ask Olga about his outdoor activities. Maybe he was being shaded too much for fear of getting him sunburned. In any case, it had been a bruiser of a day for both of us. I didn't even want to look at myself in the mirror; I had to be twice as haggard as Henry.

"O.K., big guy," I said, after I put Henry in the high chair. "Here's the deal. You need to chunk up, my friend." I put the box of rice cereal, wrapped in cellophane, on the tray in front of him. He was mesmerized by the shiny wrapping. He didn't quite have the dexterity to pick up the box, but if he had, he would have tried to eat it. There was a bit of irony in the notion that he could choke to death from eating the packaging for his food. Mild panic set in as I mentally digested that, and I gently wrassled the box away from him.

As he slapped the high chair, he started to make some new sounds that I hadn't heard before. A couple of low gurgly noises punctuated by sharp, squealy barks. Weird, but cool. I was glad to know the vocal chords were working. Maybe he'd be a talker, just like his mother.

I read the instructions on the back of the cereal box. I defrosted some milk and mixed it in with the flaky cereal per the first-time solid food directions. "So, check this out Henry," I said, as I showed him the bowl. The flakes dissolved almost immediately, leaving what looked like just thicker milk. "Well, this is supposed to be solid food. What do you think of that?" He made some more alien-inspired sounds. "Exactly," I concurred. "This doesn't look right at all."

I double-checked the instructions. The slop was the right

consistency. I took a small amount on a spoon and put it in front of his mouth. He didn't know what to do. He looked up at me and I made some goofy "yum-yum" expressions and comments. He made goofy sounds back.

Henry nipped at the cereal. I kept encouraging him and he finally took a mouthful in. He opened and closed his mouth just enough to slowly spit out the entire glob onto his bib. Which then dripped onto my pants. I reminded myself that this was why I was wearing sweats. So I tried again.

And again.

Henry was not consuming any of it. How was he going to gain any weight if he hated the rice cereal? Maybe I didn't get the right brand. Maybe I was doing it wrong. Maybe he wasn't really hungry. I needed some advice. I cleaned up Henry's face, removed his bib and put him on the floor.

I went to my computer, thinking I would check Blythe's "Even Moms Can Learn" blog for information. The closest subject had something to do with preparing gluten-free baby food. The comments following the blog described odious tales of how parents had discovered that their children were allergic to food staples like bread and pasta. I guess that was a fun surprise I could look forward to with Henry, if I could ever get him to eat any solid food.

If Blythe (via blog) couldn't help me, then maybe Angela could. I sent her a text. "Feeding Henry rice cereal 1st time. Really runny. Is that right?"

In just a few moments, my phone clinked. "Add bacon." That was her answer. She couldn't be serious. I mean, bacon was a staple of my diet, but Henry's? Then she came back with, "JK! Messy first few times. Use rubber spoon."

Rubber spoon? My mind flashed back to the baby aisle at the grocery store and I realized what she was talking about. Long silver spoons with primary-colored rubber ends were hanging off the shelves adjacent to the baby cereal. It was excellent product placement. I had just never understood what the product was for.

I felt better. And I was kind of psyched that I had a new resource besides Paola and Mom to whom I could go with baby-related queries.

Meanwhile, Dale texted me and told me that he was skipping his drink with Mike so he could help with Henry's first solid meal. I told him that his timing was great, because we needed some rubber spoons. He agreed to pick some up from the store.

Then I chucked all evidence of my failed first attempt to feed our son. "Don't tell Daddy!" I joked. At four months old, I knew that Henry could keep a secret.

29

Now That Dale and I had a baby, our entire social landscape had changed. Gone were the invites to private dinner parties at hot new restaurants in the Meat Packing District. In were elaborate celebrations honoring everything from a child's first steps to a mother weaning a baby. When Dale told me that the Macalusos had invited us to their home for a bar-be-cue, I was thrilled. And since the Macalusos' daughter was available to babysit, I, too, could converse like an adult. I couldn't wait to get out of the city.

Dale parked our car on the curb in front of his boss's home. We both stared out the window, mesmerized by the old oak trees and manicured lawns of the neighborhood. The gardens were bursting with well-nourished blossoms—blue hydrangeas, pink and white azaleas, red and yellow roses. A pair of kids rode by on their bikes. A hybrid Mercedes station wagon loaded with a mom and her children passed in the other direction. Within seconds, I felt transported, the trappings of upscale suburbia so different from Manhattan life.

I took Henry out of our 10-year-old Volkswagen. In Manhattan, having a car—any car—was a luxury. And having an expensive car was just an invitation for a carjacking or an act of vandalism. But on the curb of the Macaluso estate, where a Porsche sat in the driveway across the street, the Pedersen Family truckster looked like a beat-up jalopy.

Dale pulled a bottle of wine from the backseat and whispered in my ear. "Well, this doesn't suck."

"Yeah, no kidding," I said into the back of Henry's head, in case Bobbie was watching from his window and could read lips. "Why do I suddenly feel poor?"

"Because compared to this guy, we are."

The white door of the red brick Georgian home swung open. "Welcome!" Bobbie hastened down the steps with his arm already outstretched for the big handshake. "I'm glad you three could make it!"

Dale shook his hand back. "We are, too. Thanks so much for inviting us." Dale handed over the wine, crediting me with the selection. Bobbie nodded in approval.

Helen, wearing a French country apron over her tailored outfit, skipped down the steps. "Let me see that baby!" she cried.

We all greeted each other while Henry started wriggling around in my arms. "I think he just needs to stretch out. The poor guy isn't used to being in a car that often," I explained.

"Yes! Yes!" said Bobbie. "Well, come on in. I'm sure Helen can find a spot for him."

Dale strutted inside, completely oblivious to Bobbie's delegation of child duties to his wife. I had a feeling that this whole afternoon was supposed to be a strange soft sell, exposing two city slickers/ now parents to the familial benefits of living in the 'burbs. But celebrating the sexist trappings of pre-feminist America wasn't going to convince me. Moving to the Island would just extend both of our commutes, and right now, that was not an option.

Once past the heavy oak front doors, it was clear that the inside of the Macalusos' home was even more impressive than the outside. The white marble floor was accented by a richly detailed silk rug. The low ceilings and heavy wood moldings were an indicator of the home's age—a time when homes were smaller, and details were much more refined. A long hallway off the vestibule connected the front of the house to the back, as indicated by the bright light glowing at the rear of the home. As my eyes adjusted, I could see a wall of windows at the end of the hall.

My urge to move towards the light was disrupted by a young woman who came bounding down a staircase off the vestibule. "This is our daughter, Leslie," introduced Bobbie. "She's home from Conn College for the summer."

Leslie smiled as she slid down the last step onto the marble floor. "This must be Henry," she said, cooing over him. "I think my mom set up one of my brothers' rooms for you upstairs." She reached out for the diaper bag. "I'll help you get set up."

"Thank you, Leslie," said Helen. "She's a C.P.R.-certified babysitter," Helen informed us proudly as I followed her daughter upstairs.

After a brief exchange of pleasantries, Leslie left me alone. I smelled something cheesy and oniony permeate through the vents into the room. If hot hors d'œuvres were being served, I hoped Helen had a warming drawer, because I was about twenty minutes away from making it downstairs. I lavished all my attention on Henry; undoubtedly, Helen and Bobbie were doing the same thing to Dale.

Once I was finished feeding Henry, I collected a few of his toys and headed downstairs. I should've just put everything in the diaper bag and brought that down, too, since teething rings and squishy toys were slipping out of my hands. Henry's favorite, the pair of plastic keys, dropped to the floor in the hallway past the vestibule. I stopped momentarily, unsure of whether to pick them up or just keep walking to the rest of the group.

The keys had fallen next to a cut in the baseboard of a long, wood-paneled wall. A small light was visible under part of the wall. Upon further inspection, I realized that part of the baseboard was actually the bottom of a door, which was camouflaged along the hallway. Leslie popped in and picked up the keys for me. I stood at the mystery door and asked, "So what's in there, the Bat Cave?"

Leslie laughed as she walked me into the bright yellow Great Room, where Dale was just finishing his first beer. "Maxine discovered your secret room, Dad," she said. Then she held out her hands, indicating her interest in holding Henry. I wasn't sure if I should hand him over or not. Then she added, "It's where Dad keeps his stash of weapons."

"What?" said Dale, standing up.

Helen chimed in. "Don't be alarmed. It's Bobbie's pet project. He's very proud of it." She motioned for me to allow Leslie to take the baby. I still didn't let go.

"Wait a second," said Dale. "I think I've heard about this from O'Shaughnessy. You've got a collection of knives and swords, right? Antique stuff from all over the world?"

This sounded interesting, and legitimate. I kissed Henry and relinquished him to Leslie.

"Would you like to see it?" asked Bobbie.

"Sure." Dale and I answered at the same time. I wasn't sure if I was invited, but I followed on as Bobbie and Dale walked down the hall.

Bobbie pulled out an unusual-looking key from a ring in his pocket. He slid a panel in the wall-door to the side, and then inserted the key into a lock. He turned the key from side to side, pushing it further into the mechanism each time. "The lock is antique," he explained. "Helen and I took this fascinating tour through Yorkshire a few years ago. We got to see all the abbeys that Henry the VIII ruined during his creation of the Church of England. This lock is reputedly from some old abbey storehouse." He made a final turn of the key and the lock opened with a heavy, satisfying clink.

Dale rubbed my shoulders and I smiled back. We felt like two young students being invited into the sanctuary of a rich, eccentric scholar. If the lock was an indicator, the room had to be loaded with strange and fascinating objects, each one with a tale all its own.

Bobbie opened the door, and the interior was impressive— with its brightness. The room alone, clearly a state-of-the-art facility, would have been fantastic even if it had been empty. Temperature and moisture gauges, as well as computerized inventory and monitoring systems, lined the wall to the left. The rest of the space was covered with thick, glass enclosed cases housing Bobbie's swords, knives and daggers. The pieces were supported by Lucite pegs, which gave the appearance that they were floating mid-air. If it weren't for the glass barriers, any sudden movement in the room could result in an unexpected haircut, or worse, a severed carotid artery. I shuffled around in the safety of my own personal space.

"Check this out," said Dale. "Give me a number." He glanced at Bobbie, who, with a nod, permitted Dale to go on.

The first item that caught my eye was a combination pistol and knife. It looked old and clunky, kind of like the worst of both weapons in one. Per Dale's request, I read off a number adjacent to the piece. "O.K. 1407."

Dale typed the number into a computer screen on the wall. Within seconds, an image of the item appeared. "Elgin Cutlass Pistol. C.B. Allen Manufacturers, Springfield, MA. 1837." Dale continued reading the data, which included details about the item's manufacture, its provenance and purchase information. Dale concluded with, "Estimated value: $15,000."

Dale and I exchanged a look of awe, which undoubtedly provided satisfaction to Bobbie. "You picked a good one there, Maxine," he said.

"What exactly is that?" And before Dale could open his mouth, I turned to him and said, "And don't tell me it's an Elgin Cutlass Pistol."

"It's a combination weapon, as you can see," started Professor Macaluso. "The Bowie knife was popular in the 1830's, so this pistol has a similar long, dagger-like blade below the barrel of the pistol."

Dale stepped closer to the glass of the cabinet. "How effective was this thing?"

"Not very," demurred Bobbie. "These pistols were ordered up for a naval expedition to the South Seas. Apparently, some of the men got mixed up with some Fijian cannibals. No one's sure who won that contest, but it had to have been bloody."

"No kidding!" said Dale.

My stomach turned. "And a few were used in the Civil War." Bobbie continued on about the technological advances in weaponry which had categorized the Civil War as America's first "modern" war. I was going to add something about it also being America's goriest, but that would have been a buzz kill for the boys.

Perhaps noting my disinterest, Bobbie called my attention to some information about the pistol. There was a scanned image of an official-looking diagram, along with some descriptions for its manufacture. A couple of tell-tale notations made me ask, "Is that a patent?"

Bobbie smiled. "I thought you'd appreciate that."

"I wonder how old it is." I magnified the image, revealing some astounding information. "Oh, my God! It says it's patent 254! That's incredible!"

"How many patents are on file right now?" asked Bobbie.

I thought a moment and said, "Over nine million."

Dale and Bobbie shared a laugh, both probably calculating the odds that they'd ever see such an early patent in a field of nine million possibilities.

I just kept looking for more treasures. A separate cabinet housed what had to be the most beautiful piece in the collection. "Would you mind telling me about 2814?" Dale started programming the numbers into the system, but Bobbie waved him off.

"I know all about this one." Bobbie slid the glass door open and removed the golden sword from its pegs. It was about two feet long, with a slightly curved blade. The handle was encrusted with cabochon rubies, emeralds and sapphires. The blade, unlike those in the rest of the collection, seemed almost pristine.

Dale was mesmerized. "What is that?"

I knew immediately. "Don't you remember? They used one at La Grenouille on New Year's when we went out with Paola and Nelson."

"Right!" Dale's eyes lit up. "It's a Champagne sabre!"

Bobbie held the sword with pride. "I bought this when I made Managing Director at Worthington." The jewels on the sword sparkled as Bobbie chronicled its historical significance. "The tradition of slicing corks off Champagne bottles is supposed to have started with Napoleon. His cavalry men used to do it with their swords. The modern-day Champagne sabre has been designed specifically to remove the cork while minimizing glass breakage." Bobbie held the sabre towards Dale. "You want to hold it?"

Dale took it with both hands, examining it with reverence. I expected him to be whipping it around the room, doing childish role-play. Instead, he seemed in awe of the item, like it symbolized what he could achieve if some day he, too, became a Managing Director at Worthington.

Gingerly, he handed the sword back to Bobbie. I would have preferred that he hand it to me, but that would have broken the spell that Bobbie seemed to have cast over Dale. I'd have to watch how much Dale drank, just to make sure he didn't do something crazy, like commit to another year of working for Bobbie, Beat the Boss-style.

30

After The Tour of the weapons cache, I wound up spending the majority of my time with Helen. I offered to help with whatever she was preparing, but she seemed to have everything well in hand. As Bobbie took Dale outside to grill up our dinner, Helen slunk off to her prep kitchen. "I have a surprise for you!" Maybe Helen had her own quirky collection stored away with the Christmas china and the extra paper towels. Did she collect gnomes? Or maybe silver souvenir spoons?

She emerged with a colorful liquor gift bag. "The gals from the society wanted to give you something special as a thank you for your help with the cocktails for the gala. We hope you like it!"

I tried to be as gracious as possible as I pulled out a tall, thin bottle filled with a dark liquid. It was definitely not a Long Island merlot, which I was expecting. A quick look at the label clarified the contents: it was a bottle of vintage Long Island port. "Helen. This is so nice!" I said, genuinely excited. "I've always wanted to try a Long Island port!"

"Well, you might not want to drink this one." Helen pointed out various scribbled signatures in metallic pen which were all over the bottle. "See this? That's Jerry Seinfeld!"

"What?!" I took a close look at the autographs. Jerry Seinfeld, as I had learned from watching his eponymous sit-com on Netflix, was super anal. Not surprisingly, his signature was fairly legible. I turned the bottle around, trying to make out the other names. I could identify Alec Baldwin's, but the rest were too scrawled to decipher. Helen informed me that about a half dozen other Long Island celebrities, including Billy Joel, Kevin James and Rosie O'Donnell, had signed the bottle. A bottle similar to mine had been entered into an auction at the Heritage Society gala. It had sold for $10,000.

I tried to hand the bottle back to Helen. "This is a very generous gift, Helen. But I think you should save it and use it for your auction next year. I'm sure the society could use the money."

Helen shook her head. "No. We all wanted you to have something for helping with the event." She put the bottle back in the bag with finality. "I mentioned it before, and I'll say it again. If you ever get bored with law, you could make a very good living putting those skills of yours to work."

"Those skills?"

"Yes. Your love of 'mixology' or whatever you call it." She sounded like my mother.

"Well, thanks for the compliment, Helen, but it's just a hobby."

I let my mind drift for a second, thinking about how much fun it would be to get paid to make up drinks for people. After about three or four events, I'd probably run out of liquors to try. And I'd most certainly have cirrhosis of the liver from all the experimentation I'd need to do.

But Helen's fundraisers weren't about my drinks. They were about Long Island—the food, the history. "Helen, does the society document the galas and other activities that you sponsor? I mean, you could have a beautiful coffee table book of your events that really showcased all the wonderful things about Long Island that the society is trying to preserve."

"See? You have so many great ideas! Too bad you and Dale don't live out here. You'd be such an asset to the community! You've got to come out some time soon for lunch with me and the girls!"

"That sounds like fun," I said, wondering just what that might be like.

On the car ride home, Dale was unusually quiet. He was slumped up next to the driver's side door, with his right hand on the top of the steering wheel. I tried to make conversation by telling him some of the details of my chat with Helen. When the car ahead of us was only going 50 miles an hour and Dale didn't bother changing lanes, I knew something was on his mind.

"So, what did you and Bobbie talk about?"

"Well. . ." Dale sat up and put both hands on the steering wheel. "Bobbie asked me if I wanted to move out to Long Island. With Worthington."

"Oh, my God," I said, clueing into the Macaluso Master Plan.

"Helen kept talking about how much I could help with the Long Island Heritage Society."

Dale looked over uneasily. "Well, Bobbie asked if I'd consider running the Worthington Office in Garden City. He said O'Shaughnessy really wants the job, since he's already out here with his family."

"O'Shaughnessy? Running an office?" I thought about it for a minute. My opinion of Patrick had warmed ever since his brother had delivered Dale to the delivery of Henry. "That actually seems like a good fit."

"I know."

"Then why did Bobbie ask you?"

Dale finally pushed on the accelerator and changed lanes. "I don't know. Right of first refusal? Maybe he thought that now that we have a family, it would be a good idea for us to move out of the city."

My head started spinning. How had this conversation transpired without my knowledge? "I don't understand this. You don't want to move out of the city, do you? We just bought the apartment with the intention of staying in Manhattan. I mean, financially, wouldn't we be losing our shirts if we turned around and tried to sell the place so soon?"

Dale shrugged. "Worthington would take care of that." Worthington took care of a lot of things, but they all came with a price. Dale's slave labor had been rewarded with financial bonuses, which were terrific. But I was now under the impression that this offer was the real icing on the Beat the Boss cake, whether Dale wanted it or not.

"Do you feel an obligation to take the job just because Bobbie asked you?"

"A little bit. Yes."

We drove by the next few exits in silence. We both knew that a move to Long Island would radically change our lifestyle. If I commuted to Manhattan and Dale ran an office, we'd most certainly need a live-in nanny. And neither one of us would have much quality time with Henry at all. The pressure for one parent to be a presence in our son's life would inevitably fall on me, and I had more than enough guilt on my conscience as it was. I dreaded the idea of putting myself in a situation where I would have to choose between my career and parenting Henry. I wanted to do both.

There were plusses. We were going to have to figure out a way for Henry to have some wide open spaces. And if we had another baby, we'd have to get a bigger apartment, which was a frightening financial proposition, even with all the money we had saved. A suburban home, like the ones in which Dale and I had been raised, did seem sensible.

Sensible, and downright conventional. Besides, there was only so much change a person could take in a year. Henry's arrival had been radical enough. "I don't want to move from the city," I declared.

Dale nodded. "That's what I told Macaluso."

"You told Macaluso that you weren't taking the job because I didn't want to leave? Like it was my fault?"

Dale reached his hand out and gripped my arm in reassurance. "No, no. I told him the same thing. That I didn't want to move from the city."

"Oh," I said, relieved. "Why?"

"Well, it's easier to leave Manhattan than it is to come back. And while running a branch of Worthington would be great and I'd learn a ton, the actual investing opportunities would suck."

"You told him they'd 'suck'? Really?"

"No, not exactly. But he knew what I meant. I don't want to

be the big fish in the little pond. I don't want to help retired people organize their investments. It's fucking boring."

I was a little taken aback by the emotion in his comments. For all the pressure Dale had been under in his tenure working alongside Bobbie, he seemed to have no interest in slowing down. If anything, he seemed even more focused on his career. We just hadn't had the time to talk about it.

Dale let go of my arm. "Maybe someday we'll live the life of the Macalusos. But we both have a good thing going right now. I see no reason to deliberately mess it up."

I leaned over and kissed him on the cheek. The Manhattan skyline loomed before us, its sparkling energy evident in the twinkling lights of the island's soaring skyscrapers. With all the chaos in our lives, at least Dale and I could agree that there was no place like home.

31

I got the news on my phone while I was pumping in the bathroom. Paul Black had called a meeting for four o'clock in the afternoon. Nancy had circulated the invite, along with an agenda. Apparently, my team's work was the main focus of the session. Since I was designated as the main speaker, I could make my presentation as pithy as possible, leaving the balance of the time for the partners to talk. If all went well, the meeting would be done in an hour, 90 minutes tops. I would be able to leave the office well before my requisite 6:00 pm.

My team met in the conference room at 3:50, ten minutes before the meeting was supposed to start. I knew Nancy Lallyberry would never allow anyone to appear more prepared than she was, so her team assembled immediately too. Harry, Deirdre and Paul all rolled in shortly after four. Seeing that we were all ready to begin, the partner group sat down quickly.

Paul Black took his seat next to his newly minted mentee, Jeffry Hsu. "Before we begin," Black started, "I would like to make a brief announcement. This will go out officially to the entire firm, but I have heard through my sources that Jeffry Hsu has passed the New York State Bar Exam! Congratulations, Jeffry!"

Everyone in the room applauded. Jeffry stood up and shook Black's hand as if he were accepting a Golden Globe award. I couldn't remember this sort of recognition after I had passed the bar. Maybe if my partner designee had been Paul Black rather than Caine Seaver, things might have been different. But I doubted it.

"O.K.," continued Paul. "Maxine, you're on."

"Thanks, Paul. And congratulations, Jeffry." Jeffry didn't acknowledge my compliment, having initiated a side conversation with Paul. There was no tactful way to break that up, and since the clock on the wall read 4:07, I proceeded with the agenda. "Per HKI's request, our team has done a thorough review of the regulations related to, um . . ." I stumbled because my phone was ringing. I couldn't remember where I put it, so I talked over it, hoping it would stop quickly. "As you can see from the first bullet point . . ."

I had barely made it through the regulatory citation when my ringtone kicked in again. Harry McCale closed his eyes in frustration. Paul Black looked like he wanted to fire me. Nancy Lallyberry leaned over and whispered loud enough for everyone to hear, "You know, we're supposed to turn our phones off during the meetings. They're supposed to be on vibrate in case of an emergency."

With Nancy's brilliant statement of the obvious, Deirdre chimed in. "Maxine, if that's an emergency, you should answer it."

The words sounded a lot more compassionate than her tone.

"I'm so sorry," I apologized. "I'm sure it's nothing." I rummaged through my pockets hoping to resolve the matter expeditiously. My heart stopped when I realized that the number in the call logs was Olga's. And not only had she called me at work, but she had texted me. She never texted me.

I excused myself, and asked Jeffry to carry on. As I walked out of the room, I heard him take responsibility for all the research that had been done. He was probably planning to add a proposal to garnish some of my wages as a bonus for all of his hard work. I'd have to deal with him later.

I buzzed Olga as quickly as possible so I could get back into the meeting and defend myself. "Olga! What is going on? I'm in a meeting!"

"I not sure. Henry look sick. I take him to hospital."

"What?!" I froze in the hallway. "Where are you? What happened? Is Henry O.K.?"

I rushed to my office, trying to understand the severity of Henry's condition. After a couple more questions, I was able to ascertain that Henry's condition was not life-threatening. But something was wrong, and Olga was unable to articulate exactly what it was. Unfortunately, my brain decided to fill in the gaps by conjuring up horrible images of infant morbidity. I grabbed my belongings and ran out of the building.

Outside, I cut about 17 people to grab a taxi and hysterically ordered the driver to Lenox Hill. I didn't bother explaining my behavior to the cabbie. *My son's at the emergency room, but I don't know why* sounded like something a paranoid, irrational person might say And maybe that's exactly how I was behaving. Had I just bolted out of an important meeting to find out that Henry had something inconsequential, like a low-grade fever?

I got on my phone and called Joy. I asked her to apologize to everyone, particularly Deirdre, Paul and Harry. I hoped that she could work some magic for me. Why couldn't I have hired her to be Henry's nanny?

In the meantime, I texted Dale. Not surprisingly, he didn't respond. I figured I'd find out what problems there were, if any, before I took on the Herculean task of trying to get him on the phone during business hours. And even though Jeffry was still in the meeting, I emailed him and asked for a full debrief. I was still his superior.

Though the cab ride itself had calmed me down, my anxiety level rocketed when we drove up to the E.R. I threw some bills at the cab driver and ran inside. I charged directly up to the admitting nurse, inserting myself in front of an elderly woman who was, as far as I was concerned, not in distress. "I'm looking for Henry Pedersen. The baby. Where is he? The nanny told me she brought him here."

Slow as molasses, the nurse batted her eyelids. "Please get in line. I will get to you when it's your turn." The old lady uttered something on the order of "You kids. . . ." while she tightened the grip on her cane. I thought she might use it to smack me, so I decamped and reconsidered my entrance strategy.

An E.M.S. van pulled up to the front door of the E.R. "Oh!" exclaimed the old lady. "That must be Gerry!" While a crew of medical professionals flocked to the vehicle, I bolted from the waiting room. I ran through the opened doors into the examination area, ignoring the calls from the nurse.

I faced a line of about a dozen curtained bays. Some were open, some were closed. All of their lights were on. I plunged into the hallway, ready to rip open all of the curtains to find Henry. Double doors boomed open behind me, and I knew someone, probably a security guard, was after me. I had to find Henry before I was detained, and the easiest way to do that was to shout out his name. "Henry! Henry!" I called desperately, as if a five-month-old infant could shout out, "Right here, Mommy!"

A man in scrubs, followed by Olga, emerged from one of the bays. He said something to Olga in Spanish, and she pointed at me and nodded. "You're the baby's mother?"

"Yes. I am Henry's mother," I said breathlessly as I shoved my way into the bay. The doctor motioned the security guard to stand down. Henry was on a gurney, his little arms outstretched. Some tubes were sticking out of his body. The beeping of a nearby machine was the only indicator that he was still alive.

My throat tightened. It felt like razors were lining my esophagus. I managed to cough out a question before tears streamed down my face. "What happened to him?" I stroked his little hand and touched his cheek, hoping his eyes would open. They didn't.

"I'm Dr. Sherman. Your son is going to be fine. Your nanny brought him in for severe vomiting. He is dehydrated, so we are administering fluids through an I.V."

I looked at Olga. She didn't make eye contact with me. She wasn't looking at Henry either, just staring at the curtain next to her chair.

"Is he unconscious?" My voice quivered when I asked the question.

Dr. Sherman rubbed my back consolingly. "No. He's sleeping. And he doesn't have a fever. So that rules out infection, which can be very dangerous."

That news didn't make me feel any better since I still didn't know what was wrong. "O.K. So what happened? Did he ingest a poison or something? Why would he just start vomiting?"

"Well, I'd like to talk to you about that." The doctor once again addressed Olga in Spanish. She left the bay, and the doctor gestured for the security guard to follow her. Then he asked me, more like a detective than a clinician, "Have you noticed vomiting before?"

I gasped. "No! Never! And Olga never said anything about it!"

"Has your son had a regular check up with a pediatrician recently?"

I took a step back and rubbed against the curtain, which startled me. I realized that I had yet to return to the pediatrician for Henry's follow-up to the awful four-month check up. Henry was eating both milk and solids regularly, so I had pushed the appointment off. "He saw her, the pediatrician, about five weeks ago for his four-month check up," I stammered.

The E.R. doctor, probably accustomed to drama, kept pressing for data. "Did she indicate that there were any problems?"

"Well, Henry was a little underweight. We started him on solids to see if he'd gain more weight. I was supposed to have brought him back to see her but my work. . . ." As I was making my confession, the scene at the pediatrician's office whirled through my mind. I remembered the shifty look on Olga's face that day. I stopped talking when I realized that, today, she wore exactly the same expression.

Something was wrong. I needed to talk to Olga. "Where did you send the nanny?" I darted to the curtain, but my urge to flee was counter-balanced by my need to stay with Henry. "It has to be her. She did something!"

The doctor put his hand on my shoulder. "I think you need to calm down. I'm sorry if I frightened you. I just think that your son might be allergic to the formula he's on, that's all. It happens, and the symptoms can sneak up on the care-giver slowly. And with your schedule, something like this might be even harder to detect."

"Formula?!" *Did this guy have the right baby?*

The doctor casually signed off on a chart and asked, "Have you switched formulas recently, Mrs. Pedersen? Or maybe you ran out and the nanny bought a different kind? I doubt it's a systemic manufacturer's problem because this is the first case we've seen."

"Henry's not on formula!" I yelled. "What are you talking about?"

The doctor put his chart down. He picked up a bottle which had been left on the stand next to Henry's gurney. It looked like one of my Avent bottles, but the liquid inside seemed different than breast milk. It was thicker, pastier. "Your nanny brought this here and said that this is what she had been feeding your son. We can run some tests on it, but it looks like formula to me."

We must have been causing some commotion because a security guard peeked his head through the curtain. "Is everything O.K. in here?"

I yanked him into the bay. "No! Go watch the nanny!"

The guard tucked his shirt under his protruding gut. "Oh, she's gone. She told me that she couldn't stay any longer because she had to pick up her kids. She said it was O.K. for her to leave."

"So you just let her go?" I wailed. "What kind of a place are you running here? That woman is a criminal! I don't know what she did, but she did something to my son!" My arms were waving all over the place until they landed on his back. I practically shoved him out of the hospital saying, "Go find her!"

The guard held onto the pistol in his holster and waddled out of the facility. With an I.Q. seemingly hovering around 60, this guy would probably accommodate a request to visit the I.C.U. by someone infected with the Ebola virus. We all knew there was no chance that he'd find Olga. At this point, she had probably inserted herself into the N.Y.C. subway system like the rat she truly was.

As much as I wanted to find her, Henry was now my top priority. He was still asleep. Dr. Sherman and I chatted quietly, trying to deduce what had transpired. We ruled out an allergy to my breast milk, as Henry had nursed successfully for the first 12 weeks of his life. And I hadn't eaten anything unusual recently, so Henry was probably not reacting to any potential irritants from me.

The doctor kept pressing for an answer. He believed that Henry's supposed cradle cap, which had migrated to his face, was an allergy-induced rash. And that his fitfulness and weight loss had less to do with caregiver confusion and more to do with a reaction to something he was ingesting. We ruled out anything strange with Henry's toys, home environment, detergent; all of these things had been static since his birth.

Whatever had come over Henry had started when I had gone back to work. I explained that I had plenty of pumped milk in the freezer, and Olga documented just how much was consumed each day. Dr. Sherman picked up the bottle Olga had brought with her. "If this is what your nanny was feeding your son," and he shook the unrecognizable liquid around, "then what happened to all of the milk you produced?"

Dr. Sherman and I locked eyes as we came to the same conclusion. "She has an infant herself, doesn't she?" he said. All I could do was nod. Olga must have taken the milk my body had produced for the health and well-being of my own son and fed it to hers. It was sick, and mean, and heart-breaking.

Worse yet, all the evidence against her was circumstantial. I could never prove that she had switched out Henry's food. Olga had betrayed me in one of the worst ways imaginable, and I was denied the opportunity to legally crucify her.

I walked over to Henry. I couldn't decide if I felt guilty for being a working mother instead of a stay-at-home, angry that my nanny wound up being a borderline felon, or grateful that, in the end, he was not significantly harmed.

I stroked his little hand and he finally started to let out some cries. I was so overjoyed to hear him that I didn't get upset when my milk came in and stained my shirt. After the doctor did a quick check of his vitals, I was encouraged to feed him. A nurse tech helped re-arrange Henry's tubes so I could hold him. Then, she lingered in the bay, ostensibly cleaning up and organizing the four by six foot space. I suspected she was monitoring my behavior, like some sort of spy for Child Protective Services, so I told her to leave.

I took care of Henry and then checked out of the facility as politely and quickly as I could. Henry and I needed to go home and try to forget that any of this had ever happened.

32

According to Dale, word of our horrifying ordeal spread like wildfire through the ranks of Worthington Investments. My inbox was flooded with forwarded emails from his colleagues, expressing concern and offering suggestions. My jaw dropped when I read one from someone who "knew the right people who could help you get that bitch deported." His tone was crude, his words were derogatory, but his sentiment was spot-on.

Bobbie Macaluso didn't send an email. Rather, Helen called to offer support. That support came in the form of a catered meal from Mesa Grill, delivered to our home. The gesture was too extravagant to be strictly professional, even for Worthington. I briefly considered how easy it might be to just quit and decamp to Long Island, since the notion of going through the process of finding another nanny was mind-numbing.

I went on auto-pilot with my communications to the folks at McCale. I garnered a handful of concerned responses, but no catered meal. I sent a separate note to Deirdre, requesting the option to work out of my apartment for the next week or so until I could find some replacement childcare. She offered a sincere measure of concern and approved my request. She also added that getting back to a regular work routine might be the best medicine for everyone. It was an interesting thought that I would consider later. At the moment, the best medicine for me came out of the vodka cabinet.

NYC Baby Prep scrambled to find an interim nanny while the search for permanent help continued. Of course, Tawny Sheen did not admit to any wrong-doing. She reminded me of the no-fault clause I had signed when I became a client of NYC Baby Prep, which basically held them harmless in situations such as mine. Why I had agreed to sign such a ridiculous document and then pay her an exorbitant fee to probably scan Craig's List for caregivers was beyond me. I just knew that next time around, I was going to be a lot more probing with my questions and demanding with my background checks.

My mother probably spent about a week in medicated isolation after she heard the news about Olga. That's the only explanation I could come up with for why I hadn't received my daily phone calls. I could have confirmed my hunch by calling the house in Westchester, but on the off chance that I was wrong, I would have had to listen to one of her surly rants. I decided to stay under the radar as long as possible.

On the night of the tenth day of the no-call stalemate, I was informed that the babysitter I had arranged for the following day had come down with the flu. Under normal circumstances, I might have called in sick to work, or used a vacation day. But I had some critical meetings that I needed to tend to, so I had to at least call into work. Besides, I had to save the vacation days for real emergencies, like when my mother wasn't available.

Begrudgingly, I called home and asked for her help. She agreed to come into Manhattan after rush hour in the morning, and stay through dinner. This didn't exactly mesh with my phone call schedule, but I accepted her offer as graciously as I could. After all, I was desperate.

I was on the phone when she arrived at my apartment. She gave me a quick hug and then made a bee-line for Henry's room. Despite the universal sign of unwelcoming—the closed door—she barged right into the nursery, waking Henry up from the nap he had started just ten minutes earlier. I put my cell phone on mute.

"What are you doing? You woke him up!"

My mother came out of the nursery, holding Henry on her shoulder. He was pounding the cloth she had placed over her pressed white shirt. She was rubbing his back trying to soothe him. "I think he's still hungry," she said. "Didn't the doctor say to feed him whenever he's hungry? Especially now?"

"He's not hungry. He's tired. I just fed him and got him all settled so I could take this call. Can you just put him back in his crib?"

I heard someone mention my name on the conference call. I ran into the bedroom, shut the door and took the phone off mute. I could hear Henry crying, so I headed into my closet, hoping my clothes would muffle the sounds of my upset child.

After the call was over, I took Henry from my mom. "Look, I will nurse him—again—but I'm going to need you to let him sleep. I have some work I have to get done right now, O.K.?"

My mother removed the blanket from her shoulder and folded

it up neatly. "I don't know why you called me into the city to help you. If I had known that Henry was going to be napping, then I wouldn't have rushed to get in here."

My phone was buzzing, undoubtedly with questions from the conference call I had just been on. Not only did I have to deal with Henry, but I had to manage my mother, who, in grandparenthood, seemed to have forgotten all of the skills she had bragged about during motherhood. "Mom, why don't you take the opportunity to walk around the neighborhood? You always complain that you never get to spend time in the city. Go shopping or something, all right?"

"But how much time do I have? It's kind of silly for me to go all the way down to Saks if I can't shop when I get there."

"Then go to Bloomingdale's!" Henry had fallen asleep again. So much for his insatiable appetite. I picked him up gently and placed him in his crib. I shut the door and sat down at my computer.

My mother was still in the apartment. "Don't you want the monitor on?"

I threw the chair back as I rushed to stand up. "Henry is right on the other side of the door. Perfectly fine. Nothing's going to happen to him. I have work to do."

My mother gathered up her things. "Maybe I should just go home."

"No! Please. I need help." Specifically, I was thinking about the four o'clock call I had scheduled, and there was no way Henry would sleep until then. I scrambled to task my mother with something. "Uh, would you mind going to the store and picking up a rotisserie chicken for dinner?" I rummaged through my purse and gave her some cash. "I don't care. Whatever looks good. It would be a huge help."

My mother took the money and folded it up carefully. "You

know, they pump all kinds of fat and salt into those store-prepared birds. You should really learn to cook." I ignored her. She was right, but at the moment, I didn't exactly have the time to master the art of French cooking, or reign supreme over anything except my skyrocketing stress level.

She left, and I busied myself with my work duties. I worked productively and tidied up all of my responsibilities about five minutes before my next scheduled call. This allowed me a few moments to reflect on the progress, or lack thereof, I had made to find a new nanny. Over the past few days, I had interviewed five candidates, all of whom had been rejected.

One middle-aged woman had been a high school Spanish teacher, so Dale and I were excited about the prospect of Henry growing up in a bi-lingual environment. Surprisingly, it was her bastardization of the English language that was the problem. Her use of the term "ain't," overuse of the word "awesome" and unabashed confusion over the grammatical status of the word "good" resulted in her immediate disqualification.

A male applicant and a 65-year-old woman were also given the kibosh purely because I didn't like them. Knowing the potential legal issues related to discrimination based on sex or ageism, I had requested that NYC Baby Prep perform a background check on sexual offenders for the first candidate, and expressed concern over the pile of prescription medications in a certain applicant's knitting bag which may or may not have been easily accessible by an infant for the second. Tawny and I agreed to move on to other candidates.

A well-qualified Hispanic woman with young children didn't even garner more than five minutes of my time because her profile was too reminiscent of Olga's.

The final candidate, a pretty Middlebury graduate with a Psychology degree focused on Child Development, had been the best hope for a replacement. She had made the cut from Skype to an interview at our apartment. During our discussion, Dale had returned home early from work. The girl held onto Dale's hand just a fraction too long as he shook hers, all while he was undoing his tie. Her lips parted as Dale smiled, and the interview, as well as any chance of her winning a position in our household, was terminated shortly thereafter.

Having gone through this mental summary, I realized that what I really needed was an asexual version of myself, only about ten years younger.

I was in the middle of an email to Jeffry when my mother returned with the groceries. I finished up so I could help her unpack.

"I decided to make you a pot roast," she declared.

"Oh. Thanks." I didn't want to push my luck, but I needed her as a babysitter, not a personal chef. I unloaded a big cut of meat, some potatoes, carrots, celery, tomatoes and miscellaneous herbs. "Should I just leave all this stuff out?"

My mother was in full food-prep mode, having unearthed an apron from somewhere in the kitchen. "Yes. You get back to work. I'll take care of dinner."

I had to push my cause. "I really appreciate your cooking, but what about Henry? I've got a call coming up."

My mother waved me off. "I said I would take care of it. I think you should go to your room, though. You can close the door. That way I can watch Henry in the living room while I cook."

Little cries were coming from the nursery. My phone rang. I couldn't respond to both, and my mother was holding a vegetable peeler. She didn't look up. "I don't get to say this anymore, but go to your room, Maxine. Multi-tasking was not invented in your generation."

33

The bustle of Lower Manhattan faded as I passed through the entrance vestibule into the minimalist and chic TriBeCa Relaxation Salon. The ceilings of the lobby had to be about 12 feet tall, the height emphasized by the polished concrete floor. Long silver beads hung the length of the floor-to-ceiling windows. Between the dimmed light and the piped-in sound of trickling water, I felt like I was standing on the inside of a waterfall.

Having discovered that we had both purchased the same half-day spa package from LivingSocial, Angela and I had agreed to schedule our treatments together. Angela was already waiting for me at the reception desk, drinking a bottle of TriBeCa Relaxation Salon mineral water.

The receptionist greeted us, checked us in and directed us to the elevator. In the confined space of the metal box, the smell was unmistakable. It was lavender and flowery with a vanilla undertone. Fresh, light, yet sensual. No doubt about it: the distinctive odor was Parfum Aix's Eau de Vie.

"Do you smell that?" I asked.

"You like it? I tried this new perfume at Macy's on the way over here. It's called Perfume X."

Most Americans botched the pronunciation of Parfum Aix, but the double meaning was part of the brand's charm. "You mean Parfum Aix, Eau de Vie, right?"

"No. I mean Perfume X. Like X-rated. Like unknown, mysterious." She sniffed her wrists and smiled. "I think it's an awesome name. I can't believe nobody's ever thought of it before."

"Somebody has thought of it before!" I said, my voice rising. The elevator doors opened, and we were handed some white robes and locker keys.

"What are you talking about?" When I explained my background with Parfum Aix, Angela became suspicious. "So you're telling me that Perfume X is some sort of a knock-off of another perfume? I don't believe it."

I started to undress, hungry for details. "Tell me what happened—you saw this at Macy's? In the cosmetics section?"

"Yeah. I got spritzed by one of those perfume handlers, you know? They had this big display and everything. A black curtain with a picture of a man grabbing a woman by her waist . . . . All the women wore black miniskirts and corsets. Totally hot."

It sounded sleazy, not hot. "Did you buy a bottle of the perfume?"

Angela reached into her purse and pulled out a box. The merchandising was uncanny. The branding and the bottle were all knock-offs of Jacques's marquis creation. I handed it back to her. "Do you mind opening that? I want to see what it smells like."

Angela ripped off the plastic cover and opened the box. She took the bottle out and pushed the atomizer so we could both inhale the scent. We both grimaced. "What the fuck?!" she exclaimed.

One of the women in the locker room glared at Angela.

I didn't care because Angela had perfectly articulated my thoughts. I wafted the smell towards me again. "Eww. That's disgusting. It smells like flavored rubbing alcohol."

"This is total bullshit," said Angela angrily. "They sprayed me with one thing, and then I bought that. What a scam!"

"Totally. I bet they are freaking out at McCale, trying to deal with this." At least I hoped that they were. Caine and company had to be threatening Perfume X with all sorts of legal posturing, just based on the name alone. But the perfume swap scheme was a different ball of wax. If Parfum Aix could prove what Angela had described, the legal ramifications for Perfume X would be criminal.

But I wasn't on the account anymore, and I had enough on my mind. Angela and I migrated to the Quiet Room so we could try to relax before our treatments. I lay down on a pea green chaise and stared at the white-washed walls. The blankness of the room didn't empty my mind. Was I supposed to reach out to Jacques? Or offer my help to Caine?

"Maxine? Angela?" called a woman in a white lab coat. "Your therapists are ready to see you now."

Our rubber spa shoes squealed on the concrete floor as we followed the woman down a hallway painted a sterile hospital-green. Teardrop lights hung from the ceiling, marking pairs of closed, white metal doors. The place looked like a refurbished sanitarium. Between the sexy spritzers at Macy's and this place, it seemed that New Yorkers would go for anything.

Angela, her face contorted, leaned over and whispered, "Did we sign up for a massage or a lobotomy?"

"Not sure," I replied. "But I'm going to decline the scalp massage, just in case."

Angela was fully splayed on one of the chaises in the Quiet Room, her eyes closed, her face content. I sat down next to her and gently tugged on her robe. Slowly, she opened her eyes. "That was awesome! I am so relaxed right now. And even better, the masseuse used some heavily scented massage oil, so I don't smell that Perfume X crap anymore."

"Well, my masseuse said that I need about 800 more massages to get the lumps out of my shoulders. She told me that I needed to get the stress out of my life. Helpful, right?"

"Not. Let's hope she doesn't quit her day job because she sounds like a lousy shrink."

We were guided to the nail room for deluxe mani/pedis. "Speaking of day jobs, how's yours?" I asked. Angela always had some hilarious story about somebody drunk at a work site or a foreman caught pilfering bricks from inventory for his home patio project.

"Did I tell you about the guy who brought his baby to a worksite?"

"No. But I can empathize with him already," I mused sarcastically.

Angela spun the Opi nail polish display case. "No. No, you can't. The guy's wife was on a trip, and since he couldn't find anyone to watch the kid, he thought the responsible thing would be to bring it into an environment with dust, nail guns and plastic tarps."

I picked out a conservative shade of pink. "He did not do that."

Angela switched out my pink for bright red. "Yes, he did. And when I called him to the office, he tried to get me to watch the kid."

I couldn't imagine doing something like that at McCale. And of late, there were plenty of situations where I would have wanted to try. "So what did you say to this guy?"

"I sent him home. And he thanked me. He thought I was giving him paid leave, but I really just deducted a day of work from his paycheck. He probably won't even notice." She pulled out a shade of neon orange for herself. "The better question is: How is your job? What is going on with the nanny search?"

Angela had listened to me complain about the interim childcare situation *ad nauseam*. She knew that I was at the whim of whichever babysitter was scheduled to watch Henry whenever I needed to go into the office. Not having a regular sitter was hard on Henry and required me to spend time, each time, explaining the ropes Chez Pedersen to another stranger. "Well, I can't seem to find anyone from the list of nanny candidates that NYC Baby Prep has provided."

"Well, I think you're just burned and paranoid. But I don't blame you. If something like that had happened to Gina, I'd have quit my job and become a housewife."

I looked down at the small pool of swirling warm water that surrounded my feet. In my worst moments of despair, I had considered quitting McCale. But I knew that the radical notion of leaving my job for a temporary respite would have a major negative long-term impact on my career. If Paola had been able to manage motherhood and a job that required travel, I could at least pull off an in-town job. "I can't quit, Angela. And I really don't want to quit. I like my job."

"Well, I'm sorry to tell you this, but if you don't get your butt back into the office on a regular basis, they're going to make you quit." Angela pulled her feel out of the water. "Seriously. They'll counsel you out."

"What? Why? Why can't I negotiate a position where I work out of the house some of the time and just go to the office for meetings?" That's really what I had been doing for the past three weeks. And I had subconsciously intended to keep doing it until someone said otherwise. I thought I was working the system, but with Angela's revelation, I realized that I might be positioning myself for termination.

Angela rolled her eyes. "Does anyone else in your office do that? Does your firm support that kind of set up?"

"No. But maybe I can be the first one. You know, set the standard for the other women at McCale."

Angela wasn't convinced. And quite frankly, neither was I. If we didn't walk around the office at McCale haggard and weary, then by all appearances, we weren't working hard enough. "It's all about expectations, Maxine. If you didn't work from home before the baby, they're never going to let you do it now."

The pedicurist started to aggressively clip my cuticles. "I never thought about it that way." I should have thought about it that way, since Deirdre Morgan had given me practically the same advice months ago. Now I was playing defense, waiting for the fallout that would inevitably come from working at home. I wasn't controlling expectations at all. I was ignoring them.

"I gotta tell you—this might be the perfect time to start looking for another job. If talking to your boss doesn't work, you could go somewhere else and negotiate your work-from-home situation on the front-end." Angela was nodding vigorously in approval of her own advice. "And besides, you should always look for a job when you already have one."

"Duly noted," I concluded, my head spinning. Angela was

probably right. But considering the fact that I couldn't even find a nanny, the odds of me finding the time to embark on a job search were slim to none.

I watched laconically as the pedicurist started to paint my toenails bright red. My fingers were next. If McCale, Morgan & Black did ever fire me, I could always audition for the part of trampy perfume spritzer for Perfume X.

34

Henry was down for a nap and Dale was at the gym. I had a rarified moment of serenity on a Sunday afternoon. I could have read a book. I could have watched television. But I eschewed relaxation for masochism. I went into my bathroom, took off my clothes and stared at myself in the mirror. My body, with the extra pounds of baby weight, was a metaphor for almost every aspect of my life: it had great potential, but I just didn't have enough time to work on it.

I turned sideways. This was the least flattering viewpoint, and standing up straight didn't help the cause. Yes, the boobs were bigger, but that didn't mean the rest of my body should have grown in proportion. More exercise and less eating were the keys to dropping the weight. And there was no hiding my need to do it, as I stood nude on a cold tile floor.

Yes, I would throw out all the junk food in the kitchen and try to order healthier meals. I would buy better snack food for the apartment. But I needed to burn calories, and relying on excreting breast milk as a means for weight control was becoming less effective now that Henry was moving to solid foods.

I reminded myself that at one time, I had actually enjoyed exercising. Maybe I should have used this moment of self-reflection to do yoga while Dale was at the gym. Somehow, with his busy schedule, he had made the time to work out. I was busier than he was—I should have been the one to go to the gym!

I spent some time being angry with him while I sucked in my stomach and flexed the vestigial muscles in my arms and legs at a flattering angle. Yes, Dale could have done more to watch Henry or help around the apartment. But basic biology required me to be the source of Henry's food. So whether I was pumping milk or nursing Henry directly, more of my time was eaten up by feeding our son.

I looked at my unshaven armpit and considered going all negative-feminist on Dale. I could demand that for every hour I nursed, he should provide some equal contribution to the household. I could calculate all the money I saved on formula from nursing and then spend it on myself. But I couldn't threaten him with that, or much else for that matter. I had no leverage. I was just pissed that I was the one who had to deal with the majority of Henry's upbringing by myself.

I put some clothes on and considered how to get my life back on track. If I just had some certainty about my professional future, I might be less mentally fatigued. I considered Angela's advice. Maybe I should look for another job. It might be the best time to do it. I could take off for interviews when I was working from home, and no one at McCale would be the wiser.

I pulled up my résumé, determined to update it, my LinkedIn account, and my alumni profile for Columbia Law by the time Henry woke up from his nap. As I started to summarize my Parfum Aix experience, Dale entered the apartment.

"Hey! What are you doing?" His hair was matted with sweat as he made his way to the refrigerator for a drink.

I pushed my chair away from the desk. "Interesting you should ask." He plopped on a chair in the living room where I was working. "I'm looking for a job."

Dale was grasping around for the remote when he said, "As what? Don't you have enough to do at McCale?" He turned on the television. The bulb in the TV monitor seemed to set one off in his head. "Wait a second. Are you looking to leave McCale? Did something happen? Did you get fired?"

"No," I said, slightly alarmed by his reaction. "It's Sunday. No one gets fired on Sunday." Dale looked at me sideways. "But I am thinking about looking around. If I can't find a nanny, things are not going to turn out well at McCale. I can feel it."

Dale sat up on the couch. "Has anyone actually said anything to you? I think you're over-reacting." Dale read the concern on my face and put the TV on mute. "Maxine. You're doing all your work just fine, right? Why should anyone at McCale care if you work part-time out of the apartment?"

I crossed my arms in front of me. "How do you think Bobbie would feel if you suddenly started to work part-time from home? How would that go over at Worthington?"

Dale raised his voice defensively. "Look. You just had a kid. It's a completely different situation."

I sat down on the couch next to Dale. Here was a guy working himself to the bone to reach his potential, to be as successful as he could be. I knew he was a driven man, a competitive man. But the notion that Henry's entrance into the world would disrupt his path in any significant way hadn't even registered with his psyche.

"I did not just have a kid. Henry was born almost six months ago. But for all the clichéd reasons, I am in a completely different situation than you are."

"What do you want me to do?" he asked earnestly. "Do you want me to talk to some nanny candidates? I can have Sabrina work some into my schedule if you think that would help."

We had tried something like this before. I had delegated babysitter identification duties to Dale for the occasion of Mike Simonson's 35th birthday party. Dale claimed that the sitter was "certified," but in what, I had no idea. When we got back from Mike's party, Henry was asleep in his crib wearing the stinkiest diaper imaginable. Not only were his clothes ruined, the sheets and part of the bumper were stained. The sitter claimed that the voluminous bowel movement must have occurred after Henry had gone to sleep.

Dale was totally blotto from the party, so I had to negotiate pay with the sitter, bathe Henry, clean the crib and get our son back to bed. It would have been easier if I had just looked for the sitter myself. And there was no doubt that having Dale screen potential nannies would just result in a straight pass-through of all candidates from NYC Baby Prep directly to me.

Deep down, I knew that the Olga debacle had scarred me. I had no faith that any hired help would be satisfactory. Now I was risking my career because I was paranoid. I knew there had to be good childcare out there. I just couldn't bring myself to trust anyone.

"I'm having a hard time with the nannies, Dale. I think I need to come clean with Deirdre. I asked her if I could work from home for a week or so. Over a month has gone by."

"I disagree. She probably hasn't even noticed. You don't need to call attention to your situation."

"I'm tired of skulking around. I need to deal with this head-on. The best thing is going to be for me to negotiate some interim set-up until Henry is over the hump."

"When's that going to be?"

"Well," I said inconclusively, "Whenever I think the time is right."

"Good luck with that negotiation strategy, Maxine." Dale put the TV back on. "If you don't know what you want before you talk to Deirdre, you're not going to get it."

35

Joy was in the elevator when I arrived for work. She, of course, knew all the intimate details of my work schedule—and my work location. She was highly empathetic towards my situation and had probably covered for me in ways I had not even imagined. The fact that I didn't bother to touch base with her before scheduling my monumental day in the office was pure stupidity on my part.

"All the partners are where?" I stammered as we walked off the elevator.

"They're at an off-site retreat for two days," said Joy. It was 8:30, and barely half of the staff was in the office. Those that were there were sporting business casual attire.

"So you're telling me that the day I decide to come in for face time, no one's here?" I threw my suit jacket on my desk, which had piles of files and mail on it.

Joy rubbed my back. "Pretty much. But Nancy will be here, so at least you'll get props with her."

"What is that supposed to mean?"

"Well, she's been not-so-subtly walking by your office each day at regular intervals to see if you're here." Joy walked towards the door. "She's probably charting it out and giving it to Deirdre for brownie points."

I shook my head, thanked Joy, and closed the door to my office. Being back *in situ* made me realize just how ridiculous it would have been to suggest my plan of working from home to Deirdre. She'd never go for it. Not because it was a bad idea, but because she'd have to deal with the wrath of Nancy Lallyberry. Nancy had barely taken any maternity leave and hadn't had a sick day since Troy had been born. I was screwed.

I sat down to read the news on my computer. Perfume X ads were popping up all over the margins of the pages I frequented. I pushed my chair back from the desk. It made complete sense. Perfume X had to have initiated a massive online campaign, buying up Google AdWords and targeting advertisements to people just like me, users who regularly accessed Parfum Aix on the internet. It would take some time to look at the ads, but if they were misleading enough, Perfume X might be duping potential Parfum Aix buyers all over the world into purchasing their lousy imitation. The revenue hit to Parfum Aix, not to mention the damage to the brand, could be devastating.

I searched through my contacts and pulled up Jacques's number in Grasse. If he was working this evening, I just might catch him in his office. After a few pulses, someone picked up the receiver. "*Bonsoir. Le bureau de Jacques Deschemel.*"

I responded in French, identifying myself, and asking if he was available. I was informed that he was in his lab. The French admin seemed to recognize my name. Maybe she was the one who had sent me all those perfume and gin samples. She told me to hold the line while she tracked Jacques down.

"Maxine!" said Jacques, about two minutes later. "*Comment vas-tu? How are you?*"

We exchanged some pleasantries. Jacques was appreciative of the photos I had sent him of Henry; I asked how his gin was coming along, etc. Then I got to the point. "Jacques, I wanted to ask you about something, not as a lawyer, since I am not on the Parfum Aix account."

"Yes, I know. I am still upset about that. I tried to talk to Caine. . ."

I had to interrupt him since that was water under the bridge. "Jacques, have you ever heard of Perfume X?"

"Perfume X?" he repeated. I couldn't tell if he hadn't heard me properly, or if he wasn't sure if he knew what I was talking about.

"Perfume X is a knock-off of Parfum Aix. And they are aggressively pushing their product. Is McCale helping you with this at all?"

"Oh, right! Perfume X. Yes, Vivienne told me about this company. She talked to Monsieur Seaver about it." I could tell that Jacques had a strong dislike for Caine because he never called him by his first name.

"O.K. Good. I assume they are taking all the requisite legal action on your behalf."

"Well, there's nothing to do."

"What?"

Jacques's tone became stern. "We were told that Perfume X would not compete with Parfum Aix because we have exclusive distribution rights in selected stores—Saks Fifth Avenue, Bergdorf Goodman, Henri Bendel. Monsieur Seaver was going to look into Bloomingdale's. This Perfume X," said Jacques with repugnance, "would be sold at other retailers, like Lord & Taylor and Macy's."

I communicated Angela's experience to Jacques, which, not surprisingly, infuriated him. But his rage was directed more towards Vivienne than Caine. "Vivienne is my local representative for Parfum Aix. She is supposed to monitor the competition! *Mon dieu!* What has she been doing? Shopping?!"

I tried to calm Jacques. "Look. I don't know how long this switcheroo thing has been going on at Macy's. It may have just started. I am sure Caine can help get this resolved expeditiously."

"Yes! Yes! Absolutely! I will talk to him," he said. "Thank you for being so conscientious. Perhaps now that you're back from maternity leave, you can come back on the account?"

I graciously avoided his question, and we hung up. I was trying to fly under the radar at work, so the last thing I had considered was approaching Deirdre and Caine for a transfer.

But I had to believe that Caine would reach out to me once he got a call from Jacques. Then I could tell him about the online marketing angle, which I'm sure he hadn't even considered. He'd have to be impressed by that. Then maybe I could get back on Parfum Aix and fix this whole mess. And if Jacques could operate from France, maybe I could work from home.

I was pulled from my daydream by the buzz of my phone. *Want me to review your resume b4 you send it out?* Another text from Angela. She had been digitally harassing me since I had arrived at the office, telling me to keep my options open. I only answered her texts because she kept sprinkling in details about one of her subcontractors who had been using prostitutes in a Porta Potty. The details were riveting.

What first seemed like a hilarious comic bit had transformed into a tale of cheap desperation. I couldn't stop thinking about how disgusting it would be to have intercourse in a hot, plastic box that housed human excrement. How did either one of those characters get to a point in their lives where sex in a Porta Potty was even remotely alluring? I guess I had to factor in some massive doses of self-loathing for one party and financial destitution for the other.

And my life was in the gutter because I couldn't find a nanny. Wow.

Oddly, this tale of base human behavior was highly motivating. With no one of importance in the office, and six more hours of freedom (from pre-paying the babysitter), I followed Angela's advice.

I updated my résumé and sent it over to Mrs. Perretti. While she reviewed it, I joined every applicable Facebook and LinkedIn group, emailed friends from law school, and scoured the online classifieds. After incorporating Angela's comments, I sent my résumé to the human resources departments of all the Manhattan law firms with departments in my specialty. I started research on consumer products companies with the intent of applying for an in-house counsel position. And just for the interviewing experience, I applied to a bunch of not-for-profits in town. By the time I was done, I had spent an entire day at the McCale offices without billing a single minute of time to a client.

36

I never heard from Caine about Parfum Aix. And no one had sent me any threatening emails about my lack of presence in the office. I just kept hammering away, billing hours to HKI and juggling life with Henry at home.

Interestingly, my job search bore almost immediate fruit. Within a week, I was contacted for an interview with the Landmark Preservation Association of Manhattan. I scheduled a sitter, re-arranged my conference call schedule at McCale and breezed through 90 minutes of chit-chat with Linda, the director. I had somehow convinced her that my knowledge of copyrighting consumer products was easily transferable to preserving architectural monuments in Manhattan. She was highly enthusiastic about my qualifications and my fit with the organization.

The next week, I had a phone discussion with one of the group's major donors. It took about five minutes of active listening, but I was able to find common ground in the fact that his third wife was expecting their first child. I couldn't relate to the multiple marriages, but I had the baby chit-chat nailed. At the end of our talk, he told me I was perfect for the position.

The job seemed to have more plusses than minuses. The schedule was completely flexible, enabling me to work from home at my discretion. The work would not be anywhere near as challenging as it was with McCale, and I was all but guaranteed a pay cut. However, I was sure to learn something new. And I would avoid breaks of employment on my résumé that might raise red flags later. When I was ready, I could return to corporate life on my own terms.

And then there were the contacts. My phone interview had been with Larry Symcox, a man who had made his fortune in the high-tech industry. Dale was practically salivating at the notion of getting intimate access to figures of this stature through my potential employment with the association. Ultimately, I might even find another job for myself through the relationships I could make.

All I had to do was nail the last interview. It was scheduled at the association's mid-town location, which is where I would report if I needed to come to the office.

Unlike the spatial offices of McCale, the mid-town offices of the Landmark Preservation Association were cramped and low-tech. Rolls of architectural drawings were shoved into any available crevice, thereby restricting the workspace for the staff. When I inquired about the possibility of converting the drawings to an electronic format, Linda informed me that many of these plans had been signed by the original architects and were treasures all to themselves. When I saw one of these little gems being used as a doorstop, I held my tongue. I could re-organize the office once I got the job.

And I was absolutely delighted when Linda offered it to me. I didn't know what the salary was, and I didn't care. An extraordinary wave of relief rolled through my body, accompanied by a whoosh of empowerment. Everything had finally come together, in a way I had never expected. Gleefully, I accepted on the position on the spot.

As Linda showed me to my office, which I was to share with a file clerk and a research analyst, I asked when she would like me to sign the requisite employment papers with the human resources department. Suddenly, her face turned grim.

"Well, Mrs. Pedersen, we're too small to have a human resources group. Brenda, here, usually handles payroll and such." She pointed at a gray-haired woman hunched over a file drawer. Wiry hairs protruded from her lip and chin, and she snuffed at me like she was blowing into a handkerchief.

"O.K.," I said, determined to minimize contact with Brenda. "Who handles the benefits, the on-boarding process, all of that?"

Linda repositioned the pencil that had been lodged in the bun on top of her head. "I think we have a bit of a misunderstanding here, Mrs. Pedersen."

"We do?" I scratched my own head. "I apologize if I was being too forward. Shall I give you a few days to compile a compensation package?"

"Mrs. Pedersen, there is no compensation package."

Yes, there definitely was a miscommunication. "I'm sorry—did I miss something?"

"The Landmark Preservation Association is a non-profit entity. The revenue we receive is used exclusively for the operational upkeep of the office. Unfortunately, we are unable to pay any of our workers. We're all volunteers. I thought this was clear to you."

I dropped my briefcase on the floor. Had I really been so desperate for a job that I had missed the signals that my best option for intellectual stimulation would be a volunteer position? "Well, I apologize for the confusion. I would love to work with your organization, but I really need salaried work." I thought I might be able to salvage the situation. "Do you offer contract work? Perhaps I could offer my services on an as-needed basis?"

Linda laughed out loud. "Can you imagine the talent we'd have lined up if people found out we actually paid our employees? You are a hoot, Mrs. Pedersen!"

My disappointment over the lost Landmark Preservation position evaporated when I got an email from the H.R. department of McCale, Morgan & Black's major competitor, Hershel & Dixon. The notion that I could make a somewhat lateral move without slashing my paycheck was an alternative I had hardly dared let myself imagine. I responded to the email immediately.

I was offered an interview slot for the upcoming Tuesday at 11:15. Not 11:30. Or 11:00. Either of which would have implied at least a 30-minute discussion. An 11:15 interview just sounded cursory. And although I knew the first discussion would be a phone screen, I was hoping for more than the duration of a sit-com episode to sell my skills as a superior attorney.

In preparation, I consulted Angela about how to handle screening interviews. She advised me to prepare crisp, concise responses to the questions I would most likely be asked. I was also instructed to list the achievements I wanted to cover before I hung up the phone. All good advice. I completed her tasks and felt confident and prepared for the call.

Interview day arrived, and at 11:10, Henry was happily playing in his crib and well fed. I had given him a brand new toy that I expected would engage him for some time while I took the call in the living room. I got myself some water and dialed the number to Hershel & Dixon.

Someone picked up the phone, but no one said anything.

"Hello? This is Maxine Pedersen, calling for an interview. Is this Hershel & Dixon?" I squeezed the handset of the receiver and winced, wondering if I had called Deidre Morgan's number by accident.

"Oh, oh," said the voice of someone in her twenties. "This is Stacy at Hershel & Dixon. I'm sorry. I thought you were calling at 1:15."

I glanced at the invite, which had positioned itself on my calendar at 11:15. She must have been doing the same thing because she said, "Whoops, you're right. This was scheduled for 11:15."

"Will that work for you?" I asked, trying to be professional, but not wanting to deal with an interview two hours from now, when my son might be crying in his room.

"Yeah. This is fine. Let's just get it over with." I heard her move some papers around. "Let me pull up your résumé here. . . ." I started scribbling on the pad in front of me while I waited in silence. "You know, I'm sorry, Maxine, but I can't find it. Would you mind emailing it to me? Maybe we should just reschedule the call."

"I'll resend the email right now. While you wait for it, I can give you some background on myself and summarize my interest in Hershel & Dixon." I hoped her company didn't have some ridiculous firewall that would delay the receipt of my email. I had a feeling that if I ever got off the phone with her, I'd never get back on.

"O.K. Got it." As she started talking, it became clear that she hadn't even read my résumé. She made fragmented comments out loud as she scanned it. "Yale undergrad. History major. Yale Debate Association, Director of Development. Club Tennis, Co-Captain." No questions about any of that. She continued. "Columbia Law. Law Review. I.P.C.?" Her voice inflected upwards until she read on, discovering that *I.P.C.* was an acronym for Intellectual Property Club. I looked at my watch. Four minutes had passed. She spent three more recounting my past to me.

When Stacy finished reading about my seven years with McCale, she dropped the bomb. "I don't understand why, after so many years of loyalty to McCale, Morgan & Black, you'd want to leave and come to Hershel & Dixon. What's the impetus for the move? Why now?"

Angela had coached me on this type of question, advising me not, under any circumstances, to volunteer anything about the fact that I had a baby. Legally, there could be no discrimination about the fact that I was a new mother, but in practice, I'd never be seen as accessible as someone without a child.

I stumbled through my prepared response. "Well, I think McCale, as a firm, has been moving their consumer products practice away from smaller organizations with unique I.P. issues and focusing on broader, international manufacturing regulations." It sounded like mumbo-jumbo, and I was banking on the fact that Stacy would not be well-versed in corporate strategy.

She was, however, well-versed in résumé reading. "Hmm. Well, it looks like you brought on some significant business to the firm.

From your description, it sounds like the company Perfume X, right?"

I stopped myself from correcting her. I wondered if she had laid a trap, purposefully asking me the wrong name of a client to test my ethics. "Well, of course I can't reveal the name of the company, due to client confidentiality."

"Of course," she said, disappointed. "Too bad. Word on the street is the Perfume X account is highly lucrative." Did she mean Parfum Aix? Or Perfume X? I didn't know what to say, so in deference to Jacques, I said nothing. But Stacy kept going. "Doesn't matter anyway since it looks like you moved off the client over a year ago. What happened there?"

"Standard staffing move," I said as nonchalantly as possible.

"That's odd. I mean, if you brought the business in, why wouldn't you work the client?" The interview was approaching the 15 minute allotment, and I hadn't controlled one minute of the discussion. So I tried to change gears.

"To be honest with you, Stacy, I have had a fantastic professional experience at McCale, Morgan & Black. But as you probably know, the transition to partner takes more than just sales. Timing, mentorship and sponsorship are all critical elements for anyone looking to achieve such a personal milestone." More mumbo jumbo. And I was in delicate territory now, since this round of verbal goo was all related to human resources. Angela would have pulled her hair out if she had heard my response.

Stacy let a few seconds pass. "Well, it looks like our time is up. Thank you for speaking with me today about your experience. We'll be in touch if something opens up at Hershel & Dixon." The phone went dead.

Dejected, I went into Henry's room, hoping he could cheer me up. Half of the foam alphabet blocks I had given him to play with had been thrown out of the crib. I viewed the disorder as a positive sign of Henry's burgeoning throwing arm, rather than a nuisance to clean up. He looked up, smiled, and handed me a block labeled with the letter F. "Thanks, man," I sighed. "I'm glad someone's tuned in to what's going on around here."

37

Paola plopped a raw chicken on a cutting board in her kitchen. She pulled a knife from a wooden block and held it in anticipation. "Hey, Nelson! I'm gonna do it!"

Dale picked up Henry and propped him in the crook of his arm. "Watch it with the cutlery, will ya, Brighton? Henry's already had a haircut." Henry's hair had come in auburn, like mine. Last week we had the long wisps cut from the top of his head, and the remaining hair fuzz seemed much darker. Now he looked more like Dale, which somehow made him even more adorable.

Amanda, loose blonde tendrils askew, came scuffling down the hallway. Like a bee to honey she lunged at the kitchen table for

Dale's unattended phone. I snatched it up before she could grab it. Then Nelson snatched her up before she could get upset. He put her on his shoulders, her head close to the ceiling of their Chelsea apartment. She pulled at the thinning hair on Nelson's head.

"We ready now?" asked Paola.

"I wouldn't mess with her," said Nelson to Dale. "She's pregnant, and she's got a knife."

"I can see that. If this is how she behaves while she's pregnant, I'd hate to see her in the delivery room."

Henry let out a laugh, even though he couldn't possibly understand the meaning of what he had heard. Then Amanda started in. "C'mon, Mommy! Do it! Do it!" She was encouraging her mother, even though she couldn't possibly understand what Paola was about to do.

Paola put the knife down and stood solemnly over the chicken carcass. She closed her eyes and started reciting something in Spanish. Nelson gazed, intoxicated by the sounds of his bi-lingual spouse.

Dale lost his composure and started chuckling.

Nelson slapped him on the shoulder. "This is sacred! Shut up!"

Paola finished her incantation. She picked up the knife with both hands, took a deep breath, and wacked the blade down through the rib cage of the chicken. The cleaved bird fell apart, with each half flopping over to one side. Paola dropped the knife, and she and Nelson cried with excitement.

As they hugged one another, Dale looked at me and said, "What the . . . ?" And then he mouthed the word "fuck." Now that Henry had started to imitate sounds and repeat words, Dale had had instituted a profanity blocker on himself.

Paola fanned herself in relief. "It's a family tradition. From my mother's side. In Mexico."

Nelson told her to sit down, shoving Dale out of the way so his wife could have some space. "It's quite amazing, actually. The women in Paola's family sacrifice a chicken or a goat each time one of them becomes pregnant to ensure a healthy baby. The act goes back for generations, right honey?"

"That's right," confirmed Paola. "My mother was very upset that I could not return to Mexico for a proper ceremony, so I told her I would do something here."

"Well, then where is your mother?" asked Dale. "I'd think she'd want to see how well you could hack up a store-bought chicken."

"Not funny," responded Paola. "She's in L.A. because my sister is expecting a baby. She's going to help out there for a while."

I gave Nelson a broad smile. "So you get to be Super Dad until Grandma gets back. How fun for you!"

Nelson took Amanda from his shoulders and scowled at me. Paola turned her back on us both and started prepping the chicken. I guess I had hit some sort of familial minefield in the Brighton household.

"Dale," said Nelson, "You want to bring Henry back to the playroom with Amanda?"

"Great idea," said Dale. He held up Henry's hands as our son stumble-walked his way out of the kitchen.

"Don't forget, honey. I'm going to need that recipe for my paper," said Nelson as he left the room.

"Paper?" I asked once Nelson was out of earshot. "What paper?"

Paola started butchering the bird. "Nelson's writing a paper about the transformation of cultural traditions in modern society. It's for his tenure application."

"He's up for tenure?" I said, surprised. "Isn't that a lot of work?"

Paola pulled a boning knife from the block. "Yes, it is," she said, as she severed a chicken leg. "We had an agreement. I was going to keep working, and he was going to stay home with the baby. Not stay home like a Mr. Mom, but be in charge. I make three times as much money as he does, but I can only do it if I can travel." Paola held up the chicken by its wing. She turned the bird as she sliced through some connective tissue.

"Wow," I said. "I thought your mom was going to help out." And as I said it, I realized that Paola's mom would probably be splitting time between her grandkids, who were on opposite coasts.

Paola rolled her eyes. "My sister's baby couldn't have come at a worse time. Nelson is swamped. He's got to write papers, do lectures, apply for grants and get this—travel! Him! He's got to travel to do research! *Qué jodienda!*"

Her face was red. Sweat was forming on her forehead, so I got her a drink of water. "Here. Come on. Don't freak out so much. It's not good for the baby."

Paola dabbed her forehead with a kitchen towel. "Sorry. This is going to be fine. I mean, if this had happened while I was pregnant with Amanda, I don't know what I would have done. At least now I know what I'm getting into, right?

"Speak for yourself," I said. "I still don't know what the heck I am going to do."

"So what's happening? Are you going to talk to your boss about working from home?"

"Yeah. I've got a meeting scheduled with her this week." I hoped this one was going to stick, as the last two Joy had scheduled with Deirdre had been postponed. "In the meantime, I had another interview. Total bust, which is a bummer, because it was Hershel & Dixon."

Paola wedged a knife between the ball and socket joint of the leg and thigh of the bird. "That's a bummer. What happened?"

"The interview lasted a whopping 15 minutes, and they haven't called me back in almost two weeks. I don't think McCale has anything to worry about."

Paola and I switched places as she opened her refrigerator. "Ouch. I'm sorry." She rummaged through the produce inside. "Take this." She handed me a red onion and some garlic. Perfect. I expected her to pull out a rotten banana next. "Here. This, too." Out came bell peppers, a bouquet of herbs and a plastic container that housed a dark, goopy paste.

I held the Tupperware up to the light. "What's in here? Is this for the chicken?"

"Yeah. I made it yesterday." She opened the container and held it up to my nose. My eyes started to water. "It's a concentrated paste made from dried peppers and chicken stock. My mother's recipe. What do you think?"

"I don't know," I said, intrigued. "It seems pretty hot."

Paola dumped the paste into the bowl with the chicken. "It is hot, but it will mellow when it cooks with the chicken." She coated the chicken parts with the paste and shoved the bowl to the corner of her counter. "That is going to sit for a bit and marinate."

"Right," I said, impressed and somewhat intimidated by Paola's domesticity. The closest I had ever come to butchering a raw chicken had been when I used a steak knife to slice a grilled chicken breast from Delmonico's. Sure, I knew my way around a bar, but Paola's culinary skills seemed much more useful, especially for a parent. "Does Amanda eat this stuff?"

"She eats what I cook—when I get around to cooking. My mother brings her all kinds of things. *Carne asada, pollo en mole,* stuff like that." She wiped off her hands on a towel and then started chopping the vegetables. "You're going to have to start cooking pretty soon. Henry's going to have to eat something besides jarred baby food."

Good. More stuff to do. "Maybe I should just hire a personal chef, and see if she does babysitting on the side. I'd probably have better luck with that."

Paola cored a red pepper. "Not a bad idea. Maybe you could get her to clean, too."

"Exactly!" This seemed like a great concept. "You know, I should post a job description on the Cordon Bleu Facebook page. What do you think pays better: sous chef or Manhattan nanny?"

"Good question. I don't know. But I love that you're thinking out of the box. Just make sure she can make mac 'n cheese," said Paola seriously. "It's an American staple."

38

Deirdre sat behind her desk, facing the doorway. Her secretary told me that I could go in, so I quietly sat down and waited for Deirdre to finish. It gave me time to get even more nervous about talking about the obvious: why I wasn't coming to the office on a regular basis.

"Good. Done." Deirdre slid away from her computer screen and got up to join me and the padded furniture. She brought over a file folder that was about an inch thick and put it down on the coffee table between us. "I'm glad you scheduled a meeting. We have a number of issues to discuss."

I put my hands on the legal pad on my lap, only to notice the veins on the back of them pulsating wildly. I took a deep breath with the hopes that my voice wouldn't shake when I started to speak. "I'm glad you are finally available. I've wanted to follow up with you in person regarding my work situation."

"I don't think you have a work situation," corrected Deirdre. "You have a childcare situation."

I wasn't expecting her to get straight to the point, but maybe that's because I didn't want her to. I wanted to dip my toe into the pool of discussion and get comfortable. Deirdre, not one for wasting time, just pushed me straight in. "You're right. Childcare has been a problem, especially after Henry's health scare."

"I can't imagine how you must have felt. You know you have the firm's full support in Henry's recovery. How is he doing?"

I unintentionally perked up. I wanted to control my emotions and discuss this serious issue in a detached manner, but talking about Henry made me think about Henry, and that made me run at the mouth. "He's great! Doing really well. He's fully recovered. Gaining weight. He can pull himself up now, which is awesome."

Deirdre stared at the thick folder without smiling. She looked up deliberately and said, "When will you be returning full-time to the office?"

"Uh. . . I'm not sure," I stammered. "That's what I wanted to talk to you about."

She slid back in her chair and put her hands in her lap. "O.K. I'm listening."

"Well, I feel like the last month or so has worked out very well, given my ability to stay on top of everything at McCale with a partial work-from-home strategy." I had practiced that as my opening line, hoping that my nervousness would abate if I could just verbalize an opening comment. It didn't. So I just blurted out what was on my mind. "I was hoping that I could keep working from home until I could get a few more things straightened out."

Deirdre crossed her legs and asked non-confrontationally, "And how long do you think that will be?"

My face went blank. I should have listened to Dale. I had come into this session without a negotiation strategy. I didn't know what I was supposed to ask for except something that Angela had warned me that I was not going to get. Lost, I just replied, "I don't know."

Deirdre picked up the folder. She opened it up, flipped through some pages and then asked, "Do you know what this is?"

"I'm guessing it's not HKI-related, since we're not discussing client work."

"No. It's not client-related," said Deirdre, her tone resolute. "This is your Performance Improvement Plan from H.R. They call it a 'PIP,' which is a cute-sounding name for something administrative and bureaucratic."

McCale tacitly espoused the "up or out" theory, meaning that employees were either promoted up or counseled out of the company. I sat in shock as she held a document framing me in the latter category.

"On paper, you are doing your job. As you just indicated. You haven't missed a deadline since you returned from maternity leave. You have participated in all of your meetings—sometimes remotely—but you have been involved nonetheless. If I had to check off boxes summarizing a list of tasks and whether you had completed them, every box would be checked." I nodded. "The issue is that no one else at McCale, Morgan & Black works remotely. So from H.R.'s perspective, there's an inequity."

"With all due respect, Deidre," I started, my confidence growing out of weeks of pent-up frustration, "I think H.R.'s policies are antiquated. They should be updated. And this is the perfect opportunity to do so."

Rather than challenge me, Deidre applauded me. Literally. "I couldn't agree more, Maxine. But Morgan is only one of three names in McCale, Morgan & Black." She waited a few moments, so my brain could process her coded support for my cause. Now I understood why I hadn't been told to return to the office. But that folder was still on the coffee table.

"So. . . what does this mean?" I asked meekly.

"I'm supposed to give you a series of warnings, have you review your sins with H.R., and then have you swear you'll get back to the office by a certain time frame; or. . . your employment with McCale, Morgan & Black will be terminated."

She had to be joking. "What? Do you mean I'd be fired?"

"Yup. Fired." Then she threw the folder on the table. "But not yet."

I started rolling my pen across the pad in my lap. "I'm confused, here. Am I supposed to talk to H.R. or not?"

"No. There's something more important that you need to handle, and this *is* client related." Deirdre got up to retrieve something else from her desk.

I was fully prepared for her to give me a year's worth of casework so I could avoid going to H.R. This whole scene brought me back to the extra book report about Molly Pitcher that I had to write in lieu of going to the principal when I was in middle school. That was my punishment for standing up on the school bus to tell the driver that he was going the wrong way home. Some things never change.

Deirdre handed me a full-page newspaper ad from the *New York Post*. "This is about Parfum Aix. Or rather, Perfume X."

The problem was immediately obvious. A well-dressed man's hand was gripping the hip of a woman in a mini dress. That alone would have been plenty suggestive but Perfume X was going raw. The woman's dress was cinched up and the man's forefinger was under the string of her "underwear." "Wow!" I exclaimed. "What's the next ad going to be? I mean, where's the line between art and porn here?"

"That's the point, obviously," said Deirdre.

I threw the paper down in revulsion. "I know that's the point." I glanced at the ad again. It was tasteless, but I could see the allure. Angela would have loved it. "Well, it is a fantastic ad campaign for Perfume X. But Jacques must be freaking out."

"Exactly. And that's where you come in."

"You want to put me back on the account?" I could barely contain my excitement at the notion. But before I could get my hopes up, Deirdre brought them down with the weight of an anvil.

"Well, no. We just need you to talk to Jacques and smooth everything over."

"What do you mean?" I leaned over in my seat.

Deirdre sat back in hers. "Well, Caine kind of dropped the ball on this one. He does not have a good relationship with Vivienne, and I think their lack of communication allowed this thing to snowball into this piece of trash."

I thought about what she had said. I was embarrassed with the care—or lack thereof—that my firm had provided Jacques Deschemel and the entire Parfum Aix team in France. The brand of one of our flagship clients was under siege, its product fraudulently represented, and apparently, we had done nothing to stop it. "What do you expect me to say to Jacques? Where do we stand on all of this?"

"Say whatever you need to say. Something along the lines of how feverishly we're working to file the appropriate lawsuits, restraining orders, and complaints to shut this thing down."

"We are?" I said, in disbelief.

Deirdre stood up, the meeting apparently over. "We just need you to fix this. And then that," she said, as she eyeballed the thick file on the table, "will go away."

39

It was a sunny Saturday morning, the kind of day that inspired New Yorkers to lay on beach towels in Central Park in order to work on their summer tans. I was too agitated to undertake such a lackadaisical pursuit. Over a week had passed since my discussion with Deirdre, and I was still generating enough nervous energy to set my hair on fire.

Dale was on the golf course with Bobbie, so I resolved to resume a regular regime of my favored form of exercise, running. It had been over a year since my last jog. I had no idea what my fitness level would be, but I was hoping to make it around the park at least once without embarrassing myself. My only source of encouragement was that my running shoes still fit.

I wheeled through the entrance at 79th Street with Henry in my collapsible jogging stroller/backpack. Pilots of this celebrated item were finally available, and I was one of the lucky few to own one. Its collapsibility was enabled by a clever ball-and-socket mechanism attached to each wheel. Unfortunately, the stiffness of the plastic component impeded the shock absorbance of the stroller itself, resulting in a bumpy ride for Henry over Manhattan's uneven sidewalks. A small nylon pouch and two padded straps were all that accounted for its designation as a backpack.

While interesting in concept, the jogging stroller/backpack was an attempt to combine two great ideas into one superior product that ultimately downgraded the utility of both original components. It reminded me of the Elgin Cutlass Pistol Dale and I had seen at Bobbie Macaluso's house. The positioning of the knife under the barrel of the gun had ruined the accuracy of the pistol. Like the stroller I was pushing, there had been no synergistic union of ideas.

The last time I had been on a jog, I had had two great jobs that went well together. I had lived what I believed was a perfectly enriched existence as a wife and a lawyer. With Henry added to the mix, the delicate balance had collapsed. Rather than redistribute the finite amount of energy I could commit to my responsibilities, I had tried to just add on the function of motherhood. As a result, I had multi-purposed myself to the point where I didn't feel like I was particularly good at anything anymore. Yes, I, Maxine Pedersen, had become a human version of this ridiculous stroller that I was pushing.

With each stride, I could feel the flesh on my thighs rumble. I wasn't sure if I was really out of shape, or if pushing the jogging stroller was siphoning the energy I could be using to get up the hills on the east side of the park. In need of a break, I veered off the main path to show Henry something special. We weaved through some pedestrian traffic, stopping in front of a granite statue of one of New York City's most esteemed former residents, Alexander Hamilton.

I kneeled down next to Henry, who was sucking on the teething toy attached to the side of his seat. "You're named after this guy, Henry. That's where the 'Hamilton' comes from." Henry's eyes twinkled when I said his name. "This guy lived in our neighborhood almost 250 years ago. Isn't that cool?" A couple paused next to me to read the plaque at the foot of the statue. They had to be tourists, since anyone else would have known about the monument or would have been too busy to care. With my bonding moment interrupted, I swung back onto the main path and continued my run.

Every now and then I thought about what day-to-day life on Manhattan Island must have been like for the early colonial settlers. Today's conveniences were luxuries for folks of that era, or more likely, they hadn't even been invented. And yet these men (and some women) are revered for their bravery, intellect and fearlessness in creating a nation founded on democratic principles that are admired the world over.

How I longed to be inspired by these revolutionary figures. Yet my only connection to that bygone era seemed to be the natural childbirth I had endured bringing Henry into this world.

I rounded the top of the park, the foot traffic decidedly reduced. Unencumbered by the worry of colliding with another jogger, I finally hit my stride. More importantly, the endorphins kicked in. It was a huge relief to know that I had some residual aerobic capability. I picked up speed and saw another jogger, a few yards ahead, pushing a state-of-the-art jogging stroller that Henry should have been sitting in. As we came down a long slope of pavement, I surged past her. And I just kept going.

The landmarks of West Side flew by. The Dakota. Strawberry Fields. And of course, Dalehead Arch. These sites had been my daily companions during my pre-baby jogs. The sight of them had become prosaic from years of over-exposure, but with Henry in tow, they were now fresh and new. I couldn't wait for him to get older so he could ride the carousel or search for turtles at Turtle Pond.

As I reached the southern end of the park, I whizzed by the ornate gables of The Plaza. Over the past 40 years, the landmark had changed ownership at least five times. At one point, it had closed down completely for renovations. Some of its rooms were sold off as condos. Nonetheless, the soul of The Plaza had survived. It would always be a New York icon. In fact, if Henry had been a girl, tea at The Plaza would have become a sacred mother-daughter ritual.

I sprinted north, weaving through the thickening masses. The jogging stroller/backpack was not as responsive as I needed it to be, given the speed at which I was running. I had to continually pick up the handle, elevating the back two wheels so I could re-orient the stroller on the axis of the single wheel out front. Each time I did, I felt that poor Henry was going to slide right onto the pavement. No doubt improvements to the stroller's maneuverability would have to be incorporated in future models, or the manufacturer would go bankrupt.

My lap around the park complete, I walked out onto Fifth Avenue. I headed past the grand staircase of the Metropolitan Museum of Art. It was packed with people from all walks of life, from Upper East Side dowagers ascending the stairs, to tour groups huddled en masse, to members of the ubiquitous homeless population corralling their belongings. Then I heard someone yell, "Is that the new stroller I saw on Pinterest?"

From the corner of my eye, a woman stood up, waving her arms to flag me down. I stopped and waited for her as she carefully wound her way through the crowd. I could appreciate her deliberate pace as she looked to be about seven months pregnant. "Hi," I said, as I waited for her to catch her breath.

"Sorry to bother you," she started. She looked down at Henry who was pumping his legs like he was doing imaginary reps on a Nautilus machine. "Oh, he is so cute!"

I smiled with pride. "Thanks. His name is Henry. He's almost nine months old." None of this information was any of her business. But I was a full-fledged member of the Mom Club, the ground rules of which were to over-share interesting factoids about our children to complete strangers.

"Oh, I'm having a boy! He's due in about seven weeks!" Perfect. This future mom was already exhibiting the attributes of a seasoned member of the club.

"Well, you look great," I said.

"Thanks." She kept eye-balling the stroller. "How did you get that? They're totally sold out at Babies "Я" Us and I can't find any online."

"I pre-ordered a year and a half ago." I considered her timetable and wondered why she was in such a hurry. Then I remembered that all future moms were infected with this uncontrollable disease called "nesting." "Don't worry. You probably won't need a jogging stroller for another year. And by that time, I'm sure they'll be back in stock."

"Well, you should see our apartment in Brooklyn. It's tiny. A jogging stroller that can collapse and then be used as a backpack would be awesome. I think it's genius."

That's what I had thought. But at this point, I had no further use for the contraption. "Well, if you like it so much, then this is your lucky day."

"Huh?"

I fished around the stroller pouch for my keys and slipped them into my running shorts. Then I started to unhook Henry. "You can have it. Seriously."

"What do you mean? You don't want it?" The surprise in her tone was accompanied by an undercurrent of concern. She started to give the stroller the once-over, as if she were considering whether or not to buy it.

"There's nothing wrong with it. The collapsing mechanism is great." I detached Henry's toy and then pulled him out of the device. "If you want it, it's yours." I rolled it towards her, concluding the transaction.

"You don't want any money for it?"

"Nope."

The woman put her hand on the handle and started pushing the stroller back and forth. "You're just giving it away? Are you sure that's a good idea?"

"Oh, I'm sure." With my body exercised, my mind was finally clear. "And I've got plenty of other ideas where that came from."

40

I arranged the tables in Conference Room B into a triangle. I stood behind one, a single manila folder resting in front of me. To my right sat Jacques Deschemel and Vivienne Suivant. To my left were Caine Seaver and Deirdre Morgan. Identical manila folders were positioned in front of everybody in attendance.

I sat down, ostensibly to start the meeting, even though I was the least senior person in the room. It seemed like only yesterday that I had walked out of Deirdre's office, tasked with salvaging the Parfum Aix relationship in order to keep my job. Not sure what to do, I had consulted some experts.

Dale suggested some cut-throat corporate tactics—the sort of undercutting, competitive shenanigans that unfortunately helped make the world go 'round. Paola advised me on business strategy. She was the queen of "quantifying value" or putting a dollar figure on every major business initiative she undertook. And of course, Angela made sure that, from a human resources perspective, my ass was covered (her words). I went back and forth on a game plan, which was finally culminating at this very meeting. I adjusted the cuffs of my lavender blouse and took command of the room.

"*Merci* to everyone for coming together on such short notice." All parties murmured in consensus as they shifted uneasily in their seats. "I have been in touch with each of you over the past few days and I appreciate your cooperation and patience. I think a reasonable solution has coalesced, one that will be satisfactory to everyone here."

I stared at the folder in front of me. It seemed so plain, so mundane, so familiar. Knowing what it contained, I smiled. I opened it deliberately, noting that in doing so, I would close a major chapter of my life.

Everyone followed suit, girded to absorb the customary set of technical business points a manila folder might ordinarily contain. Although my head was tilted towards the folder, my eyes focused on the McCale table.

Deirdre, more of a quick study, looked up within seconds. Caine had to read the full three paragraphs before reacting. Rather than look at me, he glared accusingly at Vivienne. She sat up haughtily in her chair. Jacques gave me a wink and a nod.

"The first sheet is my resignation from McCale, Morgan & Black." I spoke as respectfully as I could in addressing Deirdre and Caine. "It has been a fantastic experience working with you both at McCale." Then I forced myself to add some flowery words of appreciation that later I would be glad that I had mentioned.

Later, like when I realized that having my professional and personal life turned inside out was probably the best thing that could have happened to me.

I thanked the McCale team so enthusiastically because if I were talking, then Caine was not. He had started to sweat and had begun to clean his glasses. I knew that his unchecked maladroitness had undoubtedly, and probably unintentionally, enraged Vivienne. The last thing he needed to do right now was open his mouth and try to defend himself. He put his glasses back on, my cue to move on.

I flipped to the next memo in the folder and summarized it before anyone could read it. "I will be joining Parfum Aix as the interim liaison between the company and McCale, Morgan & Black."

"But what about Vivienne?" blurted Caine.

"I will be returning to France," she said, inconclusively. During my discussions with Jacques about my Benedict Arnold-inspired move, we never covered the ultimate disposition of Ms. Vivienne Suivant. And I really didn't care.

I had negotiated virtual *carte blanche* in dealing with McCale, Morgan & Black on Jacques's behalf. Working at Parfum Aix, directly for the President, would help mitigate the wasted time I would need to spend defending my position from work-related political attacks from people like Nancy Lallyberry and Jeffry Hsu. I was thrilled about the notion of having the freedom to perform under the umbrella of a trusted, distinguished innovator like Jacques.

Although I had resigned from corporate America, so to speak, I wasn't naïve. I had no plans to retreat under cover of a foreign company's protection in dealing with firms like McCale, Morgan & Black. I had a reputation to maintain, and a new boss to impress. Which brought me to my next memo. This one had numbers on it.

"We are all disappointed about how the situation with Perfume X was handled. And despite the fact that efforts have been made to fix this thing," I said, staring demonstratively towards Deirdre, "some aspects of the relationship should have been handled differently." I picked up the sheet that referenced the information, which had been branded in my brain. "Parfum Aix has sustained considerable financial loss as a result of McCale, Morgan & Black's mismanagement of the Parfum Aix account. The figures you have before you represent two categories of damages." Caine was fidgeting wildly in his seat. Deirdre grabbed his forearm as she read the memo intently. As she did, the grip on Caine's suit jacket became tighter and tighter.

"The first figure is the estimated loss in sales, both past and future, from the mismanagement. The second figure represents punitive charges as a result of the damage sustained by the Parfum Aix brand. We propose a cash payment to Parfum Aix for half of the sum, with the remainder to be deducted from future billings by McCale, Morgan and Black to Parfum Aix."

The sum on the memo totaled over eight figures. Nonetheless, the amount was still less than the total value of the Parfum Aix account for McCale. Deirdre was well aware of this fact, but of course, had no intention of just rolling over to the terms I had proposed.

She removed her glasses. "Maxine. Jacques. We regret the developments from this situation, but we at McCale, Morgan & Black can accept no wrongdoing with regard to these accusations." She glanced down at the paper. "These figures are very threatening. I don't believe that this is the way a professional relationship should be conducted."

"We do not believe that this is the best way to handle a professional relationship either." I called her bluff and flipped to the final memo in the folder. "This is a Letter of Intent from Hershel & Dixon, offering to assume the role as lead counsel for Parfum Aix."

"What?" exclaimed Deirdre. Her eyes were bulging. This was the first time I had ever seen Deirdre Morgan lose her cool. I refused to lose mine, especially because I hadn't finished delivering the news.

"In fact," I continued, "due to the notoriety of Perfume X, Hershel & Dixon is more than anxious to serve Parfum Aix. They have agreed to cut their rates by a third for the first three years of the relationship." That wasn't the entire truth. I had actually negotiated the rate cut with Hershel & Dixon on the condition that they would provide legal representation for Jacques's new endeavor *Créneau*, the gin.

Deirdre was speechless. Having served my retribution, I, too, was at a loss. And so the only person who had yet to say anything finally spoke up.

Jacques Deschemel got up out of his chair. Ever the gentleman, he preferred to address the McCale team while standing. "Deirdre. Caine. I want you to know how much I value the work that your firm has completed for my company over the past year and a half. Maxine may have won me over," and he smiled graciously in my direction, "but the rest of the team, including Monsieur Seaver, handled some very delicate matters with extreme professionalism."

"Thank you," mumbled Caine resolutely.

"I would like this relationship to continue. This company, Parfum Aix, is my identity. I have spent decades building and maintaining a reputation. Perfume X is not the first to attack my brand, and it won't be the last. I need to know that Parfum Aix will be protected aggressively. And that we will be protected with integrity."

Deirdre gathered up the pages from the folder and stood up

as well. "We, too, would like this relationship to continue. Would you give me until the end of the week to discuss the terms of your proposal with the partners at our firm?"

"Of course," said Jacques.

As the rest of the group collected their belongings, Deirdre worked her way over to Jacques. I heard her apologize again and make some genuine-sounding admissions of regret. I also heard her add, "You got a good one there in Maxine. I am looking forward to watching her career unfold."

I knew which career she was talking about. But Maxine Pedersen, attorney, was just one of my jobs. There were others, which required varying levels of energy and commitment. Mother. Wife. Daughter. Friend. I, like so many before me and so many to come, would have to juggle these roles to find a personal equilibrium. At least now I knew that the best way to achieve this balance was to invest in the vocation most critical of all: the job of being me, Maxine Pedersen.

epilogue

Henry took his first steps today. He pulled himself up on the ottoman in the living room and lunged to the couch. When he got there, he realized that he didn't need to hold on, and he just kept walking. He was so proud of himself. I sent a video to Dale and I think he was tempted to hijack the monitor in the trading room at Worthington so everyone could bear witness to his son's extraordinary athleticism. Maybe I needed to get Henry a toy cash register so Dale could help him learn math by counting fake money. How *apropos*.

McCale, Morgan & Black lost the Parfum Aix account. The key partners voted two-to-one not to pay the financial penalty that I had demanded. Deirdre Morgan voted against McCale and Black and was over-ruled. Again. But she didn't lose; she went with the Parfum Aix account to Hershel & Dixon, which is now Hershel, Dixon & Morgan. I hear they have a newly instituted work-from-home program that's the envy of the city.

Caine is still with McCale. Apparently, he is trying to persuade Nancy Lallyberry to join him for his business meetings. I'm sure their collective charisma has clients beating down the doors. At least that's what Joy tells me. She sends me updates regarding Jeffry Hsu's outrageous requests, now that she's become his admin. Joy is just about the only thing I miss about McCale & Black. But she seems content to stay, which is probably for the best. If she left, the organizational infrastructure of the firm would probably collapse.

I am in professional bliss managing Jacques's myriad projects. I've been more than busy, given the lack of legal know-how that characterized Parfum Aix before my arrival. I've also been structuring deals for the production of *Créneau* gin. And as a side stream of revenue, I have been concocting cocktails designed specifically for his liquor. We're working on a special promotion for the release of *Créneau*, so be on the lookout at your local spirits shop!

Dale is happier than ever now that his Beat the Boss tenure is up. He's got more contacts than he can manage, but with the browbeating demands of Worthington Investments, it's tough for him to carve out his own niche. Not surprisingly, Bobbie Macaluso is moving to semi-retirement over the next few years. In preparation, Dale and Rajeev have been in secret talks to start their own company. Rajeev just got married, and Dale wants to spend more time with me and Henry.

And the next addition to our family. . . .

CPSIA information can be obtained at www.ICGtesting.com
Printed in the USA
LVOW06s1230191013

357620LV00002B/3/P